Praise for the novels of Lee Tobin McClain

Also by Lee Tobin McClain

The Off Season

Cottage at the Beach
Reunion at the Shore

Safe Haven

Low Country Hero
Low Country Dreams
Low Country Christmas

Look for Lee Tobin McClain's next novel
in The Off Season miniseries,
available soon from HQN.

For additional books by Lee Tobin McClain,
visit her website, www.leetobinmcclain.com.

LEE TOBIN McCLAIN

christmas
on the
coast

HQN

ISBN-13: 978-1-335-08066-0

Christmas on the Coast

Recycling programs
for this product may
not exist in your area.

HQN
22 Adelaide St. West, 40th Floor
Toronto, Ontario M5H 4E3, Canada
www.Harlequin.com

Printed in Spain

For Grace

christmas
on the
coast

CHAPTER ONE

AMBER ROWE WOKE up to the sound of a child crying and pushed herself to a seated position on the couch. "Hannah?"

Heart pounding, she looked around the living room of her little beach cottage and then checked her phone. Just 11:15 p.m.

Outside, a dog barked, and something, maybe a cat, yowled over the rattling November wind. Amber shoved her fingers through her hair, reflexively pressed at the scars on her abdomen and sucked in a deep breath, let it out. She'd been sleeping so heavily, dreaming.

It hadn't been her daughter crying. Hannah wasn't a small child anymore, but a thriving college freshman two states away.

She heard the dog bark again, closer, and the same howling sound. It couldn't be a child, could it? Had to be a cat, or... She cocked her head, listening.

Was that a cat or a child?

Shoving her blanket and travel books aside, she crossed the living room, flipped on the porch light and opened the door. "Hello?"

Silence for a moment, and then one deep, baying bark, shockingly close, made her jump. She peered into the darkness just beyond the porch light's circle and saw a big, dark dog.

Then the wail of a child pierced her heart, and she rushed

onto the porch. She made out a small form hugging the dog's neck.

"Hey, buddy, what's wrong?" She kept her voice warm and soft, knelt to make herself smaller and less frightening. "Do you want to come in?" She held out a hand, too concerned about the child to be afraid of the large dog.

The child—a little boy in superhero pajamas—buried his face in the dog's neck and continued sobbing, flinching as a gust of cold wind ruffled his hair.

This wouldn't do. "I have hot chocolate," she said, leaning forward enough to touch the child's arm.

The dog growled.

She pulled her hand back. "Don't worry, big boy, I have a biscuit for you, too." She kept a canister of them for Ziggy, her sister's goofy goldendoodle, and King, her brother-in-law's German shepherd.

"His name's Sarge," the boy mumbled, turning his head sideways on the dog's neck to look at her.

That rang a bell, but she couldn't stop to think about why. "Come inside and we'll find your parents." She held the door open and gestured, and the boy came in slowly, the dog beside him. Both of them had muddy feet. The boy, who looked to be four or five, politely wiped his Spider-Man slippers on the mat before following her across the room.

They reached the kitchen and she was glad to note that his sobs were slowing down. "You have a seat and I'll start some hot chocolate. And we'll get Sarge a biscuit." She filled a cup with water and stuck it in the microwave, then shook her tin of dog treats.

Sarge, who appeared to be a bloodhound, lifted his head and sniffed the air, but didn't leave the boy's side.

She extracted a large dog biscuit and held it out to the dog, and he took it delicately despite the strings of drool hanging from his saggy jowls. He flopped down on the floor and started to crunch. Apparently, he'd decided she wasn't a danger to his charge.

"I'm Miss Amber," she said, smiling at the child. "What's your name?"

"Davey." He studied her with big teary eyes. "I'm cold."

"Of course you are." She stepped into the living room, grabbed an afghan off the couch and wrapped it around his shoulders. Then she fumbled in the cupboard and found instant hot chocolate and some stale marshmallows, and pulled almond milk from the fridge. The microwave dinged and she fixed a steaming, chocolaty mug for the boy, cooling it down with the milk.

She sat down catty-corner from him, the dog between them, and slid the mug close. She'd made it too full—it had been a while since she'd had a little one—but he knew to lean forward and slurp rather than picking the mug up. He'd stopped crying, though his face was still wet with tears.

"Where are Mom and Dad?" she asked.

He pointed to the sky.

Oh, no. "In heaven?"

"Mommy is," he said, and slurped again.

"Where's Daddy?"

His lower lip trembled. "Daddy was scary."

Her hands tightened into fists. "Did Daddy hurt you?"

He shook his head vigorously.

Amber blew out a breath and tried to think. Even if the child's father hadn't hurt him, a father being scary was cause for concern. And the boy was obviously lost. Calling 911 made the most sense, unless a junior officer who liked to use lights and sirens responded, waking the neighborhood and scaring the child all over again. She pulled her phone from her back pocket, scrolled and tapped her brother-in-law's name.

He answered immediately, his voice hoarse with sleep. "Amber? You okay?"

"I'm fine, but I have a...situation." She explained what had happened, keeping her voice calm and quiet, aware that the little boy was listening.

"I'll be over," he said, and ended the call.

Suddenly, footsteps pounded up her front steps. "Davey! Davey, are you in there?" came a man's frantic yell.

"Daddy!" Davey ran to the door and Amber hastened after him. Scary Daddy wasn't coming in here without an explanation.

Davey tried to open the door, but she put a hand on his shoulder. "Step over there a minute," she ordered firmly, and opened the door a crack.

There was a wiry man, barefoot, flannel jacket open over a thermal, dark hair disheveled.

He cleared his throat. "I'm trying to find my son." He looked past her, scanning the room.

"What makes you think he's here?" She tried to keep her voice steady.

"Yours is the only light on in the neighborhood. If he went outside, he'd go toward somewhere that was lit up."

The bloodhound brushed against her leg on its way to the door, tail wagging.

"Daddy!" Davey pushed past her, too, and reached for the storm door handle.

She stilled his hand. "Davey said you were being scary."

The man let out a big breath, his tense face and shoulders relaxing, and she realized she knew him. She tilted her head to one side. "Are you..." She frowned, trying to remember his name.

"Paul Thompson. You interviewed my wife a while back."

"That's it." The husband of her interview subject had seemed like a nice guy. And she remembered...yeah. She knew way too much about his personal life, but right now, that wasn't relevant. "Come on in." She held open the door.

He walked in and swept his son up into his arms. "Davey, Davey, Davey. You know you're not allowed to go outside after dark." He rested his cheek on the top of the boy's head. "You scared your old dad."

"Sorry, Daddy." The boy looked totally relaxed in Paul's arms.

"Come on into the kitchen," she said, leading the way. Somehow, she didn't want little Davey to go off into the darkness with the man who'd been scary, even if Paul seemed like a perfectly decent guy. She gestured them both to the table. "Davey was having some hot chocolate. Want some?"

"Uh, sure." His eyes skimmed over her and then he quickly looked away, leaning down to scratch the bloodhound behind his big, droopy ears.

At that point, Amber realized she was wearing a skimpy crop top and leggings. Nothing to hide her bony, boyish form. She started another cup of hot chocolate and then ran out to the coat closet, grabbed a hoodie and pulled it on. As she walked back into the kitchen, she heard father and son murmuring together.

"You were yelling loud," Davey said. "You said, 'Get down, get down, get help!'"

"I *did*?" Paul pressed his lips together.

"I'm sorry I watched a shooting show. But you were 'sleep on the couch and it came on and I—I just wanted to see the soldiers." Davey started to cry again.

"Hey, hey, it's okay," Paul said, grabbing a napkin and using it to wipe Davey's tears, cuddling him close. "I wasn't mad. I was having a bad dream."

"Some dream," Amber commented as she pulled boiling water out of the microwave and stirred hot chocolate mix into it. No marshmallows for Dad; she'd put them all into Davey's cup.

She was pretty sure Paul was telling the truth. There was no guile in the rugged face, and his body language was open. He was obviously able to be affectionate with his son, who seemed to adore him. There was no way to fake that.

Davey picked up his half-empty mug and guzzled hot chocolate.

Amber met Paul's eyes over the boy's head.

"Thank you for taking him in," he said. "I panicked when I woke up and he wasn't there. We just moved in today, and he doesn't know his way around at all."

"He had a good escape buddy in Sarge," she said lightly, smiling at the dog who'd flopped down onto his side. It looked like he'd decided the humans could take over for now.

A car pulled into the driveway beside the house, spewing gravel, and then she heard heavy footsteps, this time coming up the back steps.

Paul leaped to his feet and pushed Davey behind him. In his hand was a gun she hadn't known he was carrying, and her heart gave a great thump.

"Put the gun down," she forced out through a dry throat.

Davey knelt on the floor behind Paul, wrapping his arms around his knees. "I don't like this," he fretted, rocking back and forth.

Sarge stood, the hair on his back bristling as he watched the door.

"Amber? You okay?" Trey's voice outside the door sounded loud, concerned. He must have seen her and Paul through the window.

Heart pounding, Amber stepped in front of the door. She was facing Paul and directly in his line of fire, but she was praying he wouldn't shoot a woman. "Everything's fine," she said to the rigid man whose eyes were glued on the door behind her. "It's my brother-in-law. I called him when Davey came over. He's a cop," she clarified when Paul showed no sign of relaxing his fighting stance.

Davey was sobbing quietly.

"Everything's fine," she repeated.

"Amber! Open up!" Trey pounded on the door again.

"Just a minute," she called over her shoulder and then she frowned at Paul. "I'd appreciate it if you'd put your gun away."

His eyes narrowed. He slid his weapon into a holster inside his jacket but kept his hand on it.

"Why don't you just sit down," she said quietly. "You're scaring your son." For whatever reason, she didn't want Trey to come in and find this man an utter basket case, someone who should have his kid taken away from him.

Paul's head drooped for a minute and pain crossed his face. "Sorry," he said. He looked back at Davey and it was as if a switch flipped; he knelt and picked the boy up and held him close. "It's okay, buddy. Everything's okay."

Curiosity licked at her. She waited until he'd sat down, Davey on his lap, before opening the door to her very tense, angry brother-in-law.

THE FEEL OF HIS SON in his lap—safe, warm, *alive*—helped Paul get his heartbeat back to something resembling normal.

He tried to make his face look normal, too, to stop sweating, but the big guy at the door was a cop and clearly on high alert. He'd almost certainly seen Paul's weapon, because he was watching Paul with narrowed eyes. So was Amber.

Of course they're watching you. You acted like a madman.

Just as he'd done on the job, leading him to be here in a little shore town in a program designed to help him heal.

At least Davey was calming down. Paul focused on his son, used a napkin to wipe his tears and held it to his nose. "Blow. Real hard. There you go." He wiped Davey's nose. "You're fine. We're all fine. Okay?"

Davey looked up at him and nodded, and Paul's heart seemed to warm and grow. He didn't deserve the trust in his son's eyes, but he'd try to live up to it. He stroked Davey's hair.

"Everything okay here?" the guy asked Amber.

"Yeah. I think so." She backed away from the door and beckoned the guy to come farther in. Her hand was shaking. "Sorry to call you out so late, but Davey, here, came to visit me, and then his dad showed up a few minutes later."

"Hey, buddy." The cop walked slowly in their direction, smiling at Davey. He stopped a good eight feet away and knelt down, hand subtly near his waist where, almost certainly, a weapon was concealed. "My name's Trey. I'm a police officer, just making sure everything's okay."

Davey looked up at Paul, his face solemn, and then back at Trey. "It's okay. My daddy's a cop, too."

Paul blew out a breath and tried to smile at the officer. He shifted slowly, held out a hand. "Paul Thompson. Just moved into the cottage next door, and Davey took a notion to come outside while I was dozing on the couch."

"Trey Harrison." The officer stood, stepped closer and shook his hand, looking directly into Paul's eyes. Then he refocused his attention on Davey. "It's late to be outside by yourself. You're, what, five?"

"Four." Davey held up four fingers. "I have a birthday coming. Then I'll be five." He held up five fingers now, to illustrate.

"Wow," Amber said, moving over to the counter and leaning against it. "Five is big."

"Sure is," the cop, Trey, agreed.

Davey nodded, his face solemn. "Daddy said I can have a party."

Now that the immediate danger was past, shame licked at Paul's insides. He was a poor excuse for a father, scaring his son like that, but he was all Davey had. And Davey couldn't take another loss, not after losing his mother two years ago.

Paul's whole life centered, now, around protecting his son.

"Daddy, you're squeezing me," Davey said.

Paul loosened his grip. "Sorry, kiddo. You had me scared." He let Davey slide to the ground and watched him as he cuddled against Sarge. Thank heavens for his loyal former K-9 dog. How terrifying might Davey's late-night excursion have been without the big bloodhound for company?

"Sit down, Trey. Want some coffee?" Without waiting for an answer, Amber turned and reached high for a cup, her sweatshirt rising to reveal a thin slice of skin above those skimpy leggings. Women shouldn't wear them, Wendy had always said; she'd thought them too tight and revealing. Paul had agreed, just to keep the peace. He hadn't been the best husband in the universe, but he'd known enough not to defend other women's revealing clothing choices to his wife.

He looked away and realized that Trey had seen him

checking her out. He hadn't been, not really. He'd just noticed what any guy would notice, probably including her
brother-in-law. Still, his face heated. He didn't need to add
"creepy old guy" to the list Trey was no doubt making in
his head.

Not that he was that much older than Amber. Ten years,
at the most.

But ten years could be a lifetime.

Amber put coffee in front of Trey and then looked at
Paul. "Want a refill of hot chocolate? Or some coffee?"
She glanced down at Davey. "I'm thinking he won't need
a refill."

Indeed, Davey was resting his head on Sarge now, his
eyelids fluttering like he could barely keep them open.

"Thanks, I'll just finish this off." He wrapped a hand
around the still-warm mug.

Trey pulled out his phone and started texting. Apparently, he'd decided Paul wasn't an immediate threat. "Letting Erica know everything's settled down," he said to
Amber. "She's worried."

"Take a pic so she knows I'm okay," Amber said, and
struck a pose, her own coffee cup lifted in a toast, pasting
on a big smile. "And then I'll fix you some eggs because I
know you're always hungry. It's the least I can do, calling
you out in the middle of the night."

That last was directed at Trey, and again, Paul felt shame.
"Sorry to get you up, man," he said.

Trey shrugged. "Goes with the territory." He snapped a
photo and went back to his phone, and Paul once again had
to tear his eyes away from Amber. She was a character, all
right: hair frizzing out wildly behind a colorful headband,
tattoos up one arm and rings on most of her fingers. And
those bright flowered tights that fit her so well.

It wasn't just her clothes or hair, though. He remembered thinking her a little eccentric, in a good way, when she'd come to interview Wendy. Then, she'd worn a dress and some kind of jacket and boots, all professional.

But she'd gotten Wendy laughing more than he'd heard her laugh in months, and when he'd looked in on them, he'd seen that Amber had pulled off her wig of long hair and was showing it to Wendy. Her head had been completely bald, just as Wendy's was.

Amber had beckoned him in and showed them both pictures of her variously styled wigs in all different colors, suggesting which would best suit Wendy.

Now Amber's hair was chin length, and he had to assume that it was natural, since she was wearing it home alone in the middle of the night.

She pulled eggs and a loaf of bread out of the refrigerator and turned as if to ask them something. Then her eyes fell on Davey, now asleep. "Want me to put him to bed on the couch for a little bit?"

Paul didn't want his son out of his sight. "He's just as comfortable sleeping on Sarge. Do you have a blanket, though?"

She nodded and reached around him for an afghan lying across a kitchen chair. Before Paul could take it from her, she'd knelt and tucked it around Davey, as tenderly as any mother would.

Paul swallowed. Davey needed a mom. Maybe after Paul pulled himself together—if he ever *did* pull himself together—he'd try to meet someone. Another Wendy, sweet and steady and pure.

Amber rose gracefully to her feet and kind of danced over to the counter, set a frying pan heating with a chunk of butter in it and then broke eggs into a bowl with one hand.

"So, you two know each other?" Trey's voice was friendly, but Paul could hear the wariness underneath. Trey was still evaluating whether Paul was a risk to his son.

And the man was well within his rights. It was Paul who'd done something wrong. "Not well," he said. "Amber interviewed my wife for her book."

Amber beat the eggs to a froth with a big silver utensil, poured them into the pan and pulled a small bundle of something green out of the fridge. She snipped pieces into the eggs, then turned to face them. "Davey said she's in heaven," she said quietly. "I'm sorry for your loss."

"Thanks." He flashed back on Wendy, fixing eggs for breakfast. Not like these eggs—just plain ones—but it had been sweet to have someone cooking for him.

"Sorry, man," Trey said. "How's Davey handling it?"

"He's resilient, like all kids." Paul looked down at his son. "But it's taken its toll."

"On both of you, I imagine." Amber turned back to the counter and sliced thick pieces of brown bread.

What could he say to that? "How'd the book do?" he asked Amber. "What with all that's been going on, I haven't had time to look for it."

"It did great," Trey chimed in, sounding proud. "In fact, she has an offer to do another one. You going to go for it?"

Amber stirred the eggs and turned off the burner. "Pretty sure I am."

"This next book project seems kind of risky to me," Trey said. He reached across the table and started reading the spines of a stack of books. "Nepal, Tibet, the Himalayas..."

"Well, mostly Delhi and Calcutta," Amber said, smiling, "but I do hope to squeeze in some side trips. They want me to do a book on cancer patients in South Asia," she clarified to Paul. "How they do with non-Western medicine."

"Wow. So you're going to, what, live there?" Paul couldn't fathom it. He'd wanted to travel, a lifetime ago.

"More like a couple of long trips," she said. "I'm excited."

"Cool." Amber was way far from his comfort zone and his type. The odd little flutter of heat he'd felt was just one of those opposites-attract things.

Amber scooped eggs onto two plates, added slices of bread to each and brought them over to the table.

"You're not eating?" Paul asked.

"She never eats." Trey took a big bite. "Even though she's a great cook."

"I do so eat," she said in a play-whining tone that told Paul she and Trey were close. "Just not in the middle of the night."

Paul dug into the eggs, flecked with spices and rich with cheese, and realized he hadn't had dinner. Had he fixed something for Davey? Geez, what kind of…yes. He'd cut up a hot dog, stirred it into some mac and cheese. Not exactly healthy, but at least he wasn't starving his kid.

Amber sat down at the table with them and pulled out a big map. "See, I want to start in Delhi. That's where my publishers have some contacts. But I'd like to get out into the countryside, too, see how people manage disease when they don't have access to modern medical centers." She was running a red-painted fingernail over the map as she talked. "And then I'll be so close to Nepal, I have to make a side trip there." Her eyes sparkled.

"I don't like the idea of you traveling alone," Trey said. "Neither does Erica."

"I'll start out alone," Amber said, "but I doubt I'll be alone for long. There's a big expat community in most of these places, so it's easy to find friends to travel with."

Trey shook his head.

Paul kind of admired that loose attitude toward planning a trip, especially to the other side of the world. "I don't think I could do that," he admitted.

"Well, you couldn't. You have responsibilities here." She nodded down at Davey. "But my nest is empty, and except for helping out with the Healing Heroes cottage, I'm free to pick up and go anytime." Something flashed across her face and then was gone.

Maybe some of her enthusiasm could be bravado. Maybe she was traveling alone because she didn't have anyone to go with.

For just a minute, that wide world of adventure beckoned. He'd never even left the country.

But no. His job was to be safe and keep his son safe, not go globe-trotting.

"So you're staying in the cottage?" Trey asked, and Paul realized the man was still observing him in the guise of making conversation. Probably deciding whether to call child protective services.

Paul couldn't blame him. What had happened tonight hadn't just scared Amber; it had scared Paul as well, badly. It made him wonder whether he was, in fact, fit to parent a child.

Paul couldn't let something like that happen again. And he also couldn't jump up and pull his weapon every time someone knocked on the door.

He looked directly at Trey. "I had a nightmare, and that's what scared Davey. I'm getting counseling for PTSD and I'm to do volunteer work here in town. That's the deal with the cottage. My old boss set me up for it." He hated revealing even that much, but his symptoms were too obvious to ignore. He couldn't act like he didn't know he had a problem. He cleared his throat. "I'm thinking maybe I should give up my weapon for now." He pulled it out, slowly, and laid it on the table.

Trey had tensed, but as soon as Paul's hands were away from the gun, he nodded and scraped the last of the eggs off his plate. "I can hold on to it if you'd like."

Paul didn't like it, not one bit. But he couldn't risk carrying when he was so obviously out of control. "Thanks."

"Think you're okay to take care of him now?" Trey asked, nodding down at Davey.

Paul rubbed a hand over his face. "I have to be. I'm all he's got." His own words made him straighten his spine. He had to buck up because he could lose everything. Worse, Davey could.

He needed help, and he had to get it here, or else.

CHAPTER TWO

LIGHTHOUSE LIT WAS a comforting place, like any bookstore. Mary Rhoades, its owner and manager, tried to take in that comfort Thursday evening as she knelt beside a box of new dog-related books and fought back tears.

The lengthening shadows outside reminded her it would soon be time to close. She could indulge in her emotions after she was alone.

"I told you I'd make that display!" Julie, her best employee, came over and took the book featuring dogs in costumes out of her hands. "Though I still don't understand why you even need to have a display about pets just three weeks after losing Baby. We've got great-looking fall displays. Leave it at that."

The mention of her ancient, beloved Maltipoo tightened Mary's throat, but she swallowed her emotions. "Pet books sell like hotcakes. People will love them."

She stood, gripping the edge of the display table for support, her knees complaining. She needed to get back to her exercise class. When you were nearly seventy, aches and pains were inevitable, but exercise did help.

"I'll finish this," Julie said in a mother hen tone. "You unpack the self-help books. And take a couple of them home to read, while you're at it."

"Who's the boss here, anyway?" Mary complained mildly, but she did as Julie said and went over to start unloading the box Julie had been working on. Julie, a fif-tysomething redhead, was way more of a friend than an employee, and had every right to call Mary on her mistakes, like mooning over books full of cute dog photos.

Mary knew that her grief over Baby was complicated. A counselor had once told her that every loss she had would bring back the biggest loss of her life, especially if Mary didn't resolve her grief about that. Which, she supposed, she hadn't; she tried not to think about it.

What Mary really needed to do was to start a new char-ity project. Helping others, that was the only thing that filled the empty places inside her. She'd been thinking of an expansion to the Healing Heroes program. Maybe now was the time to stop thinking and start doing.

The bells on the shop door jingled, and Mary glanced over as a familiar man strutted in. Completely bald and roughly Mary's age, Kirk James wore a sport coat, pressed jeans and dress shoes. He looked like a man on a mission.

Mary ducked behind the shelf.

"Hi, beautiful," Kirk said to Julie. "Is Mary around?"

Mary caught Julie's eye and shook her head, making a zipping motion over her lips.

"She's right over there, and she's feeling blue," Julie said without a moment's pause, the traitor. "Maybe you can cheer her up."

"Great idea." Kirk came over and smiled his charm-ing smile. "What do you think, babe? Take a spin with a younger man?"

She snorted. Kirk was only a couple of years younger than she was, but he was quite the ladies' man, at least in his own mind. "I'll pass today, but thanks. Maybe I can inter-est you in a self-improvement book, though?" She held up a religious text, *The New Purity and Why It Works.* "This one seems like it could do you some good."

He squinted at the title and frowned. "You know I'm not much of a reader."

"And you're in a bookstore because..."

"Because I was hoping you'd join me for a drink down at the Gusty Gull," he said. "There's a band tonight."

She raised an eyebrow as she continued shelving books. "There's that Olson kid playing his harmonica and guitar. Which takes some talent, but it's not exactly a band."

"We could drive into Baltimore," he offered. "I know you're used to the finer things."

"Thanks, but no." She'd moved to Pleasant Shores to escape the finer things and make a fresh start. Which didn't include dating. Men were amusing creatures, but she had no interest in getting involved with one.

"We'll drive up the shore tomorrow." Kirk ignored her refusal as only a retired real estate agent could do. "There's a guy I know who's got a litter of new puppies almost ready to find homes."

"You should go, Mary." Julie came over to join the conversation. "At least take a look."

"It's sweet you're worrying about me," Mary said, meaning it. "But I'm not ready for a new dog. And I'm perfectly fine, or I will be."

It was true. She had a wonderful set of friends, work she loved and plans for the future.

"Life is short," Kirk said. "It's meant to be lived."

She glanced down at her watch—she was a dinosaur for wearing one, but she didn't like to carry her phone everywhere—and saw that it was closing time. Normally, she wasn't glad of that, but if it would get these two off her case… "I'm sorry," she said to Kirk, "but I've got to start closing up. Anything I can help you with before you go?"

He threw up his hands. "Aside from taking me up on one of my offers sometime? No." He turned on his heel and walked out of the shop.

"Now you've hurt his feelings," Julie said.

Mary felt a twinge of guilt; Kirk was her next-door neighbor and a nice man, beneath all the posturing. "He'll recover."

"Sure he will," Julie said, "but men have their pride. I remember when Earl got upset and stayed away for weeks before I finally called him and apologized."

Mary put an arm around Julie's shoulder as they walked toward the register. "And I'm glad you did. He's perfect for you."

"Thank you." Julie turned and gave Mary a quick hug. "I just worry about you."

"Don't worry," Mary said. "I've been thinking about my next venture."

Julie was gathering her things, but she paused and raised an eyebrow, clearly interested. Julie was one of the few people who knew that Mary was the money behind several philanthropic projects in the town. "Healing Heroes has been a big success so far. I saw that the new guy has a little boy."

"Yes. It's up and running smoothly now. And little Davey seems sweet."

"Trey is doing great. And you know I'm thrilled about Drew's comeback." Trey and Drew had been the first two participants in the Healing Heroes program.

Trey had ended up marrying a teacher in town, and they were deliriously in love. Drew was Julie's son-in-law. Thanks to the Healing Heroes cottage, Drew and Ria,

Julie's daughter, had reunited. They and their two teenage daughters now seemed like a happy family.

Mary was pleased with the Healing Heroes program. She was doing valuable work with her wealth, but it wasn't enough. The cottage could only accommodate one resident at a time, which limited the scope of the program. She had the time and energy to do more. "I'm thinking of expanding Healing Heroes," she said.

"More police? There's a need," Julie said. "Although it can be hard to find officers who are able to pick up and move here for three months."

"Yes, and that's why I don't want to just build more of the same." Mary had been pondering things, thinking about the past, really, and how to continue making amends. "I'm thinking of doing something for victims of violent crime, their families."

Julie's head tilted to one side, her eyes steady on Mary. "Why that? I mean, it's obviously a worthy cause, but... what's your interest?"

And that was exactly why she had to tread carefully. She didn't want Julie, or the other two or three people who knew about her charitable endeavors, to start asking questions. No one had been more shocked than Mary when her abusive first husband had left all of his money to her. Combined with what her second husband had left, it was too much, undeserved, a burden. "I was just watching a documentary about crime victims," she said. Which wasn't a lie.

"If you're still in the exploring stage," Julie said, "the town really needs a library."

"That's true." Mary adored libraries, even though they were a sort of competition for bookstores. "I mean, there's a library up the coast, but that's not the same as having one right here in town." She sat down in one of the comfortable chairs lining the wall and propped her elbows on her knees. She'd love to do something so in line with her interests as a library. Books had been her friends for so many years.

But making amends came first. She wasn't nearly done with that.

"I'm sure you'll figure out what you want to do. I'm always here to talk." Julie grabbed her purse and headed out the door, then paused. "You should think about going with Kirk to see those puppies."

Alone at last, Mary locked the door behind Julie and heaved a sigh. She liked solitude, found it relaxing, except when it got lonely. Automatically, she looked at the heart-shaped dog bed beside the counter, now empty, and sadness weighed down her shoulders. Baby hadn't just been any dog and couldn't be replaced by some puppy Kirk wanted to show her. The Maltipoo had gotten her through a lot of hard times, had stuck around when Mary had been truly alone in the world.

She'd flicked off the lights and was heading toward the cash register when she heard a sound from the far side of the store.

"Victims of violent crimes, huh?" The voice was female and oddly familiar.

Heart pounding, Mary moved behind the counter where she kept her handgun. "Who's there?" She hadn't done her nightly walk-through yet, but the store was small. She hadn't thought any customers were present.

A fortysomething woman strolled out from behind the shelf of cozy mysteries. Dressed in a plaid shirt and jeans, with dark dyed hair cut in an outdated shag, she approached Mary. Maybe she was more like fiftysomething, because she had deep grooves beside her mouth and wrinkles between her eyebrows. She looked... Mary's heart nearly stopped.

She looked like Imogene. Different hair, stockier, older, but...

She *was* Imogene.

Mary sank down onto the stool behind the register, sliding her handgun back into the drawer. "I never thought I'd see you again," she rasped out.

One side of the woman's mouth quirked up in a sarcastic smile. "You'll be thrilled to know I'm in town for a few days." She turned toward the door, then looked over her shoulder. "I just wanted to let you know I'm around. We'll talk soon, *Stepmommy dearest.*"

AMBER KNELT IN the sandy dirt outside her cottage, using the little trowel she'd brought out, trying to open a package of bulbs and to ignore the nervous feeling in her stomach.

"There she is, Daddy!" Davey's voice drifted from the cottage next door, and she turned to see him walking beside Paul, nearly hidden by the huge bouquet of flowers he was carrying.

She watched them come in her direction. Davey was chattering about something, and Paul's head was bent to the side, listening. Paul wore jeans and a polo shirt, but he managed to rock the plain, conservative outfit because of his impressively muscular frame. One of those triangle ones—broad shoulders tapering down to a narrow waist. Not that she was looking, really.

She hadn't seen the pair of them at all yesterday, which had been just fine. After their late-night visit on Wednesday, she'd slept in and taken it easy. Stamina still wasn't her strong point. And she had to admit she'd been disconcerted by the whole episode. Unable to figure out if Paul was cool and attractive or a complete basket case. Well, he was obviously attractive—Amber had a weakness for the handsome, haunted ones—but that didn't matter. There was no way she was getting into any relationship, especially not with Paul. Not when she knew a secret he could never, ever find out about.

The pair of them came up her front walkway. "We brought flowers to 'pologize!" Davey thrust the big bouquet at her.

"Wow, thank you!" She buried her face in a mix of mums, sunflowers and minicarnations in fall colors. "I love flowers. That's what I'm planting now." She looked up at Paul. "But you didn't have to."

"We intruded the other night, kept you up late. It's the least we can do."

Davey sat down beside her and picked up the trowel she'd been using. He poked at the dirt a few times and then, when he saw her watching him, put it down. "I'm sorry."

She blinked. "Don't be sorry, buddy. Dig a hole for me. Dig a whole row of them if you want."

"Really?" Davey looked at his father as if he needed a second vote of approval.

"If you're sure," he said. He sounded almost as surprised as Davey had.

"Of course! Hold these a second." She handed the bouquet to Paul and then leaned over beside Davey. "Just dig a little hole, about as deep as the shovel is, like this." She dug one to demonstrate and then handed the shovel to Davey. "We'll put one of these lumpy brown balls in each hole, and cover them up, and next spring, they'll grow into beautiful flowers."

"Cool!" He got to work immediately.

"It's the Tom Sawyer strategy," she said to Paul as she

retrieved the flowers. "Why do your own work if you can get someone else to do it for you?"

"You'd better tell him where to dig, or you'll get a hap-hazard mess."

She lifted a shoulder, curious about his apparently rigid set of standards for someone else's garden. "Haphazard is fine. They're daffodil bulbs." She stood. "Let me get these into water. I'll be right back out."

Inside, as she found a vase and cut the stems, she found herself smiling. She did love flowers, and it was sweet of them to bring them over. She poked the flowers into the vase, arranging them until they looked balanced, and set them on her kitchen table.

A glance at the wall clock stole her smile. Twenty minutes until she had to make her call. And she shouldn't worry, wasn't supposed to be worrying, but she couldn't help it.

She squared her shoulders and walked back outside, determined to enjoy every moment of rare November warmth and sunshine. Davey and Paul were still digging—holes in neat rows, she noticed—and a big dark pickup had pulled up in front of their cottage. As she walked down her porch steps, a silver-haired man got out and hurried around to help a woman climb down from the passenger seat.

"Looks like you have company," she commented to Paul and Davey.

Davey looked over. "Grammy! Grampa! Over here!" He waved the shovel back and forth, flinging dirt onto Paul.

"They said they were coming for the weekend, but I didn't know that meant Friday morning." Paul stood and brushed himself off, a muscle tensing in his face. "Come on, Davey. Let's get cleaned up and go see them."

"I wanna dig more holes," the child protested.

"They're welcome to come over here and sit on my

porch," Amber offered, since they were already headed this way. "I'll go inside and you can visit while Davey digs."

"No, it's okay," Paul said, but the older couple had already reached her sidewalk and were headed toward the house.

She guessed, from Paul's reaction, that they weren't his parents, but Wendy's. They were older than she would have expected given Wendy's age, the man with fully white hair, the woman blonde but walking carefully, holding her husband's arm. He wore beige slacks and a sport coat, while she was chic in white pants and a sweater that looked like cashmere. Country-club clothes.

"Look, Grammy, Grampa, I'm diggin' holes!" Davey stood to greet them, gesturing with his shovel, flinging a little more dirt. He didn't hug them.

"So you are," the woman said, and leaned down so he could kiss her cheek. The man ruffled Davey's hair. Then they both looked expectantly at Paul.

"Ferguson, Georgiana," he said, "I'd like for you to meet Amber Rowe."

Amber held out a hand. "It's a pleasure," she said, and after a slight hesitation, Ferguson shook her hand. Georgiana didn't offer her hand at all.

"Thought your place was next door," Ferguson said to Paul.

"It is," Paul began.

Davey had gone back to digging, but he looked over his shoulder. "This is Miss Amber's house," he said.

"Oh!" Georgiana sounded taken aback.

Paul's face reddened. "We're just here for a quick visit," he said. "We can head over and you can see our new cottage."

"Da-ad," Davey whined, "I wanna dig!"

"Seems I may have created a monster," Amber said when

none of the others spoke up. "Tell you what, Davey, you can come back another time and dig me more holes."

Davey's lower lip stuck out.

"You were a big help." She smiled at him and held out her hand for the little shovel.

"Come on, Davey," Paul said. "We need to show Grammy and Grampa your new room. And find out about that new truck they're driving."

Davey thrust the digger into Amber's hand and turned, still sulking.

"I know who you are," Georgiana said suddenly. "You're the woman who wrote that book."

Amber smiled. The publisher had insisted on putting her picture on the book's back cover, and there had been a few small news stories about the book. Georgiana must have seen one of them, or else picked up the book—which would make sense, given that her daughter's story was in it. "That's right, I am. Did you read it?"

"Yes." Georgiana's voice was stiff, and then she pressed her lips together.

Okay, then.

"Of course, you didn't really know her." Georgiana frowned. "I shouldn't be surprised the section about her was so off base."

Heat rose up Amber's neck. But then she remembered that this was a grieving mother and father. "I'm sorry for your loss," she said. "Wendy seemed like a lovely person."

Georgiana's chin quivered. "You couldn't possibly understand."

Amber bit her lip to keep from spouting her credentials: she'd lost a family member to cancer, had gone through treatment herself, not once but twice, and now...realization jerked at her and she slid out her phone to check the time.

"I'm sorry," she said, "I have a phone call to make." She was ten minutes late, and she could only pray she hadn't missed Dr. Weber. "It was nice to meet you," she added over her shoulder as she hurried up the stairs and inside.

She called the doctor and learned, with relief, that she was still in, but with a patient. "Yes, I'll hold," she said.

Through the open window, she could hear arguing.

"It was all so negative," Georgiana was saying.

"Our Wendy wasn't like that," Ferguson added.

"C'mon, let's go see my room!" That was Davey's loud voice, and when she looked out, she saw that they'd headed off, their voices fading as they continued to argue.

She fingered through her travel brochures. She was going to get away from here, and that little family and its arguments and sorrow would be a thing of the past for her. By the time she returned from her trip, Paul and Davey might well be done with their three-month stint at the Healing Heroes cottage.

"Amber?" came Dr. Weber's voice on the line. "Good news and bad news about the biopsy."

Her stomach twisted. "Tell me."

"The good news is, it's not invasive carcinoma," she said. "It's what we call atypical endometrial hyperplasia. An accumulation of abnormal cells, which isn't cancer, but can be a forerunner. Given your history…"

Amber pushed out words through a tight throat. "Can the cells be removed?"

"No need, right now, since it was an excisional biopsy. Everything is probably fine. But we'd like to keep an eye on it and do regular retesting, that's all."

Amber cleared her throat. "I've been planning a trip overseas."

"I don't see why you can't go. Where and how long?"

She cleared her throat again. "India and the Far East, for several months right after the holidays."

"Hmm." The doctor was quiet for a moment. "We could retest again right before you go. And of course, there are doctors and hospitals everywhere." But there was reservation in her voice.

"Be honest with me. What do you think I should do?"

Dr. Weber paused. They'd been through a lot together, and knew each other well, and Amber appreciated that the other woman wouldn't dismiss her concerns, but neither would she argue the most conservative route just to be safe. "You should give it some thought," she said finally. "If the travel is a bucket list item, then you should go. But you also want to consider your daughter, and—"

"I have to do the safest thing possible, for her sake," Amber interrupted. "Which would be staying stateside. Right?"

Dr. Weber sighed. "Right. Especially since your chemo caused some compromised lung function. You're in good shape now, but if you were to contract a virus…well, as I said, give it some thought. Maybe there's a modified type of trip you could take."

"I'll look into it," Amber said, disappointment pressing down on her. She already knew the answer. She'd have to stay home.

CHAPTER THREE

PAUL LED HIS IN-LAWS back toward his cottage, worrying about Amber. She'd hurried off so fast. Had she been offended by Georgiana's remarks about her book?

It looked like he might have another apology to make to Amber, and truthfully, he didn't hate the thought of that.

He lifted his face to the warm fall breeze and let his gaze rest on the bay. Sunlight from the east slanted over it, making its surface like a mirror. He could see a fishing boat, and beyond that, a little hummock with what looked like a duck blind built atop it.

"I just don't like that woman," Georgiana said, making it clear that Amber was still on her mind, too. "Those tattoos and that attitude. Keep Davey away from her."

"Now, Georgie," Ferguson said. "You know all the young people have tattoos nowadays. And what attitude? She was perfectly friendly."

"Of course *you'd* like her," Georgiana said, causing Ferguson to roll his eyes. Paul had no idea what that was all about.

He hated that Georgiana had been rude to Amber, but he couldn't bring himself to make an issue of it. Ferguson and Georgiana had been so good to Davey, especially in the months right after Wendy had died. Davey's grandparents had set aside their own grief to spend extra time with Davey and make sure he was okay. They'd paid for a well-known child therapist to have several sessions with Davey, and while Paul usually tried to avoid taking money or expensive gifts from them, in that instance, he hadn't protested. They'd been right: whatever would help Davey was what they should do.

Overhead, geese honked their mournful cry as they flew in a neat V shape. A cool wind whistled through the pines next to his cottage. It all sounded lonely.

Or maybe that was just him projecting his own feelings. "I'm glad you came to see Davey," he said, pausing to give the pair a chance to catch up with him and Davey.

"We didn't just come," Ferguson said. "We brought Davey a present."

"I like presents," Davey said promptly. "Where is it?"

"It's in the back of the truck."

Which meant it was big. Ferguson and Georgiana didn't even own a truck, so they must have borrowed or rented this one.

Davey ran toward the truck, but Ferguson called after him. "Uh-uh. You wait beside Grandma and close your eyes. Paul, give me a hand here."

Paul smiled, even though he was half groaning inside. What had Davey's indulgent grandparents bought him now?

Ferguson opened the back tailgate and slid a ramp out, and Paul grabbed the other side. Ferguson was known for overdoing it with his already-bad back. They eased the ramp to the ground and then Ferguson grabbed some kind of remote from the truck's bed and started pushing buttons. "You can open your eyes now," he called to Davey.

Davey and Paul gasped in unison as a child-sized, cherry-red ride-on jeep made its way down the ramp. "For the beach," Ferguson said.

Most grandparents would have bought their grandchild a bucket and shovel for the beach.

"Can I drive it now?" Davey asked.

"You sure can," Ferguson said.

"Wait a minute," Paul said. "It's beautiful and we appreciate it, but I'm not sure it's safe for a boy as young as Davey."

"I'm big," Davey said, a sulky edge entering his tone. "I'm almost five."

"An adult can control everything through this remote," Ferguson explained, holding it out so Paul could see.

"But I'll need to supervise him every second," Paul said as Davey climbed into the jeep and started examining it. "Because he'll definitely want to ride it every second."

And it's way too expensive, he added to himself. But that was par for the course.

"You're just here to do some rehab, right? So you'll have plenty of time to supervise him." In Georgiana's voice was a slight edge of disapproval. They didn't really understand PTSD, didn't think it was a legitimate illness.

Paul hadn't, either, not really, until he'd experienced it for himself. "I'll be doing a volunteer gig here. I'll find out more about it in the next few days." Things were still a bit up in the air, from what he understood. "Davey will be going to prekindergarten, just like he did back home."

"Public school?" Georgiana asked, her eyebrows shooting up.

"Actually, no," he said. "Not that there's anything wrong with public school, and that's likely where Davey will get most of his education. But there's a private school connected with the program I'm doing, and they provide free tuition as part of the package."

Georgiana considered that while Ferguson showed

Davey all the details of the little red vehicle and got him driving it, slowly, up and down the driveway.

Sarge let out a loud, deep baying bark from inside. "Uh-oh," Paul said, glad for a moment's escape from his mother-in-law. "I'd better bring Sarge out so he can join the fun." He opened the front door and Sarge ran out.

After lifting his leg by a clump of weeds, Sarge trotted over to the jeep. He was so well trained that Paul didn't keep him on a leash, especially in this low-traffic neighborhood.

"Can Sarge ride?" Davey called out.

"No, buddy, it's not safe," Paul said. "He can watch." Standing in front of the cottage, beside Georgiana, Paul watched Davey and Ferguson laughing together, Ferguson walking beside the vehicle, Davey grinning widely from the driver's seat. Their voices drifted back on the bay's cool breeze, the *tik-tik-tik* of the little vehicle's motor punctuating their words.

Georgiana looked up and down the cottage-lined street. "It's a pretty spot," she admitted. "Wendy would have loved it here."

"Yes, she would have." It was partly true. In the last year of Wendy's life, she'd stopped aspiring after the wealthy lifestyle adhered to by her parents and friends. She'd figured out that money couldn't buy the important things, like family and love and most of all, health.

That Wendy, the wiser one who'd seen the bigger picture, would have loved it here. Leave it at that.

"How did you get to know that Amber woman?" Georgiana asked.

He definitely didn't want to describe *that* episode in detail. "Davey wandered over there, and she was kind to him," he said. Which was true, although not the whole story.

"I think she wants something from you."

"Like what?" Paul couldn't fathom what a woman like Amber would need from a washed-up cop like him.

"Some women are always on the prowl," she said darkly. "She's probably lonely and looking for companionship, maybe more."

"Like my huge bank account?" Paul said lightly. It was a sore point with his in-laws, his humble lifestyle and lack of ambition to earn a big salary. It had been a *big* sore point with Wendy, once the initial infatuation had worn off.

"Maybe she thinks you have more than you do."

"I doubt she needs money, Georgiana. And I doubt she wants anything from me." Some part of him wondered what Georgiana had seen to make her think Amber was interested in him, but most likely it was just her suspicious mind.

His own surprise attraction to Amber was nothing more than a physical reminder that he hadn't gone out on a real date since Wendy's death. He'd had lunch with a couple of women who friends had set him up with, but nothing had come of that because he just wasn't ready. One night last spring, he'd gotten talked into a night of drinking with a few teachers from the school; loneliness had pushed him into a hookup with one of them, but they'd both agreed afterward that it had been a mistake and they were better off as friends.

It had seemed then, though, like he was waking up a little, getting ready to date. Over the summer, he'd started noticing pretty women more often and had considered asking out the mother of one of Davey's friends.

And then the awful incident and its aftermath had happened and he'd died inside again.

"I know you're going to find someone else sometime," Georgiana said, reading his mind. "But I hope, for Davey's sake, it'll be someone more like Wendy. Someone appropriate."

I can make my own decisions! But he knew what Davey represented to them: their grandson was all that remained of their beloved daughter. He put an arm around Georgiana's shoulders. "I'm a long way from that," he said, "but you can be sure I'll put Davey first if it ever happens."

A vision flashed into his mind: Amber encouraging Davey to dig holes wherever he wanted, then gently guiding him to go with Paul and his grandparents. She'd been great with him, today and the other night, as well.

Sarge let out a woof and took a few steps toward the street, and Paul smiled to see a woman walking a big, fluffy poodle mix. Come to think of it, the woman looked something like Amber, and Paul wondered if this was the sister married to Trey, the cop.

The dog spotted Sarge and lunged playfully in their direction, pulling the woman a few feet before she spoke sharply to him and regained control. "Sorry," she said. "Ziggy is friendly, but he's a big goof."

"All dogs are." Paul moved forward to let Sarge greet Ziggy. "What kind of dog? He looks bigger than a standard poodle."

"Goldendoodle," she said. "I'm Erica, and I think you met my husband, Trey, earlier this week. I'd stay and talk, but we're just taking a quick spin and then I need to get back to my son." She gave Georgiana a friendly wave and then continued down the street.

Paul wished he could just hang out in the yard without the complication of Davey's grandparents, especially Georgiana. But when he dutifully turned back to her and realized she looked teary-eyed, he felt ashamed. "Are you okay, Georgiana? What's wrong?"

"I just hate the thought that you'll replace Wendy, and Davey will get other grandparents, and we'll lose him, too." The words seemed wrenched out of Georgiana, who was normally more rigid than sentimental. "You sold your beautiful house, and I don't even know where you're going to end up after your time here."

"Hey." He pulled his mother-in-law into a hug, and surprisingly, she let him. He felt her shake with a sob. "Don't you worry about that. I'm not going to replace Wendy, ever. She'll always be Davey's mom, and you'll always be his grandparents."

"You say that now, but things change." She looked up at him, her mascara making black smudges beneath her eyes.

"That can't change," he said.

And his own determination to choose the right woman, when he started to date again, grew stronger. Georgiana was right about one thing: Amber Rowe wasn't the right person, although for different reasons than Georgiana had expressed.

Not only was she colorful and bold, not his type at all, but she was a cancer survivor. That meant she had a good chance of recurrence.

He couldn't put Davey through that kind of loss again. Better to rein in his attraction now and avoid the whole situation.

That meant he needed to stay far, far away from her.

SATURDAY AFTERNOON, MARY waited anxiously in Goody's ice cream and sandwich shop. She needed to get her new program up and running, fast.

Imogene hadn't shown up again for the talk she'd threatened, and Mary hoped she wouldn't, but life didn't work like that. You had to prepare for the worst.

Imogene would come back, and she had enough on Mary to get her way. And her way was taking a big chunk of Mary's money, if the past was any indication.

Before that happened, Mary absolutely had to get this new program for victims of violent crimes underway. And as she'd thought about volunteer work for Paul, the latest resident of the Healing Heroes cottage, her ideas had crystalized. It would be perfect for him, given his background and because he needed something flexible so he could manage care of his son. He didn't know the ropes or the town, but Amber would help with that.

Amber walked in first, and Mary waved. "I already ordered milkshakes," she said when Amber approached the table. "Presumptuous of me, I know, but everyone loves Goody's milkshakes. We can get a late lunch, too, if you're hungry."

"I'm not going to turn down a milkshake," Amber said, hugging her and then picking up one of the cups. "Mmm, chocolate. How are you? You look great."

"So do you," Mary said, although that wasn't strictly true. Amber did look much healthier than when she'd arrived in Pleasant Shores almost two years ago, but she had dark circles under her eyes now, and somehow lacked the spring she usually had in her step. "What's the latest on your international travels?"

"Postponed," Amber said, the corners of her mouth turning down. "Medical stuff. Nothing serious, I hope, but I have to stick around."

"I'm sorry about the travel," Mary said, and pressed her lips closed so she wouldn't express her real concern. Cancer had a way of sneaking back in. Amber had already suffered so much.

Mary shot up a quick prayer: let the problem be minor and easily solved. Keep the cancer away.

"Life can stink," Amber said, shrugging. "Paul! Over here!"

The handsome former cop waved and strode across the little café. He smiled, but it looked forced.

Mary hoped her idea would help these two young people regain their enthusiasm and energy. "Sit down and have a milkshake," she said to Paul, passing one over to him.

"Thank you!" He sucked some up through the straw and smiled. "Fantastic stuff. I'd heard stories, but this is better than I imagined."

"Good. Now, I know you're both busy, so let's get right to it. Amber," Mary said, patting the younger woman's arm, "you've been doing a terrific job running the Healing Heroes cottage since Ria turned it over to you."

"Thanks. It's been easy."

"Good, because what I'm about to suggest isn't going to be easy at all. Paul," she said, turning to him, "you need a volunteer gig. So, I'd like for you both to work together on an extension for the cottage."

"What do you mean?" Paul asked.

"I mean, another similar cottage on the same street."

"To do what?" Amber stirred her milkshake with the straw. "Make Healing Heroes bigger?"

"I want to start a new program," Mary said, "for victims of violent crime."

Paul coughed and sucked in big gulps of milkshake. It made Mary realize, abruptly, that the topic might cause him pain, given his background.

"You mean a place for them to stay?" Amber asked. "A rehab, like for the Healing Heroes?"

"Yes, exactly."

"Paul could do that," Amber said, "but why me?"

"Because you're a great organizer and you know the town. You can talk people into anything. I've seen you raise funds for cancer research." Indeed, Amber had talked Mary into making a sizable donation.

"If what's involved is buying a property and raising funds, I'm not sure I could be of much assistance." Paul rubbed the back of his neck. "Not much experience with either thing."

Mary studied him. "You're quite familiar with crime victims, aren't you?"

"What do you mean?" he asked sharply.

Embarrassment washed over Mary. As the benefactor of the program, she had access to all the files, so she did know some of Paul's background. But she didn't want him to feel his privacy had been invaded. "I know you're a former police officer, of course. So you'd be able to make sure the place had all the safety features needed, help us make contact with police departments, that kind of thing."

Goody walked over to their table, wiping her hands and looking out the window. Her habitually dour expression was darker than usual. "That dog is a menace," she said.

"What dog?" They all looked out in time to see Erica walking by with Hunter in a baby backpack, her giant goldendoodle trotting along beside her.

Amber tapped on the glass and waved to Erica, then tilted her head and studied Goody. "You're calling Ziggy a menace? He's just kind of silly. He wouldn't hurt a flea."

"Maybe not a flea, but a beautiful poodle in heat is another story." Goody glared at the dog as it continued on toward the bay, heeling perfectly beside Erica.

"Ziggy's improved from his puppy days," Mary said, trying to be diplomatic, "but he's definitely got a lot of energy."

"*That's* an understatement." Goody snorted, turned away and headed back to the counter where a couple of new customers had gathered.

"What victims would want to come to a place like Pleasant Shores?" Amber asked. "I mean, it's a great town, but don't most people have their homes and neighborhoods and support systems, and wouldn't they feel bad without them?"

"For some," Paul said slowly, "it's a reminder of pain, staying at home."

"Exactly," Mary said, remembering. Until she'd come to Pleasant Shores, she'd moved so many times she'd lost count. "So what do you think?"

Amber blew out a breath. "I gotta say I'm not enthusiastic," she said. "I'm hoping to travel and write, and it sounds like this project will take a lot of time and energy."

Hmm, she'd have to figure out how to get through to Amber. "Paul?"

He frowned. "Can you tell me more about what you have in mind? Do you need me to babysit victims on-site? Is there a way to work it around Davey?"

"Of course, we can manage around Davey. The hours would be flexible. For now, I just want you to help choose the right property in terms of safety and layout." *Come on, come on*, she silently pleaded with the pair. This had to get going before Imogene kicked her money campaign into full gear.

Paul lifted his hands, palms up. "I don't see that I've got a lot of choice," he said. "The Healing Heroes program requires a volunteer gig, and if this is it, I'll take it and be glad to do it."

"I'm sure there are other possibilities," Amber said. "Trey worked at the school. You could do that."

"No." Paul held up his hand like a stop sign. "No way. I'm not good with a school, with kids."

Interesting, since that had been his job before, a school police officer. But of course, he'd had that awful experience.

It was time to put pressure on Amber. There was no room for her to hesitate and waffle, no time. "I'm really motivated to get this project started now," Mary said. "It can do some real good for people in need. Change lives. I know that's important to you."

"It is, but—"

A commotion outside the window drew their attention. Why was Kirk James knocking on the glass?

And then he held up a squirming white puppy. He was pointing at it and grinning and beckoning to her.

"I can't believe…" Anger coursed through Mary's body. "Look, I have to go. Just think about it, okay? Talk to each other, and I'll be in touch in a few days for your decision."

Right after she'd strangled Kirk James.

She marched outside. Amber and Paul trailed behind her, but she didn't have the energy to worry about them.

In front of the café, Mary faced Kirk down, hands on hips. "I told you, I don't want a puppy!"

Kirk struggled with the squirming creature, no bigger than a guinea pig, white, with a black button nose and eyes that were still baby-dog blue. He winced as it nipped him. "Ouch! Little brat. Those teeth are like needles!"

"Oh, for pity's sake," Mary said. "Here. Wrap my scarf around him so he can't bite you or get away." Kirk wasn't even a dog person; he knew nothing about taking care of a puppy. "You didn't buy it, did you?"

"I just borrowed it for now, but I can buy it for you in a heartbeat." He tried to hand the dog to her.

She took two big backward steps, hands raised in front

of her like stop signs. "No. No way. I'm not touching him. Take him back to his mama."

"Puppy!" came a child's ecstatic voice, and then Davey ran toward them, closely pursued by his grandparents.

"You show the child the puppy, and then take it back where it came from," Mary said. "I'm not ready." Her voice choked a little on the last words.

Somewhere inside, she recognized that Kirk was trying to do a good thing. It was just that he was relentless and controlling, and Mary didn't need another pushy person in her life right now.

She didn't need to break her heart with another dog. Not until she'd assuaged her guilt and gotten Imogene soothed and sent away.

It seemed like that could take a long, long time.

CHAPTER FOUR

AMBER REACHED OUT and squeezed Mary's shoulder. Mary was normally so poised, but right now, she seemed ready to fall apart. "You should take all the time you need before getting another dog. You're the only one who can know when it's time." Mary had been deeply attached to her little dog, Baby. Kirk probably thought he was going to get in her good graces by giving her a puppy, but if she wasn't ready, it wouldn't work.

"What are *you* doing here?" Georgiana asked, frowning at Amber.

Amber lifted an eyebrow. "I do live in Pleasant Shores."

"No, I mean, with Paul." Georgiana's eyes skimmed over Amber's ripped jeans and Cancer Sucks T-shirt.

What a rude woman. Wealth obviously didn't buy manners. Amber hadn't even agreed to work with Paul, but just to spite them...without answering their question, she turned to Paul and plucked at his sleeve. "You know, I think I just made a decision. I'd be glad to work on the new project with you."

Georgiana's brows drew together and she looked at Paul, clearly trying to formulate her next impolite question.

Amber turned to Mary. "It's a little chaotic here," she said. "Wonder if the Gusty Gull is open yet?"

"I certainly hope so." Mary took Amber's arm, and the two of them headed down the street.

Pleasant Shores' downtown—if it could be called that—

consisted of a few shops and cafés along one side of Beach Street. Across the street was a bike path that ran for half a mile along the shoreline, dotted with green benches facing the water. Now, in November, the path was empty, and the few people out hurried toward their destinations. Beyond the bike path, docks jutted out into the bay and a few fishing boats were visible near the shore.

The Gusty Gull was the only bar that remained open throughout the entire off-season, and its owners took their mission seriously: they were not only open, but fairly busy. "Thank heavens," Amber said as they made their way to a table in the back. "Davey's grandparents hate me and I have no idea why."

Mary waved at a few people and then took the chair across from Amber. "I know they're around my age, but please tell me I'm not that kind of old person."

"You're not, believe me. I admire you."

"Why, thank you, dear. Just for that, I'll buy the first round." They ordered fruity drinks and turned down food for the moment but kept their menus, since the fried fare smelled so good.

It was the first time the two of them had been together solo, but the conversation flowed and Amber soon found herself telling Mary some of what was going on with her. "I'm wanting an adventurous life," she lamented, "but because of my health, I have to stay close to home for a while."

Their drinks came and they both took long draws, and then Mary patted her hand. "I'm sorry you can't take off traveling like you want to. But you know what Proust said? 'The real voyage of discovery consists not in seeking new landscapes, but in having new eyes.'"

Mary was really smart, and it made sense that she was well-read, given that she owned a bookstore. Amber took another delicious sip. "The problem with the whole seeing with new eyes thing is that I see this hot family man, with nasty relatives and a troubled kid and problems of his own. That's the kind of close-to-home adventure I can do without."

"And I'm guessing that's exactly why Paul's parents were questioning your presence. They can see the way he looks at you and they don't like it."

"You really think he's looking at me that way?" Amber asked, and then felt embarrassed that she'd blurted out the question. "Not that it matters," she added. "And they're his late wife's parents, not his."

"Even more understandable they'd be resistant to you." Mary beckoned to the waitress and ordered fried shrimp and clams for them to nibble on. "He looks at you like forbidden fruit. Tempting and way too appealing."

"Right? It figures." Amber sighed. "I've always been *that* girl, the one men chase after for a fling, but don't bring home to mama." She shrugged. "I've come to terms with it. Sometimes, it's a blessing."

"With as fun and funny as you are, a man would be lucky to have you in his life, and so would his mama for that matter," Mary said. "But I can't blame you for wanting to keep your distance. Every problem I've ever had came from a man."

Amber stirred her drink with her straw. "Yeah, they're trouble. But of course they flock around you. You're gorgeous." She wasn't exaggerating, either. Mary was model thin, with shiny white-gray hair that fell below her shoulders in waves that looked natural. She dressed simply but stylishly, mostly in white or gray, and she had that knack of adding a pop of color—red shoes, or a bright pink scarf—

that made her look Parisian-chic. Her eyes were sharp and usually sparkling with a joke or a plan.

As if to confirm her judgment, a man Amber knew vaguely, Henry Higbottom, came to lean heavily on their table. "You two ladies look lonely," he said. "Care to sit at the bar with me?"

"Thank you, but we're having a confidential conversation," Mary said quickly.

"That's a little harsh," he said, but his tone was philosophical. He shrugged and turned back toward the bar.

As he walked away, Mary added to Amber, "I know that sounded rude, but you have to be firm with him. He's mostly interested in younger women—in fact, he probably was looking more at you than at me—but he's also in the market for a nurse with a purse."

"Hmm, maybe I should look into that, given my health and the fact that lots of men are nurses now," Amber joked. "Sorry, dark humor."

"Don't apologize to me. Sometimes you have to laugh or you'll cry."

That was for sure. In fact, it was pretty much Amber's philosophy of life, these days.

The waitress brought their food and they dug in. The seafood tasted delicious, fresh and fried and hot.

"I don't think a nurse with a purse is what Kirk James wants," Amber teased, leaning back with a jumbo shrimp in her hand. "He's a pretty active guy, and he's always talking about you."

"Not interested, dear." Mary dipped a fried clam into the Gull's distinctly mediocre cocktail sauce. "I wouldn't mind being friends with the man, especially since we're neighbors, but I don't want anything more, and he does."

"And he's persistent. I mean, he tried to get you a puppy,

which was dumb, but it must have taken some thought and effort on his part."

Mary blew out a breath with a *pfft* sound. "I *told* him I didn't want one, but he didn't listen. And that's typical of men, especially of my generation. Your age-mates are better."

Amber thought of Georgiana. "Men don't have a monopoly on being obnoxious. And Kirk's basically a nice guy. He ended up being a big help to my sister when she needed funds for the academy."

"True, he did." Mary shrugged. "Regardless of that, though, he wants more than I do. Not hard when I want nothing." She smiled at Amber. "How about you? Are you dating?"

"Trying not to," Amber said. "My chooser's broken. I never pick the right guy."

"We have that in common." Mary leaned forward, suddenly intent. "So since you can't leave the area right now, and you're not interested in getting involved with a man, you have some time to do the project I described, don't you? Was your 'yes' just to get those people's goat?"

Amber sighed. "I guess there's a need for a project like that. And you're right, I may as well try to do some good in the world while I'm waiting for my next move to unfold."

"Then you'll do it?"

Slowly, Amber nodded. "I'll do it."

IT SHOULD HAVE been a happy thing, registering Davey for prekindergarten at a highly recommended, popular program in their new town.

Davey was certainly excited. He bounced in his booster seat all the way from the Healing Heroes cottage to the school, and when they pulled up to the Coastal Kids building next to the elementary school, he practically exploded out of the car. "Is this it? Are we late? Where's my teacher?"

"We're not late. Our appointment is in ten minutes." Clearly, Paul had made the right decision getting Davey started in school right away. He needed to be around other kids and to make new friends while they were here.

But when they walked up to the school and were instantly buzzed in, hairs rose on the back of Paul's neck. The secretary didn't know him. Why wasn't there some sort of security check?

To test the place, he walked right past the glassed-in office, holding Davey's hand. No one came out to stop them or check his credentials.

"Where are the kids, Daddy?" Davey bounced on the balls of his feet, looking to the right and the left.

"I don't know." He wanted to urge Davey to be quiet, wanted to focus on the place's level of security, but he knew he shouldn't squelch his son's obvious joy.

As they got closer to the big central stairway, the sound of children's voices came from upstairs. Davey tugged at his hand. "They're up there, Daddy. Do you hear them? Can we go see my teacher?"

"Let's look around here for a little bit first."

No one stopped them as they strolled around the downstairs area. A brightly decorated lunchroom was set up with two long, low tables surrounded by kid-sized chairs, next to a kitchen that smelled of freshly baked cookies. There was a library with shelves of picture books, a big rocking chair, and mats and pillows scattered around the floor.

At the sight of the library, Davey did a little hop. "I like it here."

Paul pressed his lips together to keep from saying something derogatory. Maybe there was an explanation for the fact that anyone could walk into the place. Although he couldn't imagine what it would be. Didn't the school administrators know what the world was like now?

Paul's head pounded and sweat broke out on his forehead. "Let's go talk to the people in the office."

Before they could get there, though, the front door opened again. Paul spun toward it, putting a hand on Davey's shoulder, ready to push his son behind him. But the person entering was a colorfully dressed woman of about fifty, no more than five foot three and slender, obviously no threat. He sucked in quick, short breaths.

Nothing happened. Don't scare Davey.

"Are you Paul Thompson?" the woman asked, approaching them and holding out a hand.

"Yes." He took her hand in his own sweaty one, shook it.

"And this must be Davey." She shrugged out of her jacket, knelt to child level and held out her hand to Davey. "I'm Miss Meg."

"Pleased to meet you," Davey recited as he'd been taught, shaking her hand. "Are you my teacher?"

"No, but I can take you to see her. Let's go upstairs." She stood and looked at Paul. "If that's okay with Dad. He and I can talk while you meet your teacher and the other kids."

Sweat trickled down Paul's back. He didn't want to get Davey excited about the place if it was hopelessly unprotected, but one look at his son's eager face and he knew that had already happened. "Sure thing," he forced out through a tight throat.

They followed Miss Meg up a stairway with a mural of swimming fish on one side and a shiny, red-painted railing on the other. At the top were two big classrooms. A glance told Paul that younger kids were in the left-hand one—about ten of them sat in a circle listening to a teacher

talk—while kids closer to Davey's age were in the right-
hand room, set up with small tables and chairs on one end
and a large open area on the other.

Miss Meg led them to the classroom on the right, where
a slightly bigger group of children, maybe fifteen, seemed
to be getting organized for a game. A few words were exchanged between the fresh-faced teacher and Miss Meg,
and the younger woman held out her hand to Davey, smiling
at him. "I'm Miss Kayla. We're just about to play Bluebird
through My Window. Would you like to join in?"

Davey hung back, pressing into Paul's leg. "Can I,
Daddy?"

"Sure can." He smiled at Davey and squeezed his shoulder. "It looks like a fun game."

"Okay." And Davey followed the teacher into the room-
ful of kids.

As Miss Kayla told everyone to welcome their new
friend, and Davey joined the circle of kids holding hands,
Paul drew in big breaths of air and let them out slowly.
He was overreacting to the lack of security, or rather, his
body was.

"Oh, good," Miss Meg said as they watched Davey, who
was already joining in the simple song. "He seems to be
comfortable in new situations."

I'm not. Paul tried to smile and listen to the woman as
she described the half-day program and the option for extended care if he needed Davey to stay during the afternoon.

In the classroom, a girl tapped Davey on the shoulder
and he joined the short line of children weaving in and
out of the other kids' upraised arms, led by the teacher.
He was smiling, and when a couple of kids got tangled up
together—which seemed to be the point of the game—he
laughed along with the rest of the group.

Davey needed this. It was important for him to play with other kids. "I'm concerned about security," he said when Miss Meg took a breath. After one more glance at Davey, he moved to where he could better see the stairs. "We were able to walk right in and past the office. No one stopped us."

"Didn't the buzzer work?" she asked.

"Yes, but we were buzzed in right away. No one checked IDs or frisked us."

"*Frisked* you?" She tilted her head to one side, studying him.

Okay, so maybe preschools didn't frisk guests. "I could have been anyone."

"We can go down and look at the camera system," she said, frowning. "I'm pretty sure you were admitted because our secretary knew you and Davey had an appointment with me, but we can double-check that."

Footsteps came up the stairs and Paul tensed, watching. When the woman who'd been at the reception desk in the office appeared, smiled at them and went into the other classroom, his muscles relaxed a little. But his heart rate was still way up, and sweat rolled down his back.

Miss Meg looked at him more closely. "Is everything all right?"

He sucked in another breath. He wanted to grab Davey and leave, but some sane part of him knew he was in the grip of his illness and shouldn't make decisions. "I'm not feeling well," he said, and then, recognizing the immediate concern on her face, he added, "Nothing contagious, and Davey's fine."

"Let's get you somewhere you can sit down," she said, her forehead wrinkling. "Is there someone I can call for you?"

Was there? His in-laws had finally gone home. His friends were all back in Baltimore.

Someone else came up the stairs and he practically exploded. Memories washed over him in waves: he'd been joking with a couple of the sixth-grade boys, his back to the door, when there'd been a loud crash. By the time he'd turned—

"Come sit." Miss Meg took his arm, but he flinched away, and her eyes widened.

"Sorry," he said. He definitely needed to get going with the counseling here, maybe even try the antianxiety meds his doctor back home had recommended. He scrubbed a hand over his face.

She was watching him steadily. "I'd really like to call someone for you before you take your son home." Implied in her words was concern for Davey's well-being. "Davey's welcome to stay and play until you get some support."

Who could he call? He didn't know a soul in this town, didn't have a phone number. Except...

Amber had been kind the last time he'd freaked out. She'd called her cop brother-in-law, sure, but she hadn't reported him to the authorities, nor avoided him afterward.

And he had her phone number because she was in charge of the cottage. "I'll make a call," he said to Miss Meg.

He didn't want to get Amber involved in his and Davey's lives, didn't want to risk it. He was in no shape for even a friendship with a woman, definitely not a woman he was attracted to.

But there was no one else. He took one more glance at Miss Meg, whose arms were crossed as her gaze scanned from Davey's classroom to Paul. And then he made the call.

CHAPTER FIVE

THAT NIGHT, AMBER pushed her plate back, admired the darkening sky through the big dining room window of the Healing Heroes cottage and rubbed her too-full stomach. "That was delicious," she said to Paul. "You're a good cook."

Paul shrugged. "Spaghetti with meat sauce isn't exactly gourmet."

"And salad," she reminded him. "Pretty healthy."

"Healthy dinner means dessert!" Davey pumped his fist in the air.

Paul frowned. "Sorry, buddy. I didn't have the chance to stop at the grocery store today. No ice cream."

Davey's lower lip thrust out.

Uh-oh. "I think I can solve this problem," Amber said. "Davey, do you like chocolate?"

"My favorite!" He nodded vigorously.

"Mine, too," she said. "And I have some yummy brownies at my house. You help Dad clean up, and I'll run over and get them." She grinned at Paul. "See what I did there? Now I don't have to help."

"Tricky." He smiled back at her, his face more relaxed than it had been earlier today. When he smiled—when he wasn't looking like he carried heavy weights on both of his shoulders—he was very appealing.

And she didn't need to be thinking about that. "Be right back," she promised, and headed to her place.

Paul's softer side was a surprise, but not as much of one as getting that call from him had been. He'd sounded desperate, and she'd dropped everything and come to the Coastal Kids School right away.

There, she'd reassured Miss Meg that she would help Paul and Davey get home and settled, and then driven them to the cottage in her car.

Two high red spots on his cheekbones had showed Paul's embarrassment as he'd apologized and thanked her. She'd thought that would be the end of it, that he'd probably avoid her now that she'd seen his weakness, but on the contrary, he'd invited her over for dinner as an apology.

Come to think of it, the man was very skilled at apologies. First flowers, now a home-cooked dinner. Had he had a lot of practice apologizing in his life, and to whom?

She pulled out the pan of brownies she'd made for Hannah's care package. Like always, she'd made way too many. She loaded up a plate, covered it with plastic wrap and headed back over.

Twilight had given way to full darkness, but the moon cast silver light across the water, illuminating the lapping waves. She paused, breathed in the fragrance of salt water and autumn leaves, that unique combination she'd only ever smelled here on Maryland's Eastern Shore.

Grateful. She was grateful for the natural beauty around her and the chance to share a meal with new friends. When life's big milestones and pleasures seemed out of reach, it was best to concentrate on the small, everyday blessings.

She tapped on the door and walked back in to find Davey on the couch under a blanket, watching a movie featuring talking dogs and cats. "Here, buddy," she said, and handed him a big brownie. Only when crumbs fell onto the blanket did she realize her error. She hurried to the kitchen and found a napkin to spread over him.

Paul came down from upstairs and raised an eyebrow.

"I'm sorry," she said. "You probably don't allow him to eat on the couch, but by the time I'd thought of that, I'd already given him a brownie."

"They're good, Daddy," Davey said around a mouthful, dropping more crumbs.

Amber winced and went for another napkin, but Paul stopped her with a hand on her arm, stepping backward until they were out of Davey's hearing. "Don't worry about it. I appreciate your bringing dessert, but mostly, I'm sorry about today."

"You more than made it up to me with that dinner." She waved the plate of brownies under his nose. "Want to try my contribution, so I don't feel like such a freeloader?"

He picked one up, took a bite and nodded approvingly. "Excellent."

Amber felt an absurd sense of pride that he liked her baking. What was wrong with her? Everyone liked brownies.

He went back into the kitchen and poured a small glass of milk, then held up the carton. "Want some?" When she shook her head, he carried the cup to Davey. "Drink up, buddy, and then you can finish this movie before bedtime."

"'Kay." Davey obediently gulped the milk and then handed the empty cup to Paul.

"He's fading," he said in a quiet voice as he carried the glass and napkins back to the kitchen.

She followed. "Big day for him."

Paul nodded. "The other thing I have to apologize for is my in-laws. Former in-laws. Wendy's parents." He sighed, leaning back against the counter. "I'm sorry they've been so rude to you."

"Yeah, what's that all about?" she asked as she sat down at the table, propping her feet up on a chair. "Usually, it takes at least a couple of encounters before people take a dislike to me. Your in-laws don't even know me."

He scrubbed a hand over his face. "Yeah, I wondered that, too, but after talking to Georgiana, I think I know the problem." He looked to the side.

"What is it?"

"They're afraid I'll replace Wendy and they'll lose Davey."

She tilted her head to one side and looked at him while she processed that. "They're afraid you'll replace Wendy with me?" Thinking about that made Amber uncomfortably aware of the secret she was keeping from Paul.

"I know. It's ridiculous."

His words were like a bucket of cold water poured over her. Why was it so ridiculous? Was it entirely out of the question that he'd be attracted to someone like her?

He was still looking off to the side as if he were uncomfortable. It gave her the chance to study him, to notice his one-day growth of beard that had made him look a bit disreputable at the school today, the careless cowlick in his hair, the way his shoulders stretched his polo shirt.

Oh, those shoulders. She had a thing for shoulders, and Paul's were spectacular. "Why is it ridiculous, the idea that you'd date again?" she asked, deliberately depersonalizing it because she did have an ego and it could be crushed. "Are you some kind of a monk?"

He looked at her then, really looked at her, and the intensity of his gaze made her next quip die on her lips. There was a lot going on under the surface with this man.

"I'm far from a monk, Amber," he said softly, his gaze never leaving hers.

She suddenly realized he knew his way around women. "So," she said, blowing out a breath and casting about for a way to change the subject. "What was going on today, over at the school?"

He blinked, and his face went back to its usual tense lines, and she almost regretted not following up on the meaning that had been in his eyes. Almost wanted to be the person who helped Paul lighten up and smile. And maybe more.

"I don't know how much they told you about me, why I came into the Healing Heroes program," he said.

She lifted her hands. "Nothing. I'm just, like, the manager of the cottage itself. It's Earl who sets up the volunteer work, and Mary reads the applications."

He nodded. "I'm sorry I brought you into all of my problems, then." He drew in a breath, then let it out in a sigh. "It's the PTSD thing."

"What's it from?" She really wanted to know, even though it was probably a rude question.

He glanced toward the living room, then stood, walked over and looked in. Had she offended him that badly, that he was going to just leave the room?

But no, he was just checking on Davey. "He's asleep," he said as he came back into the kitchen. He leaned against the counter. "I try not to talk about it in front of him."

"Look, if you don't want to discuss it, it's fine. I shouldn't have asked."

He waved a hand. "No, the counselors say it's good for me to talk about what happened. And I owe you, after you bailed me out today."

"You don't—"

"I was involved in an...an incident." He cleared his

throat. "At a school." He paused, then spoke again. "It was a shooting."

She gasped, her heart and stomach twisting. "Oh, no." The reasons for his issues were suddenly crystal clear.

"I was supposed to protect everyone. I…couldn't." He paced over to the window and looked out into the darkness. "I don't want to go into the details. I tried to go back to work again after my required leave, but…" He shook his head. "I was a danger. Too jumpy. Couldn't even talk to the kids. I tried to give my resignation, and instead, they sent me here."

She wanted to stand up and hug him, but she just didn't know him that well. "I'm sorry. That sounds absolutely horrible."

He looked back at her, then away. "I could have handled everything better."

She wasn't going to argue with that, even though she figured he was probably beating himself up without cause. The level of support he needed was beyond her pay grade. "Did you get counseling?"

He nodded. "Yeah. They mandate five sessions, and I did them."

"Do you think you might need more?" She spoke hesitantly, not wanting to insult him.

To her surprise, he smiled. "Yeah. After the way I reacted at your place, and then today, I'd have to be stupid to think I could fix this just by gutting it out."

"Counseling can be a godsend," she said.

"You sound familiar with it." He pulled out a chair, spun it around and straddled it, crossing his forearms over the chairback.

"I've had my share." She wasn't going to talk to him

about it, though. She was going to enjoy looking at those muscular arms.

The dishwasher hummed, and from the living room, Davey's movie was barely audible. Paul took another brownie and then shoved the plate toward her. "Take these away from me or I'll eat the whole plate."

Amber smiled and pulled the plate closer. She selected a small brownie and took a bite, and rich, dark chocolate practically exploded in her mouth. Heaven.

But Paul didn't let her off the hook. "Was your counseling because of the cancer?"

"Yeah." She noticed a couple of crumbs on the table and wiped them away with her napkin.

He tilted his head to one side. "Come on. I told you my story."

Good point. "It's been tough at times, worrying about whether I was going to make it, and how having a sick mom was affecting my daughter, Hannah."

"You have a daughter?"

She nodded. "She's in her first semester of college."

"Wow. You must've had her young." Then he waved a hand. "Sorry if that's too personal of a comment. Not my business."

"Hey," she said, "as long as it means I still look young, I'll take it as a compliment. Anyway, I had trouble coping with all of it by myself so I got some help. It's not a shameful thing to do."

"Is your cancer in remission?"

"We think it still is," she said. "But they're, quote, keeping an eye on some abnormal cells. Which feels scary, as I'm sure you recall."

"Yeah." His face went bleak, as bleak as she felt when she thought about the possibility of getting sick again. Of treatments and tests and doctor's visits consuming all of her time. Of the major pain and minor discomforts of surgery. And most of all, the fear that she wouldn't make it, that she wouldn't get to do all the things she wanted to do, that she'd leave her daughter to grow the rest of the way up alone.

Their eyes met, and it was like Amber could see the sadness in his soul, a sadness that echoed her own. It wasn't often she felt understood, but she did now, in this moment.

It felt a little too intense. "So," she said, wanting to distract both of them, "I've decided I need to live it up while I can."

"With your travels?"

"No." Her stomach twisted. "My doctors don't think I should go. So I'm gonna have to live it up here," she said. "I had cut back on the partying, but now that I have an empty nest and I'm tied to the area…"

His face got stern and his eyes narrowed. "Don't do something you'll regret."

"Okay, Dad," she said.

"I mean it. You have so much to live for."

"So much living to do, too." She met his intense gaze, and suddenly she wasn't sure exactly what they were talking about.

The moment lasted longer than it should have, but she couldn't look away.

His gaze flickered down to her lips, and then he sat up straighter and rubbed his hands together. "Well. We should talk about the program Mary was proposing. Are you on board for it?"

"I told her I'd do it."

"Then we should figure out first steps." His voice sounded tight, and when he got up and grabbed a pad and pencil, he dropped it twice. "So. Look for properties?"

So. Calm, collected Paul Thompson wasn't always in perfect control of himself. She liked that. And she couldn't resist teasing him. "I'd love to go house hunting with you."

He glared at her. "Why do I have the feeling you're playing with me?"

"Would that be so terrible?" Her breathing hitched a little, but that was fine with her. Much more fun than thinking about the hard stuff.

He frowned, but he also moved closer. "Stop it." His eyes crinkled at the corners, which only emphasized their stormy expression.

Her heart rate accelerated. "Stop what?"

"Stop flirting. Or I'll…"

"You'll what?" She raised an eyebrow.

He leaned on the table in front of her, and suddenly their faces were just inches apart. "You know exactly what I'll do," he said.

She sucked in a breath, staring at him.

"But it wouldn't be wise, and you know that, too."

"Right." She scooted her chair back a little then, flustered.

"Daddy, what are you doing?" came a small, sleepy voice.

Amber didn't know how to feel about Davey's untimely appearance, but she *should* be grateful. The secrets she was carrying nixed the chance of any relationship between her and his way-too-appealing father.

As Mary approached the first potential site for the new program she wanted to fund, her steps slowed. Would this be the right spot for victims of violent crime to heal?

Three doors down from the Healing Heroes cottage, this place was a little bigger and had neighbors on each side. That was good. People who were still suffering fear wouldn't want to be off on a lonely spit of land somewhere.

Importantly, it was pretty and appealing. Even someone in the depths of despair couldn't help but be charmed by the yellow Cape Cod–style home with a picket fence surrounding the yard and a front porch that would encourage residents to sit outside and meet people, become part of the neighborhood.

Looking around the side of the cottage, she could see that a decent-sized yard led down to the bay, and that was good, too. Who could look out at the deep blue water, painted with whitecaps on this breezy, blue-sky day, and not get at least a little bit of healing?

Gulls flew overhead, along with a V of geese. The birds honked and cried, and some neighborhood kids shouted and ran in the backyard next door, their moms chatting on the back step. The occasional car drove by. It was a quiet place, away from the noise and hectic sounds of the city. Again, that was healing. Victims needed to be able to hear their own thoughts if they were to find a way forward.

So maybe this would be the place. She hoped so. She had to get this project off the ground before Imogene decided to come back and make demands.

Amber and Paul appeared from behind the cottage. They walked oddly far apart. Mary knew what that meant, and it made her smile. Paradoxically, they were far apart because they were drawn to each other. She'd experienced the same a few times. What was it with the human resistance to connection?

They saw her and waved, and she walked up the little flagstone path to meet them. They exchanged greetings and then started immediately to discuss the property.

"It's pretty secure, or it can be made so," Paul said. "That is going to be the biggest priority."

Mary glanced at Amber, who was frowning a little. "The biggest priority is healing, I would think," Amber said.

"Which involves safety and security first," Paul said firmly. They glared at each other, and then simultaneously looked away. Interesting.

As they walked inside, Mary observed the outdated wallpaper, the stained carpets, the windows that rattled in the breeze. But they were big windows looking out on the bay, and that was important. They could easily be restored to look more modern and hold out the weather. The decor could be refreshed, too. Mary would enjoy doing that. She got a little burst of excitement at the thought.

Paul moved ahead and started examining the window casings while Amber and Mary strolled through the old-fashioned kitchen. It was small, but a window over the sink looked out onto the backyard and the bay. There was a tiny table and an overhead fan. "It'll need some updating," Mary said as she studied the old gas stove.

"Right, but you don't want to lose the charm." Amber leaned back against the counter. "What's your interest in helping crime victims, anyway?"

That was exactly what Mary didn't want to discuss. There was no need to dig up all that old stuff—the real pain, but also the ugly, hurtful rumors and accusations. "It's a cause I've always believed in," she said, waving her hand. "It's time to do something about it. Now or never."

"Uh-huh." Amber raised an eyebrow but didn't question her further.

"Let's look upstairs," Mary said, and Amber led the way. There were three bedrooms, definitely in need of some decorating help, but structurally sound. Space for a family or visiting friends, which was nice. Being around others was key to mental health.

They met back downstairs and stood on the porch discussing the place. "It's nice," Amber said. "Cute and cozy."

"Can be made secure," Paul added, scanning the street in his cop-like way. "Could even be expanded later, if you wanted to."

"I like that idea." Mary looked at the surrounding cottages. The one on their right belonged to the family who'd been outside earlier, but the tiny, royal blue one on the left she wasn't sure about. She turned to Amber, who was looking in the same direction. "Know anything about that place?"

"The blue house? It's a rental, I know that," Amber said. "Want me to look into it? See who's renting it and whether it's long-term or short-term?"

"Perfect." Mary loved having Amber in charge of this program. She was so competent. Made everything look easy.

"I like the area," Paul said. "Safe, and I think it would be important to have any place we choose be fairly close to downtown. That's been a lot of fun for me and Davey, being able to walk a few blocks to get dinner or ice cream."

"One of Goody's milkshakes could heal a lot of problems," Mary agreed.

Amber did a silly little dance. "We may have a winner! I'll get on the research this afternoon."

Paul smiled, obviously enjoying Amber's enthusiasm, and then looked past her down the street. His eyes narrowed. "Don't look now," he said quietly, "but there's a woman who's been lurking around. I think she's coming this way."

Mary's heart did a great thump, and she felt her shoulders tighten. "What does she look like?"

"Dyed black hair, medium build, wearing jeans and a

T-shirt. About fifty-five years old, and height of maybe five-six."

Mary's head started to swim as Paul described Imogene. Just thinking of her stepdaughter catapulted Mary back into the most awful time of her past. A time she didn't want to think about, losses she tried to push out of her mind, but Imogene wasn't going to give her any choice.

The fact that Mary couldn't stand being around Imogene just made her feel more guilty. Imogene had lost so much through no fault of her own. It had all been Mary's fault.

And it was Mary's problem to deal with. "I'm pretty sure I know who that is. I need to talk to her. Can you two take it from here? And write up a little report on what you find out?"

"Of course." Amber was studying her. "Are you okay? Do you want us to stay with you while you talk to her?"

"No!" Mary responded too rapidly, making them both stare. "I need to speak with her alone. But I'm fine. Don't worry about me."

Amber put an arm around her. "I *am* worried. And I'm going to call you later, whether you want me to or not."

"Fine, fine," Mary said as she extricated herself from Amber's half embrace. If Imogene saw Mary happy and close with someone else, it would just make her angry.

She sucked in a deep breath, turned and there was Imogene standing on the sidewalk behind them, closer than Mary had expected although not close enough to hear what they'd been saying. "Hello, dear," she said, and walked toward her stepdaughter, determined to take the high road. "I wasn't sure if I'd see you again."

"You were hoping not, right?" Imogene said, her face— a face that had once been so pretty—twisting into a sneer.

Mary sighed. "Let's go down to Beach Street and walk

along the bay. We can talk there." And hopefully, the serene water and fresh breeze would give them both a little more insight and compassion.

As they walked toward the bay, Imogene started talking and didn't stop. "I've got to get some relief here," she said. "I've been going under and it's gotten really bad. I have a lot of bills due and I can't pay them. I need your help."

"Of course, dear, I can help," Mary said, even as she wondered what she was getting herself into. If she helped out with a little now, would Imogene continue coming to her every time she had a need? "Just show me your bills and we'll take care of the most urgent ones. And then I can help you figure out a payment plan for the rest."

"I don't need financial counseling, I need money," Imogene said. "A lot, and soon."

That didn't sound good. "I can help you out with your smaller bills," Mary clarified, "but I can't give you a big sum of money."

Imogene opened her mouth, obviously intending to protest.

Mary held up a hand to stop her. "That's what got you in trouble before. It's really what sent you down the path to using, and I don't intend to facilitate that happening again."

"I've changed," Imogene whined. "And I'm flat broke."

Mary needed a strategy. "I can give you a small amount now to tide you over," Mary said. "But I'm not going to be able to support you. You need to get things figured out yourself. If you need money, you'll have to find work." *Not here. Please, not here.*

Imogene's lower lip stuck out the same way it had when she was fifteen. "How much will you give me?"

"Let's talk about it as we walk back to my place," Mary said. "Or better yet, to the shop. I have a lot of work to do."

"How would your customers like to know about your history, what you did?" Imogene said in a snotty voice.

Dread washed over Mary. Her ears seemed to ring with avid, curious questions from the neighbors, and her head hurt with the remembered effort to decide the least hurtful things to say about what had happened. All while she'd been coping with the loss of her precious daughter. Or not coping, really, because how could you ever cope with that? Even brushing up against the edge of that pain made Mary spiral down into the darkest despair.

She had escaped the past, just as she longed to do. That had saved her. Now the past was nudging her again in the form of a very needy, very seedy woman, and Mary had no idea how to handle it.

CHAPTER SIX

THE WEEK AFTER they'd looked at properties sped along, busy with preliminary plans for the program they were calling Victory Cottage, and therapy sessions for Paul, and all the ordinary school and shopping and cleaning of daily life. Suddenly it was Thanksgiving week, and Paul hadn't thought about what to do for the holiday, except that he didn't want to go to his in-laws' house like in years past. Wendy had been the youngest of three, and her sisters had older kids. Georgiana and Ferguson wouldn't be alone.

He and Davey needed to establish new traditions—that was one thing his counseling session had helped him to clarify last week. He just hadn't figured out exactly what those traditions should be.

As it turned out, he didn't have to make a decision and do it all himself, because Pleasant Shores wasn't the kind of place where you could spend a holiday alone. Half the people in town went to a community Thanksgiving dinner at one of the churches, and since he and Davey had attended services, they got called and nagged and harassed into coming.

As soon as they walked into the Fellowship Hall in the church basement, two little girls ran up to Davey. "We're playin' in the gym," one of them said. "Come on!"

"Go ahead," Paul encouraged.

But Davey held on to Paul's hand. "Come in with me?"

"Sure." Paul followed his son into a big room set up for

children to play, with a ball pit, low basketball hoop and easels for painting. At first glance, the place seemed chaotic, packed with kids and teens. But Paul soon figured out that the teenagers were helping the little ones under the supervision of Trey, the cop he'd met on his first awful night here in town, and his wife, Erica.

Had they really been here almost three weeks already? The time had flown by.

Davey clung to Paul's leg, obviously intimidated by all the noise and action, so Paul knelt down beside him. "Want to just watch for a while?"

Davey nodded and leaned into Paul, and a sudden wave of love for his son made his chest hurt. Whatever happened here in town, whatever happened with his career, wherever he ended up, Davey was the center that governed it all. For the hundredth time he vowed to himself to protect his son at all costs, help him grow up strong and happy.

"C'mon, Davey!" This time, a little boy ran over and stood in front of Davey and Paul. "We're playin' cops." He held out his finger and thumb like a gun.

"Cool!" Davey pulled away from Paul and followed the boy toward a cluster of kids on the far side of the room.

Paul's gut twisted a little, but that was what kids did: they tried on roles, pretended to have weapons, played fighting games. He didn't want to make that type of play forbidden fruit, and he couldn't let his own issues stand in the way of Davey growing up like any other kid.

"Looks like you've gotten settled." Trey had come over and was standing beside him.

Paul stood and shook his hand. "Getting there. Davey likes his pre-K class and I've started working on a project for Mary Rhoades." He hesitated, then added, "Listen, thanks again for what you did for us when we arrived in

Pleasant Shores. I'm seeing a counselor and Davey may get some play therapy, too. I'm working on my issues."

"Good man." Trey thumped him lightly on the back. "Go relax, mingle. We've got Davey until dinner starts."

Paul didn't like to leave his son—not only for Davey's safety, but because Davey could be a buffer against people who wanted to know his business or get too friendly. He knew he needed to loosen the strings, though, so he waved Davey over and told him he'd be next door, and that Davey could stay and play until dinner was ready.

He walked through the Fellowship Hall and into the kitchen. Both places were abuzz with people talking and laughing and working together. Nice. Pleasant Shores was too small to hold anything for him long-term, whether he returned to police work or started a new career, but it seemed like a good place to regroup. On Thanksgiving Day, he needed to remember to give thanks for the opportunity.

"Give me a hand with these tables?" a bald man asked, and Paul realized it was Kirk James, the man who'd tried and failed to give Mary a puppy. Paul found himself setting up a whole row of long tables while listening to the man, who kept up a running commentary on all the women they saw. "There's Ria. Pretty, but married. Kim Johnson, she's cute and loves to go out. A little too young for me, but I have her number and I can give it to you. Goody, she runs the ice cream and sandwich shop and I wouldn't advise messing with her. Have you met Lisa Bates? She just went through a breakup and would really appreciate some attention from a man."

"I'm, uh, really not interested in dating just now," Paul said.

Kirk waved a hand. "Heard you lost your wife. Sorry about that. Get back in the saddle, that's what I always say." He grinned. "It's always been my philosophy. All I ask is you stay away from *her*." He gestured at Mary, and his expression went moody. "She's mine. She doesn't know it yet, but she's mine."

Mary *was* one of the most attractive older women Paul had ever seen: slender, with classic bone structure and flowing silver hair. "Pretty sure she's out of my league, anyway," Paul said.

"You're too young for her. Tell you what, you go for the under fifties, and I'll go for the overs." Kirk frowned. "Actually, I'll go for as low as forty-five. Nobody ever believes I'm sixty-eight."

"You don't look it," Paul said truthfully. "Listen, thanks for the tips. I'm going to see if they need help in the kitchen."

"Go ahead," Kirk said magnanimously. "Lots of women in there, too."

Paul chuckled as he went through the door. Kirk's statement proved to be true: the kitchen was full of women stirring and dipping, talking and tasting.

He stood inside the door, feeling a little out of place, but then someone gestured him over to a counter where giant bowls of salad stood ready to be distributed into individual serving bowls. Paul donned the gloves handed to him and then started scooping.

He'd just finished the job when there was a prickling in the back of his neck and at the same time, a baby let out a squawk. He turned, and just as he'd sensed, there was Amber. She was holding a baby, cooing at it, and Paul's breathing hitched. He couldn't take his eyes off her.

She looked up and saw him gawking. "Well, hey, happy Thanksgiving," she said, coming over to him. She gave him a casual hug and a kiss on the cheek.

Once again, his breath seemed to be sucked out of his chest. "Whose baby?" he managed.

"My sister Erica's. This is baby Hunter. He's four months old."

Paul remembered when Davey had been this age. He'd worn a similar pair of tiny overalls, too. Paul took off his glove and held out a finger to the baby, who squeezed it.

A teen girl who looked to be about eighteen marched over and held out her arms. "My turn," she said, and lifted Hunter out of Amber's arms. She walked away, bouncing the baby and whispering to him.

"That's Hunter's biological mother," Amber explained. "She lives in town and is friends with all of us. She gets to see the baby pretty often."

"You looked good holding a baby," Paul blurted out, and then heat spread up his face. What a thing to say.

Amber didn't seem to notice his embarrassment. She sighed. "I loved having a baby," she said. "But I was even younger than Sophia is." She nodded at the young woman who'd taken Hunter. "So it wasn't exactly the right time of life to savor those moments. Everything was a scramble."

The smell of roasting meat filled the air now, as people started pulling turkeys out of the big industrial ovens. The sound of voices from the hall got louder.

Paul and Amber leaned against the counter together, and despite the hustle and bustle going on around them, they seemed to be in their own little bubble.

"You can't have more? You're still young."

"No." She waved a hand at her abdominal area. "The cancer." She looked away from Paul, and then her face softened. "Hi, honey."

A teen about the same age as the one who'd taken the baby put an arm around Amber, and Paul immediately saw the resemblance.

"You're all hot." Amber touched the teen's sweaty curls.

"You've got your work cut out for you, helping with the kids, huh?"

"They're wild. I had to take a break."

"Paul," Amber said, turning toward him, "this is my daughter, Hannah. She's a college student, home for the Thanksgiving break." Her voice was full of pride. "And I didn't make her come and help today. She volunteered."

"I'm glad to meet you." He held out a hand, stepping out of the way of someone who'd started putting salad bowls on a big tray.

Hannah shook hands, but her eyes were narrowed.

"Our neighbor for the moment," Amber explained. "He's in the Healing Heroes cottage, along with his son, Davey."

"You might have met Davey in among the wild kids," Paul said. "Ravens shirt and freckles. Last I saw, he was playing cops."

"I saw him. Cute kid." Hannah tilted her head to one side as if she was sizing Paul up. Her gaze flickered to her mother, then back to him.

"Not as cute as you are." Amber gave Hannah a quick hug. "I'm so glad you're home."

"Me, too," Hannah said. "We'll do some fun things together this weekend, right? Just us girls."

To Paul, it sounded like a marking of territory, and that was fine with him. Amber *should* spend time with her daughter. Not with him. Because Amber as a mother was just as compelling as adventurer Amber was, though in a completely different way.

HE'S ACTING WEIRD. Amber didn't know what to make of the way Paul kept looking at her and then looking away. So after Hannah had gone back to hang with the young people, Amber nudged him and led him over to the turkeys.

"I think we need a man to start carving," she said, looking up at him. "Are you up for it?" Even as she said it, she was aware that she was both flirting *and* being sexist. A woman could just as well carve turkeys as a man could.

His gaze dropped to her lips for a fraction of a second, so quickly she wasn't sure if she'd seen it. "Sure, I can do that." His voice was matter-of-fact.

Yeah, she'd imagined it. "I can help, but I'm no good with knives," she said. "You carve and I'll make it look pretty."

They worked, with Paul cutting thin slices and Amber piling them into the metal trays to go back in the oven and stay warm.

For whatever reason, she was curious about this man. With her hands busy, she felt freer to ask him questions. "Did you and Wendy hope to have more kids, before she got sick?"

She glanced up in time to see the corners of his mouth turn down. "I did," he said slowly, "and I think she did, too. But we were having some problems."

The reality of what she'd thoughtlessly asked hit Amber like a giant rock, almost taking her breath away. She pretended to drop something on the floor and bent down to pick it up, trying to compose herself.

Paul didn't actually have *any* biological children because Davey wasn't his biological child, if Wendy's confession was to be believed.

Wendy had confided in Amber because she'd been near the end of her life, thinking about dying. Amber hadn't invited the confidence, but she hadn't been able to bring herself to cut off Wendy's halting words, either. And when Wendy had called her the next day in a panic, regretting what she'd revealed and begging Amber to keep the secret, Amber had readily agreed.

The request, the whole situation, had made her sad. Despite her wild reputation, Amber had always been a one-man woman. She knew, of course, that there were people who cheated on their partners. But Paul had seemed like a devoted husband and good father, even in the few minutes she'd talked with him. Why would his wife seek out someone else? It didn't make sense.

But she'd heard the pain and remorse in Wendy's voice, understood that the woman's conscience was sharpened by her imminent death. Wendy's actions weren't hers to judge. Amber would never have published the information in her book, of course, which seemed to be what Wendy had feared.

Anyway, Amber hadn't expected to see Wendy or her family again.

What were the odds that she'd end up living next door to Paul, knowing Davey, and truth to tell, being incredibly drawn to both of them?

"Daddy?" The small voice came from the kitchen door and Paul wiped his hands and headed in that direction immediately, with that radar all parents seemed to have.

Amber watched as he knelt to talk to his son, listened, laughed and then swung Davey into his arms. She wasn't the only female watching the scene with appreciation, either. Was there anything more appealing than an involved daddy and a cute little kid?

Mary came up beside her to finish the carving, and she was watching Paul and Davey, too. "He seems like a good man," she said.

Amber nodded. "I think so." It was true. And not only was he good, but he was getting better; he already seemed much calmer than the first time they'd met. "The Healing Heroes program is working, it seems."

"I'm glad." Mary smiled, looking satisfied. "The Healing Heroes program means a lot to me. Makes me happy to see an officer getting his life back."

The intensity in Mary's voice caught Amber's attention, and she was glad to look away from Paul and Davey. "I never thought to ask," she said, "but what made you decide to start the Healing Heroes program?"

Mary smiled, but her face was a little sad. "Police officers have been a help to me several times in the past. I wanted to give back." She gestured toward Paul. "I don't suppose he'd be willing to let me watch Davey while he carries these trays for us, would he? He seems very…strong."

"He does." Paul's muscles were on display as he picked up Davey again, and Amber had to force herself to look away. "But I'm sure that, between us, we can carry the trays."

"Good point, dear. We're hardly helpless." So they each took an end of a tray and carried it over to the oven.

Determinedly, Amber turned the conversation away from Paul. "Whatever happened with the puppy Kirk brought by?" she asked.

"He took him right back. I don't want another dog." Mary didn't sound convincing, but Amber was all too familiar with having people interfere in her life. She wasn't going to do that to Mary. She was really getting to like the woman. Mary seemed to have managed single life well for a long time, and it was obvious there was real depth behind the older woman's glamorous exterior.

"If you don't want a puppy, what *do* you want?" she asked Mary. "What's your big dream?"

Mary dipped her chin and raised her eyebrows. "Not

everyone acknowledges that someone my age could have a dream, so thank you, dear." She hesitated, then added, "As for my dream, I'm just trying to clean up the past."

It was hard to imagine what a woman like Mary would need to clean up, but from her work interviewing people for her book, Amber knew that people held all kinds of secrets beneath the surface. "Is that anything to do with the woman who was stalking us the other day?"

Mary heaved a huge sigh. "It's everything to do with her," she said, "but unfortunately, I can't tell you any more than that."

Amber nodded and busied herself arranging plates of dessert for the buffet line. She wasn't going to pry. Mary had the right to her secrets, like anybody else.

Except maybe Amber, who was keeping a secret that wasn't her own from the person to whom it would matter the most.

CHAPTER SEVEN

ON THE SATURDAY after Thanksgiving, Mary held her cell phone away from her ear as Imogene ranted on. It was the third call in a week and a half, and this time, in addition to needing money, Imogene was claiming to be upset that Mary hadn't cooked a Thanksgiving dinner. "I'm family, after all," she whined. "I was all by myself, all day."

Mary sighed. Actually, she had invited Imogene to the community dinner. Not because she'd wanted her around, but because she'd felt sorry for Imogene. The younger woman was a stranger in town, alone, with nowhere to go for the holiday. But the fact that it was held in a church had turned Imogene off.

Mary didn't point that out, though. She knew from experience that arguing with her stepdaughter didn't work. In that regard, Imogene hadn't changed a whole lot from the hormonal, angry teenager she'd been when Mary had married her father.

Besides, Mary was tired. Yesterday had been a huge shopping day, of course—Black Friday happened in Pleasant Shores, just like it did in cities—and she'd been in the store for twelve hours. She'd done two story times for the kids, giving their parents a chance to shop in peace. It had all been fun, but exhausting.

A knock sounded at her door and when Mary looked out, she saw Erica Harrison and her big white goldendoodle, Ziggy. Just seeing the pair lifted Mary's spirits, and she felt a smile cross her face. "I'm sorry, Imogene, but I have to go."

"Why? We haven't finished talking." Imogene continued explaining why she needed money, now in particular, at least a little, because she was broke.

Mary listened for another minute, wondering where the five hundred dollars she'd given Imogene just before Thanksgiving had gone, while she beckoned Erica in. "No, really, my answer hasn't changed and I have someone here at the house I need to talk with."

"But—"

"Bye, Imogene," she said gently. She ended the call, blew out a breath, and then hugged Erica and rubbed Ziggy's ears. The dog was so big she didn't even need to bend over to do it. "It's great to see you two. What brings you to Sunset Lane?"

"I was walking by, trying to give this big boy some exercise, and I realized I haven't seen Mr. James in quite a while. Wondered if you could watch Ziggy while I have a short visit with him? It's hard to focus when I'm making sure Ziggy doesn't knock the poor man over."

"I would be honored. You know I love dogs."

"Don't tell him," Erica whispered, holding her hands over Ziggy's floppy ears, "but he's having surgery tomorrow. It's past time to neuter him."

"Oh, dear. Extra treats today." Mary went to the cookie jar that still held Baby's treats and pulled out a handful. "These are tiny, but they're gourmet."

"He'll love them. Thanks so much," Erica said. She looked out Mary's front door. "Oh, look, there are Kirk and Mr. James right now."

Mary stepped backward into the kitchen. "I'm kind of

hiding from Kirk. Don't tell him I'm home." It made her feel like a bad neighbor, but seriously, the man hadn't stopped bothering her since he had taken a notion to ask her out.

"My lips are sealed. I'll wait till they get inside before I go over there."

They both watched out the window while Kirk helped Mr. James up the steps, pausing with him to rest, then saying something that made them break out in identical, loud laughs.

It was a good sound, a good sight. "I shouldn't fault Kirk," Mary said. "I should be nicer to him. He takes care of his father without a word of complaint."

"Not many men can do that. How old is Mr. James, do you think?"

"At least ninety-three. He served in World War II. And he's in great shape for his age, but he doesn't drive anymore and he has trouble with stairs."

A thought flashed through Mary's mind: Who would take care of *her* if she were lucky enough to reach her nineties? She shook it away, though, as something to think about at a much later date.

"Okay, they're inside. I'm going to head over, but I'll be back in half an hour."

"Take an hour. I love having Ziggy here."

As soon as Erica left, Mary looked at her cell phone to see three messages from Imogene. Her stomach curdled.

The woman wouldn't take no for an answer, and she was downright nasty about it. Mary sank onto the couch, and Ziggy leaned against her, panting.

The love of a dog. She remembered how Baby had always known when to jump into her lap, how comforting she had been. If only Baby were here now.

Her eyes ached with tears she was determined not to shed. Crying didn't solve anything. And she needed to solve this problem. She needed to figure out what to do about Imogene, who seemed to be settling into town.

Her threats to reveal everything about Mary's past were getting more pointed. She was endangering Mary's place in this cozy home and warm community that Mary loved, the business she'd built from the ground up.

A nasty inner demon bit at her. Yes, Imogene was endangering her life here, only that life was fake. No one in Pleasant Shores knew what she was really like, what had happened.

Ziggy gave her hand a delicate lick. He looked at her with big, brown, nonjudgmental eyes, and she leaned down and wrapped her arms around him.

She did let a few tears fall then. Couldn't help it, and she had a good sympathy companion in Ziggy, who just sighed and leaned harder against her. It was probably healthy to let out her sadness and worry in the safety of the big gold-endoodle's company. He would tell no tales.

Suddenly, an idea came to her, and she lifted her head, thinking, putting it all together.

That little blue cottage next door to the soon-to-be Victory Cottage, which Amber had discovered was a short-term rental. She'd been thinking of using it to expand the program in some way, but she hadn't figured out how.

Now, she thought about how comforting Ziggy was, and how comforting Baby had been.

Maybe this was something else to spend more of her money on and help people, before Imogene found a way to take it all.

Erica knew all about therapy dog training from going through it with Ziggy. Come to think of it, so did Sunny, a teenager who lived on the waterfront, Bisky's daughter.

Creating a therapy dog program to go with the program for crime victims couldn't happen right away; that would be too much. But she could lay the groundwork, make the initial purchase.

Protect the money from Imogene.

And eventually, if everything fell into place, they would have a therapy dog program at Victory Cottage.

ON THE SUNDAY after Thanksgiving, Amber and Hannah stopped at the local general store to pick up a few things Hannah needed for college. Amber tried not to think about the fact that Hannah was leaving.

It's all good. Hannah was doing well in school, making friends, gaining independence. She had terrific scholarships that were paying most of her tuition. True, the house would feel empty once Hannah had gone back. True, Amber would have fewer hugs and fewer laughs and no one to binge-watch reality TV with when she couldn't sleep.

Don't impose those feelings on Hannah.

So Amber focused on this moment, what she could do now. "It's so much colder up in New York. I know we got you the basic clothes, but what about these thermal gloves? You're going to be walking across campus a lot and I don't want you to freeze."

Hannah shrugged. "I don't care."

Amber tossed the gloves into her basket. "Hot chocolate mix, canned chili, ramen noodles. Stuff to keep you warm when you don't feel like going all the way to the cafeteria."

Around them, the store bustled. Parents tried to keep kids from touching the toys in the little toy section, and a couple of guys in work clothes seemed to be in a hot discussion of nails and screws and bolts. A white-haired woman carried a box of canning jars toward the checkout counter, struggling a little under the heavy load. Amber took a step toward her, but before she could offer to help, a store employee hurried over and took the box out of the woman's hands.

Amber led Hannah over to the area that housed yarn and thread and buttons. "Do you ever use that little sewing kit we bought?"

Hannah had followed her, but she didn't answer. When Amber looked over she saw immediately that her daughter was trying to hold back tears. "What's wrong, honey?"

Hannah made a squeaky little sound and her face twisted.

"What is it?" Amber put a hand on her daughter's arm, her own heart hurting in response to Hannah's emotion.

"I don't want to go back," Hannah choked out. "I want to live at home and go to community college."

"What?" Amber had been so focused on managing her own feelings that she'd had no idea Hannah was ambivalent about going back. "Where is this coming from? You love school!"

"B-b-but I want to come back and live at home." Hannah was openly crying now.

Amber put down the shopping basket. Warm gloves and hot chocolate mix would have to wait. "Come on, let's go over to Goody's and talk."

Hannah didn't protest, and Amber led her to the restaurant and directly to a table in the corner. Goody gave them a sour look, probably because they didn't immediately order food, but Amber made a thumbs-up sign to her. "We'll order in a minute," she said, and Goody nodded without smiling.

Goody had been particularly grouchy for the past couple of weeks, which was strange. But for now, Amber couldn't wonder about it. She needed to figure out what was going on with her daughter.

Amber pulled a couple of tissues from her purse and handed them to Hannah. As Hannah blew her nose, Amber tried to read her body language. Was this a serious issue, or was Hannah just having a clingy moment?

But Hannah's upset was definitely lasting more than a moment. "Is there something wrong at college that you're not telling me? Something with your friends, your studies? A boy?"

"It's not that." Hannah blew her nose again. "I just miss you. I miss Aunt Erica, and baby Hunter is going to grow up without even knowing me, and I'm afraid…" She broke off.

"What else?" Amber asked, though she had a feeling she knew.

"It's just that…you're sick. What if you need me and I'm not here?"

Amber's heart ached. How she hated it that her daughter had to deal with her mother's serious illness at such a young age, when she should be focused only on herself, her studies, her friends. "I'm doing really well now. I'm fine." At times like this, she wished Hannah had a dad. Of course, Hannah did have a father, but Amber hadn't heard from him in years and had no idea of where he was. Off the grid somewhere if he was even still alive. She'd liked the rebel type, back in the day.

And she wouldn't change a single aspect of Hannah's father's personality, because she wouldn't change a single aspect of her sensitive, smart, thoughtful daughter.

"I'm worried about you," Hannah said. "People were talking in church about how skinny you are."

Amber could have strangled whoever was insensitive enough to speculate about Amber's health in front of her daughter. "Who was talking about that?"

"Well, Primrose was," Hannah said. Primrose Miller was the church organist and a major gossip.

"Consider the source. You know I'm doing really well. And I have Erica here to help me if I need anything."

"But she's busy taking care of Hunter." Hannah sniffed. "And he's growing up without me, and you put off your trip, and I'm afraid you're going to die!"

Amber's stomach tensed, but then she processed her daughter's words, her sudden, extreme emotion. "First of all, I'm not dying. Are you having your period?"

"I can't believe you said that!" Hannah said indignantly. And then she let out a rueful sigh. "But yeah. I am."

Amber stifled a smile. "Then why aren't we eating chocolate? Let me go get us a couple of milkshakes while you blow your nose and wipe your tears." She handed over the pack of tissues from her purse—did any mom ever stop carrying them?—and left Hannah wiping her eyes and checking her makeup on her phone.

Amber brought two large milkshakes back to the table and they both sat quietly drinking them for a few minutes as befitted their rich, creamy, deeply chocolaty glory.

Reluctantly, Amber pulled herself out of the pleasures of the milkshake to address Hannah's one legitimate concern. "I did put off my travel, honey," she said. "I talked with my doctor, and she thought it was safer for me to stay home where I can get the tests I need, when I need them. It's just a precaution. I wish I didn't have to be careful, but I do. It's what's going to keep me healthy."

Hannah studied her face. "You're not hiding something the doctors found?"

"Nope." Although Amber hadn't shared every detail, she felt she could say that much honestly.

Hannah sucked down more of her milkshake. "So tell me about Paul," she said out of left field.

"What about him?" Amber tilted her head to one side, confused. "He lives in the Healing Heroes cottage with his son, Davey."

"I know that." Hannah looked at her with narrowed eyes.

"I also know he likes you. And I think you like him, too. Are you guys seeing each other?"

Amber let the question hang in the air too long. Around them, more customers were coming into the shop, the late-Sunday-afternoon rush before the place closed. The smell of crab cakes frying joined the fudge and baked goods fragrances.

"Well?" Now Hannah looked more suspicious.

"Are you kidding? You know me. I don't do in-depth relationships. I want to focus on—"

"You can't use that excuse anymore—that you just want to focus on me. I'm away at college most of the time."

And God willing, she'd go back to school tomorrow and this worried phase would be short and sweet. "True," she said, "but you're still my focus. Or maybe I just don't do that kind of relationship regardless."

"Mom. What kind of role model are you for me? What if I said I didn't do serious relationships?"

"*You* should do long-term relationships, when you're ready. You're so lovable and beautiful and smart." She reached out and squeezed Hannah's hand. "Any boy would be lucky to even go out on a date with you, let alone have you for the long-term."

"And are you saying you're not lovable?"

The question startled Amber. "Well… No. Of course not." But the reassuring words weren't quite true. Amber had had plenty of relationships—too many—but men liked her for how she looked or how fun and carefree she was. And now, when she was a little more haggard and a little less carefree, she probably wasn't going to have even those kinds of relationships.

Which was fine. Absolutely fine. She was growing beyond them. She liked her independence.

"Back to Paul. The way he looks at you, it's not just for your gorgeous body."

Amber frowned down at her skinny self, pictured the scars beneath her shirt. "Oh, right, so gorgeous." Then she tilted her head to the side and looked at her daughter. "Wait, how does he look at me?"

Hannah snickered. "Like you're a chocolate milkshake and he's on his period," she said. "I wish someone would look at me like that."

That made Amber giggle. "Drink your milkshake," she said. She opened her mouth to explain that she couldn't get involved with Paul, or any man, due to the cancer threat, but she didn't want to say that to Hannah, because she didn't want Hannah to worry about her mom's illness.

"When I next come home," Hannah said, "I want you to be dating someone seriously. If not Paul, then somebody else." She sucked up the last of her milkshake.

"Who's the mom here?" It was a joke between them, because Hannah had a major responsible, maternal side and liked to take care of her mother.

Love for her beautiful daughter filled Amber's heart. "You're going back to school, okay? I don't think you really want to go to the community college with half the kids you went to high school with." Hannah had inherited a little of Amber's own sense of adventure, and she was considering study abroad, which the community college didn't offer.

Hannah smiled. "I'll go back if you promise to do what I say. Start dating again, and not just the big dumb ones."

"Hannah!"

"Am I wrong?"

"Well…no. No, you're not." Amber had dated way too many guys whose biceps were bigger than their brains. Whereas Paul had plenty of both. "No promises, but I'll think about it."

CHAPTER EIGHT

"IT WAS GOOD of you to be willing to work over here," Paul said to Amber Monday morning, across a dining room table full of papers and drawings. "I was surprised to find out Davey's school is closed today. Stretching out the holiday weekend."

He didn't add that it was good to have her in his home, on a casual basis, sharing coffee and working together. He didn't need to be thinking about how good that part felt.

"Mary seems to be in a big hurry on the project," Amber said. "And I'm a mom. I get that sometimes schools and day cares aren't open and you need to get creative."

Her slightly husky voice played along his nerve endings. *I'd like to get creative with you.*

As soon as the thought entered his mind, he shooed it away. Totally inappropriate. It was just that she was so pretty, the sunlight from the window playing on her hair, her full lips curving into a smile.

What was that smile about, anyway? Was she reading his mind?

Heat rose up his neck. What was wrong with him, thinking that way about a working partner, someone with whom he could never let things get personal?

Davey came over and leaned against Paul's leg. "Can we go outside?"

"Later on, buddy," Paul said. "Let me put on another

movie for you." He didn't feel great about using the screen as a babysitter, but sometimes it was the best you could do.

"I want to go outside!" Davey's lower lip stuck out.

Sarge came to the other side of his chair and nudged at him as if adding his agreement to Davey's plea.

"No whining," Paul said firmly. "We'll go outside this afternoon. For now, you can color or play quietly or watch a movie."

Davey kicked at the table leg, walked over to the living room and threw himself on the floor, head buried in his hands.

Sarge nudged Paul's hand again and then loped over to Davey and flopped down beside him.

"They're hard to resist," Amber said, then added in a low voice, "We could take them outside and let them play while we talk this through."

"Thanks. I may take you up on that once we have the start of a plan."

"Sounds good." They studied the floor plan of the cottage Mary was pretty sure she wanted to buy, the one they'd all visited the other day. It seemed perfect to Paul, with the way it backed onto the water, had a fenced front yard and was big enough for a whole family.

"You know," Amber said, "we should plan a really fun play area for Victory Cottage. Somewhere a kid would love to be. That makes a huge difference to a parent."

She paused. "Of course, the kids could be any age from Davey or younger all the way up to Hannah's age."

"Big-screen TV," Paul said promptly.

Amber shook her head. "Kids are too attached to their screens. It destroys their creativity." She looked over at Davey, who'd changed the TV channel and was watching *SpongeBob*. "I mean, I get it. We all need a break, however

we can make it happen. The cottage should for sure have a
TV. I just don't think a screen should dominate a room for
kids, especially kids who are trying to heal."

"How about a screen inside a cupboard, as a compro-
mise?" Paul suggested. "Like in hotel rooms."

She lifted a shoulder. "Okay. I can accept that, if we can
make the rest of the area so appealing that they forget to
open the cupboard."

They talked about ways to do that, including an art sta-
tion, a foosball table and video games for teenagers, and
shelves of board games the whole family could play.

Amber seemed so healthy and full of energy and life. It
struck Paul that she'd be a great person to have a family with.
She seemed like the type who'd always be up for a silly board
game, who wouldn't mind if the kids' paint spattered onto the
carpet or a carelessly thrown ball knocked over a glass of milk.

The way he was thinking about how pretty she was, the
way he was imagining being in a family with her...some
part of him was reemerging after a season underground,
like the green shoots that showed up in a garden in spring.

He looked at her, head bent over the room sketch she
was drawing, tip of her tongue in the corner of her mouth,
slight fragrance of flowers emanating from her hair. His
heart felt like it was physically reaching out of his chest,
reaching for her. Longing racked him.

Maybe this could work.

Paul's front door opened at the same time the doorbell
rang, and his fantasies dissolved into tense muscles and a
racing heart and sweaty palms. He stood, and it took him
a minute to realize he didn't have a gun to grab. He strode
to the door as a cheery "yoo-hoo" came from outside.

"Hello, hello!" Georgiana said gaily as soon as he'd
pulled the door all the way open. "Surprise!"

"Grammy! Grandpa!"

Paul put a hand on an end table to steady his suddenly sagging limbs. "Don't burst in on me like that." He pulled out the handkerchief he'd taken to carrying and wiped the sweat that had broken out on his forehead.

Georgiana stiffened at his tone. "He's angry again," she said over her shoulder.

"Not angry, just—"

"Daddy won't play with me! Will you play with me?" Davey clung to Ferguson's leg. "Can we go out in the jeep? And take Sarge?"

"We have an even better idea," Ferguson said. "We've come to take you home with us for a couple of days! We can go to the car show and the toy store and the arcade by our house!"

"Yay!" Davey raised his hands in the air and hopped from one foot to the other. "When are we leaving? Can Sarge come?"

Paul pinched the bridge of his nose. "Wait. No."

Georgiana's whole face tightened. "What's wrong?"

He held out a hand to Davey. "Why don't you run to the kitchen and get your grandparents a couple of cookies from the snack drawer." He wasn't kidding himself that Ferguson and Georgiana wanted his stale animal crackers, but he wanted to get Davey out of the room so they could discuss this.

As soon as he was gone, Paul faced his in-laws. "You can't just show up unannounced and take Davey."

"He just said you won't play with him," Ferguson said reasonably. And then he and Georgiana sidled past Paul and into the open-plan living-dining room. They both seemed to see Amber at the same time.

They glanced at each other and went still.

Paul walked into the living room, too, and looked out the

big picture window at the sparkling bay, the sailboats, the gulls, reaching for calm. "You need to call in advance," he said quietly to Ferguson. "I can't let you take him."

"Now, now, we drove all the way out here." Ferguson frowned. "Surely you're not going to tell us to turn around and go home?"

Amber stood and came into the living room area. "Sounds like you have family things to discuss," she said easily. "I'll head out."

"No need," Paul said firmly. "We'd planned to work on Mary's project together this morning, and that's what we'll do. That way, Mary can look at it tonight and make her final decision tomorrow."

Amber bit her lip, and then they were all frozen in an awkward tableau. Davey broke it by running in and thrusting a package of animal crackers at Georgiana, who took it with two fingers as if it might be contaminated.

"Look," Paul said to Ferguson and Georgiana. "You can stay and play with him for a few minutes. An hour, even. But I can't drop my work, and you can't take him along."

"C'mon, Grandpa, let's drive the jeep!" Davey tugged at Ferguson's hand. The older man shrugged and let Davey lead him toward the back door.

"I'll just be next door once you get things worked out," Amber said. Obviously, she wasn't going to listen to his plea and stay, and he couldn't blame her.

Once Ferguson, Davey and Amber had left, Georgiana beckoned to the couch. "We need to talk."

"Yes, we do," Paul said, and sat down heavily. "You can't pull stunts like this. I know you were upset that we didn't come for Thanksgiving dinner—"

"It's all part of your illness," Georgiana said. "Isolating yourself from the family, and isolating your son. It's not good, Paul." She drew in a breath. "We think we can provide better care."

Paul didn't get it. "Better care for what? What does that mean?"

"Better care overall," she said. "We've been talking to our lawyer."

A roaring noise started in Paul's ears. "What?"

Georgiana patted his arm. "We're just exploring the idea, for now," she said, "but we'd like to work toward having at least partial custody of our grandson."

"No!" He stared at her, his whole body tensing at the notion of being separated from Davey for part of each week, like some of the divorced families he knew. "Why would you even say that?"

"You have to admit," she said, "things aren't going well for you, Paul. We can provide so much more. And we think Wendy would have wanted us to have Davey." She smiled at him, a shaky, stiff smile. "Just think about it. The last thing we want is a court battle."

Paul tried to relax his fists, breathed deeply to keep his calm. They might not want a court battle, but that was what they'd get if they tried to take custody of Davey away from him.

ON TUESDAY MORNING, Mary walked toward the cottage she was already calling Victory Cottage in her mind. Paul and Amber had done background work and recommended it strongly for the new program. Today, she was to meet her real estate agent there and make a final decision. Her head was spinning, but she'd pretty much decided she wanted to go forward with it.

Paul and Amber had all kinds of good ideas for the property, and listening to them, she'd been wholly convinced that buying it and renovating it for the new program was the right move.

Too bad Paul wasn't as happy as she and Amber were at the prospect of finalizing the purchase. When they'd talked over coffee earlier this morning, Paul had been as jumpy as a feral cat.

More than that, she'd once again detected a vibe between them that was almost certainly intense attraction. She wondered where that would go, whether that was why Paul seemed on edge. Maybe he wanted something to happen between them and Amber didn't.

But there was no time to speculate on other people's romantic relationships. She had a house to buy.

It was a cloudy December day, quite chilly, and for a moment, she wondered whether the business model was a good one. Buy up property, put it to good and charitable use during the off-season, and make the money during the tourist season to support it. That was the plan, and it seemed to be working for the Healing Heroes cottage, which had been rented out steadily for the past two high seasons with rates that would pay the mortgage the rest of the year.

It would be sustainable even when she was gone, and that was her goal.

The only issue was the gloomy weather during the off-season. But most places had gray skies at this time of year, and plenty were chillier than the Eastern Shore of Maryland.

She headed up the sidewalk and tapped on the storm door. There was her real estate agent coming to the door, along with...Kirk James, holding a stack of paperwork? Really?

Heather opened the door for her. "I hope you don't mind, but since you want everything pushed through quickly, I brought my mentor. He's the one who knows how to do that."

Kirk dipped his chin and looked at her over his reading

glasses, some kind of challenge in his eyes. He knew she didn't want to work with him, be with him, of course he did; he wasn't stupid. It was just that he had a sales background, which fit his personality, and he wasn't used to taking no for an answer.

At the same time, as Julie had said, male pride was sensitive. And he was offering up his time and expertise without any real hope of a return on his investment. "I appreciate that, Kirk," she said, and suddenly her last little bit of doubt was gone. "I do want it pushed through. Let's get an inspection, make an offer, all of it."

Heather glanced at Kirk, then back at Mary. "Um, can I ask why everything needs to go through in a hurry?"

No, you can't. She didn't say that, of course. That was a small town; everyone knew some of your business and wanted to know more. "I have my reasons," she said. "Leave it at that."

"All right," Kirk said. "I'll need to make some calls. What's your deadline?"

"The sooner, the better." They walked through the cottage one more time and talked about some more of the details. Then all three of them headed into town together. The real estate office was just down the street from the bookstore; everything was close together in Pleasant Shores.

The sun was peeking through the clouds now, and Mary's mood was improving, too. This was going to work, and if it did, a weight would be lifted from Mary's shoulders. If she could get the house purchased for this project, that would be one bunch of money Imogene couldn't access. And maybe, if this worked…maybe she'd finally feel like she'd done enough and could stand up to her stepdaughter. "I really appreciate you taking the time to work on this, Kirk," she said.

He smiled. "Not a problem." In this mode, being businesslike rather than predatory, he was actually an appealing man.

Mary was feeling so good about things that it took her a minute to process why, as they got close to the bookstore, her heart was sinking. Then she froze.

There was Imogene. In the doorway, waiting for her. Mary's feeling of hopefulness faded away and the day seemed to get darker.

Kirk and Heather had walked on, but now they looked back, saw her standing there unmoving, and stopped. "Are you okay?" Heather asked.

"I'm fine." Slowly, miserably, she took a step toward the bookstore and Imogene, then another.

Imogene gave a glance toward Kirk and Heather and then focused on Mary. "Where have you been?"

Her rude tone goaded Mary out of her passive misery. "Did we have a plan to get together today?"

Imogene didn't answer her question. Her skin sagged and dark circles resided under her eyes. "I need to talk to you."

"All right." Mary squared her shoulders. "We can talk in the store."

"Now, just a minute." Kirk squared his shoulders, walked over to them and put a protective arm around Mary. "Who is this woman? Do you want to speak with her?"

No. "It's fine," she said.

"You heard her." Imogene lifted her chin, curled her lip and turned toward the door of the bookstore, bumping Mary's shoulder in a move that clearly wasn't an accident.

"Hey." Kirk grasped Imogene's arm. "I don't like the way you're treating her. Show some respect."

"To my elders?" Imogene sneered and jerked her arm

away. "I'll show respect when they deserve respect. So far, I don't see it."

"Now listen here." Kirk took a step toward Imogene, looming over her.

"No, you listen, old man." Imogene propped her hands on her hips. "I need to talk to my stepmother, and you need to step aside." As she spoke, Mary caught a whiff of alcohol on her breath.

Dread pressed down on Mary. Imogene had just revealed their stepmother-stepdaughter relationship. What else might she reveal if provoked, and with even fewer inhibitions than usual due to drinking?

She put a hand on Kirk's arm. "It's okay, truly. We have things to discuss."

He studied her with narrowed eyes. "I don't like it," he said, and gave Imogene a glare. "You have my phone number, Mary. Don't hesitate to use it. I can be here in five minutes."

"And you have mine," Heather jumped in, sounding nervous. Imogene was the type of woman who scared other women, always had been. She'd been a terrible bully in school.

"I have your numbers. Thanks for your help today." She gave Heather and Kirk each a reassuring smile. "Let's get right on the...project. I don't want to waste any time."

"Will do," Kirk said, and Heather nodded. They both walked off, Kirk glancing back over his shoulder to glare at Imogene.

"Come on in," Mary said to Imogene, feeling like a giant rock was pressing down on her. Judging by Imogene's angry expression, Kirk had succeeded in making things worse.

All the same, when she glanced back to see his square shoulders as he walked away, she felt a strange urge to run after him.

CHAPTER NINE

FROM THE CHAIR where she'd been browsing travel books—
of which Lighthouse Lit had a great collection—Amber
watched Mary cross the store with the same hard-faced,
dark-haired woman who'd bothered Mary when they'd first
looked at Victory Cottage. She frowned at Julie, who was
behind the counter. "Who's that woman?" she asked as soon
as the two had disappeared into the back room.

"I don't know," Julie said, "but she's acting weird and so
is Mary. Neither one of them even said hello."

Amber raised an eyebrow. "Should we investigate?" she
asked. Julie was always up for anything.

"I think we should." A dimple showed in Julie's cheek.
"And maybe we should split them up. You take Mary, and
I'll take the mean lady."

"Done." Amber set her book down, stood and headed to
the area behind the cash register. The stockroom was dim,
but there was a light on in the small office.

She was glad of the distraction, really. She felt at loose
ends. After their work session had been interrupted yesterday, she'd written up some plans and emailed them to Paul,
and he'd added suggestions and sent them back to her. No
personal note, no mention of his pushy in-laws; just strictly
business. They'd hammered out enough of a plan, by email,
to send to Mary. Over coffee this morning, they'd talked
things through, but Paul had been tense and impersonal.

The good news was that Mary had liked their recommen-
dations. She'd planned to visit the place one more time and
then make an offer. Most likely, that was what she'd been
doing with Kirk James and that other woman who worked
in the real estate office.

Now, with Hannah back in school, Amber needed to get
going on a new project. Probably a different book project,
which was why she was leafing through travel and medical books here in the shop.

But she couldn't get very serious about it, not yet. So
it sounded like fun to occupy herself with Mary and her
problems.

She reached the doorway of Mary's office. "Hey, Mary,"
Amber said, "sorry to bother you, but I need help with the
travel books." She looked around the office. Mary was
seated behind the small desk, and the other woman had
pulled up a chair, so close she was almost blocking Mary in.

"Julie can help you, dear." Mary's voice was strained.

"Actually, I can't," Julie said from behind Amber. "I'm
a real dolt with the ordering system, you know that. And
we've got Henry Higbottom on the line, demanding to know
when his books will come in. You know how persistent
he can be."

Mary got to her feet. Her shoulders were slumped and
she looked uncharacteristically frail. "I'll be right back,"
she said, sidling around the other woman.

"You didn't even introduce me," the dark-haired woman
said in a tone that was…disrespectful? Mocking? Amber
didn't like it.

Mary sighed. "Amber, Julie, I'd like for you to meet
Imogene," she said. "Be right back," she repeated to the
woman, and trudged toward the front of the store.

Amber followed her, hearing Julie's attempt to converse

with the woman behind her: "Pleased to meet you!" and "Would you like a cup of coffee or tea?" But Amber didn't hear any response to Julie's cheerful voice. All the more reason to check in with Mary.

"Are you all right?" Amber asked Mary as soon as they were over by the travel books.

"Of course, I'm fine. Now, what exactly were you looking for?"

"Julie and I thought you seemed upset, or something, and we're not sure we like your guest. I know you said there was no problem with her when we talked before, but she seems... I don't know. We're concerned."

Mary put her hands on her hips and glared at Amber. "So this travel book thing was a fake request?"

"I'm sorry," Amber said, although she wasn't. "Is there anything we can do to help you get rid of her?"

Mary blew out a breath with a little *pfft* sound. "I wish. But no. She's my problem to deal with, and speaking of that, I need to get back to her."

"Just wait one second." Amber put a hand on the older woman's arm. "You're not all alone, you know. You have friends who want to help with any problem you have."

"I don't want help." Mary's voice was gentle, but she stepped around Amber, lifting her chin.

"But..."

"I appreciate you and Julie, but my problems are my own to solve." Mary headed to the back of the store, straightening her spine.

A moment later, Julie came out and shook her head. "No luck," she said as she came over to Amber. "She's cagey. Wouldn't talk."

Amber's eyes narrowed. "I didn't like the way she looked at Mary, and she seemed rude when she spoke to her."

"Oh, I agree," Julie said. "But what can we do about it? Unless…"

"Tell me."

"They looked like they were going to wind up," Julie said. "When they come out, I'll grab Mary, and you try to talk to Imogene. Find out what she wants from Mary. You're…" She broke off, looking sheepish.

"Pushier?" Amber grinned. "You're right. I'll see what I can find out."

"She's going to be mad at us," Julie said. "It's not our business who she visits with in her own shop."

"True. But when friends are in trouble or sad or being mistreated…I'd rather interfere than leave them alone, and later wish I'd done something."

Julie puttered around shelving books while Amber skimmed through a couple of thrillers, looking for a distraction and not finding it.

A few minutes later, Julie hurried toward Amber. "They're coming!"

"You keep Mary busy."

Julie nodded and walked over. "Staffing emergency," she said. "Michael called in sick, so we've got no one to work the evening shift."

Amber strolled over to Imogene, who had started leafing idly—and a bit roughly—through one of the books on the pet display. "So, how do you know Mary?" she asked. "We're crazy about her."

"What do *you* want?" Imogene glared at her.

Whoa. Not only rude, but without class or manners.

Still, if Amber wanted to find anything out, she had to make nice, so she shrugged. "Just killing time in a boring town," she said. She'd known people like Imogene, and she wasn't bothered by rudeness. But she didn't like the idea of the woman harassing Mary.

"It sure is boring," Imogene agreed, sneering toward the window.

"If you're here for a while and like to go out, I'm always looking for company. There's not much nightlife, but the Gusty Gull can be fun."

Imogene raised her eyebrows and tilted her head to one side. "That might be…no, wait. I'm too broke."

"Nowhere's as cheap as the Gusty Gull," Amber said, pretty sure she had Imogene hooked, "but it's up to you. I'm headed there tonight around eight." She hadn't been, but it wasn't like she had other plans.

"I'm sorry, dear," Mary said to Imogene as she hurried up to the pair of them. "I didn't mean to leave you standing there."

This was definitely weird. Mary's usual composure had morphed into obvious anxiety. She seemed almost intimidated by Imogene.

"It's okay," Amber said, "we were making friends."

The look on Mary's face screamed *No!*

All the more reason Amber wanted to find out more. In part, she was just having fun, playing detective. But mostly, she was worried about her friend. "See you tonight?" she asked Imogene.

Imogene was looking at Mary. "Sure," she said to Amber. "See you at eight." She gave Mary a little "ta-ta" wave and headed out of the store.

"Why did you do that?" Mary scolded as soon as she was gone. "She's definitely not someone you want to hang around with, Amber. I'd suggest you run after her and cancel. Tell her you forgot about an appointment."

Amber studied Mary's tight, drawn face. "Who is she to you?" she asked.

Julie had come over as Imogene left. "Second that question," she said. "Is she an old friend? She seems kind of rude."

"That's not the half of it," Mary said grimly. "Look, I know you mean well, but I'd appreciate it if both of you would stay out of my business. Which means avoiding Imogene." She spun and marched into the back of the shop.

They both watched her go, then looked at each other. "Very strange," Amber said.

"Did you say you made a plan to get together with her?" Amber nodded. "Tonight at the Gull."

"You're amazing," Julie said. "But is it safe? She doesn't seem like a very nice person."

"Aw, it's an adventure," Amber said. If she couldn't have an adventure abroad, she'd just have to take what she could get at home.

TUESDAY NIGHT, PAUL walked down the main street of Pleasant Shores with Trey Harrison, both of them with their dogs. Trey had invited Paul to bring Sarge to a search-and-rescue event he was involved in with King, and now, they'd decided to give the dogs a quick walk along the shore before calling it a night.

Trey was doing Paul a kindness, but he was also definitely checking on Paul, seeing how he was managing, and why wouldn't he? Trey no doubt remembered that first mixed-up night when Davey had run away to Amber's house. Trey was also still holding on to Paul's weapon.

Even so, Paul liked Trey; they had a lot in common. "Thanks for taking us to the search-and-rescue demo," he said now.

"Glad you could come. Sorry Sarge didn't seem like he's going to work out. I thought, with him being a bloodhound, it would be perfect for him."

Sarge seemed to laugh up at Paul, and he reached down to rub the dog's head as the breeze lifted the bloodhound's droopy ears. The sky over the bay was purple as darkness came on, and the salty, slightly fishy smell wafted to Paul. It was a smell he was getting used to, even coming to like. "Seems like there's too much involved for me to do with a young child, anyway."

"There is, for sure. I could never have fit in six hundred hours of training if I'd gotten started after Hunter came. As it is, I'm limited in what I can do, but it keeps King happy." He glanced down at his German shepherd, who was trotting beside him. "These dogs need to work. Drew Martin—he's the guy who stayed at the cottage last year—his dog actually went into a depression. Drew's daughter Kaitlyn got the dog into agility work, and she's thriving now."

Paul nodded. "I'll have to figure that out eventually. Sarge's a little lazy, like you saw tonight, but he's too smart to just be a pet."

Across the street, noise came from a stand-alone building that looked like a restaurant or bar. As a couple walked inside, more music came from the open door. "Is that the Gusty Gull I've been hearing about?" Paul asked.

"Sure is," Trey said. "Want to stop in for wings and a beer? It's pretty basic, kind of a dive, but it's one of the only places open during the off-season."

"What about the dogs?"

"We can tie them on the patio." Trey sniffed the air, and indeed, the pungent smell of wings was appealing. "To tell you the truth, I wouldn't mind. Erica's busy tonight, so it's either this or a take-out pizza. I don't feel like cooking."

Paul checked the time on his phone. "I have an hour or so before Davey's due home, and I should get a call beforehand. I can grab a quick bite." He'd been glad Davey was invited, along with the rest of the pre-K class, to a girl's birthday party up the shore at a trampoline park. It was one of the wealthier families, obviously, because they'd rented a bus to drive the kids up and bring them home.

They walked in and sure enough, what seemed like a good chunk of the town's population was there. Music played and people talked and laughed. There was a small dance floor, empty now, and a bar that was almost full. They chose a table off to the side of the room, near the window, so they could easily check on the dogs.

Of course, they kept their backs to the wall. Always. It was a cop thing.

Paul scanned the room, searching for loose cannons and risk factors. Then he realized that Trey was looking at him, raising an eyebrow. He sighed. "It's obvious?"

"To me. How's all that going?"

Paul blew out a sigh. "Counseling is good. They've got me meditating, which, trust me, I would never have done if I wasn't desperate."

"Does it help?"

Paul nodded. "Helps me focus, calms down some of the racing thoughts."

"That's good, then."

They ordered hot wings and beers and Paul watched, idly, as the door opened and more people came in.

And then the watching wasn't so idle anymore because there was Amber.

He frowned. Amber was with the woman they'd seen kind of stalking Mary. What was that all about?

"Do you know that woman with Amber?" he asked Trey, whose eyes were also following Amber and her companion.

Trey shook his head. "Never saw her before."

"She's some connection to Mary, but I don't think it's a positive thing." He started to stand, caught Amber's eye. When she gave a subtle little shake of her head, he sank back down again. She and the woman went to a table.

"Good to see Amber out having fun, making new friends," Trey said. "She's a little lonely, now that her daughter's gone off to college."

"She's close with you and Erica, right?"

Trey nodded, smiling. "She's terrific. She's the best aunt Hunter could ever have, and she's a great sister to Erica. Helped get us together, in fact."

"How sick is she?" The question seemed to burst out of him, but once he'd asked, he held his breath.

Trey's head snapped sideways to look at him. "She's not sick."

"Well, but she had cancer, right?"

Trey nodded. "Yes. Erica worries, but she hasn't had a recurrence now in two years, so it's all looking good. Thing is, she had breast and then ovarian cancer. Runs in their family. Their mom died of it."

"Wow." Paul's gut twisted. He hadn't known it was that bad.

."Those two have had a hard time of it," Trey said. "They're good women, really good women. They deserve to be treated well." There was definitely a warning in Trey's eyes.

"Understood." Paul nodded. He got it, a brother-in-law being protective.

They talked about this and that and their beers came, and then their wings. Paul's eyes kept being drawn back to Amber.

She wore tight jeans and a sweater, nothing fancy. Her

hair was chin-length, just straight. He couldn't see from here, but he knew she normally didn't wear much makeup.

And yet, the way she threw back her head and laughed, the relaxed way she looked around the room and greeted friends, all of it made her seem fun and appealing. She had a vibrant energy and life that clearly drew people to her.

It drew Paul, too.

A tall guy dressed like a cowboy went over and stood talking to the two women. He gestured toward the dance floor, and Paul's muscles tightened.

"You like her," Trey said around a mouthful of wing.

Paul blew out a sigh. "Yeah. But I'm in no shape to do anything about it."

Amber's companion stood, steadied herself and walked to the bathroom, banging into a chair on the way. The cowboy headed up to the bar.

Paul glanced at Trey. "Think I'll walk over and see what's going on."

Trey nodded. "I'll keep an eye on the dogs."

Paul made his way across the bar to Amber's table. He was acutely conscious that he was just like any guy approaching her, wondering if he'd be rebuffed. "Having a nice time?" he asked.

She shrugged and smiled. "The Gull is always fun. Company could be better, though." She nodded toward the restroom into which her friend had disappeared.

"That's the woman who was stalking Mary, right?"

Amber nodded. "I'm trying to find out more about her, so don't mess it up."

"Doing police work?"

She grinned. "Gotta do something." She looked past him then, and the woman walked toward them, grasping the backs of chairs to steady herself.

At close range, Paul saw the red eyes and glazed expression of a user. He wondered if she'd ingested something in the bathroom. Maybe, although she'd already been stumbling a little when she'd gone back there.

"Do you need a ride home?" he asked Amber. He didn't like the idea of her hanging out with some druggie.

"I'm fine," she said. "Paul, this is Imogene. She's in town for a bit and I'm showing her a good time, as best I can."

"Like to party, handsome?" she asked Paul.

Heat climbed his face. Maybe he was a prude, but he got uncomfortable when women came on to him, even as a joke. "Not much of a partier," he said. "I'm a single dad." He looked at Amber. "And you shouldn't be partying, either, given your health."

She raised her eyebrows, staring at him. "What did you just say?"

"It's getting late. You need your rest." The minute he said it, he knew he'd taken the wrong approach. He just wanted to get her away from Imogene, and he'd said the first thing that came to mind.

"We all do, big boy," Imogene said. "But resting alone's not much fun."

"And we're all adults who mind our own business." Amber's tone was icy. "I think I *will* take off, not because I'm sick, but because I'm sick of being told what to do." She gave him a glare. "Are you staying, or heading out?" she asked Imogene.

"Think I'll stay. See if any of the guys here are friendlier than Mr. Fancy here."

Amber snickered, gave Paul a wave and left, and Imogene walked up to the bar.

That hadn't gone well, but it *had* been effective; he'd gotten Amber out of here. No way would he let her put herself in harm's way, even if she was just trying to help a friend.

CHAPTER TEN

WHEN HER DOORBELL rang the morning after her night at the Gusty Gull with Imogene, Amber pushed back her chair from the breakfast table and straightened her spine. She and Paul were scheduled to work together today, and since neither of them had canceled, she guessed they were on.

Don't let him bully you, and don't get attracted.

Amber had been highly irritated by Paul's comments last night. Who was he to tell her she should get more rest?

When she'd thought about it, though, she'd realized that he probably was just trying to get her away from Imogene. Which was a different kind of patronizing, since Amber could take care of herself in that regard, too. But the truth was, she'd been glad to escape Imogene. Before they'd started talking to other people at the bar, Imogene had said something interesting: she'd told Amber that she'd "really screwed up" in her earlier life, done something terrible. Amber had tried to pursue it, to find out what it had to do with Mary. But she hadn't been successful.

Once there were a few guys around, though, and Imogene had had more to drink, Amber's opportunity to learn anything helpful to Mary had disappeared.

When she opened the door now, her throat went dry. Paul stood there, laptop in hand, wearing faded jeans and a flannel shirt with sleeves rolled up. His face was serious, almost stern.

Her heart seemed to do a little dance, just seeing him. And it wasn't only because he looked good. The thought of spending the day with him, even working hard, made her way too happy.

"You can come in, but not if you're going to yell at me about last night." She stepped back so he could enter.

Sarge pushed past Paul and thrust his big, slobbery face into her hand.

She gladly shifted her attention to the dog, kneeling to rub his big ears. "Did you come along to help us, big boy? Did you guess I'd have a treat for you?"

At the word *treat*, Sarge gave a short, deep bark.

Paul sniffed the air, and his expression softened. "Something smells good."

"The way to a man's heart…" she began, and then heat climbed her face. She *wasn't* trying to get to Paul's heart. "Or a dog's heart, for that matter, is food. Come on into the kitchen, you two."

While she cut slices of coffee cake, Paul paced, looking out her windows toward the bay, inspecting the novel that lay facedown on the table, bending to pick up a leaf that had fallen from a potted plant.

She was way too conscious of him, and she needed to stop. Their relationship was strictly business.

"You didn't have to cook," he said as she carried two plates to the table. "I'm here to work."

"And heaven forbid we'd have any pleasure in the process," she said, and then her face heated again.

Their eyes caught and she knew he'd noticed the word *pleasure* and taken it where she hadn't meant it to go.

Consciously, at least.

Was it warm in here, or was it just her? She needed to

get her focus off Paul, no matter how handsome he was, no matter how appealing his stern protectiveness.

"I didn't forget your treat, you good boy," she said, looking at Sarge as she set the plates down. She turned and pulled out a large, bone-shaped biscuit from the canister on the counter. "Can you shake hands?" she asked, and he held up a paw, eyes on the treat, then took it delicately from her fingertips.

Finally, there was nothing else to do but to sit down at the table.

Paul did, too, but he didn't pick up his fork. "I'm concerned about last night," he said. "I don't want you spending time with that woman. Imogene."

She laughed at his tone. "Oh, Dad. You never let me have any fun."

"I mean it." He didn't smile. "I'm serious. It's not safe."

She took a bite of coffee cake and lifted a shoulder. "Even if you're right, so what? I of all people can take risks." She hadn't meant to say that; it had just popped out.

"What do you mean by that?" He still hadn't picked up his fork, but was studying her, head tilted to one side.

"Because I've had cancer twice! Do you know how likely a recurrence is?"

His eyebrows drew down and together. "No. How likely is it?"

She shrugged. "Just…it's more likely that I'll end up with it than most people." She'd talked with her doctor about the odds, had read all the statistics, and the upshot was that it was all individual.

"Whoa, whoa, whoa. You're fine taking risks because you might possibly get cancer again? What kind of sense does that make?"

She couldn't answer that. There was no answer, not a

logical one, anyway. "I just had a test that showed something my doctor wants to keep tabs on. So I can't travel because of the risks."

He shook his head. "I'm sorry to hear that. What are the risks?"

"Can we not talk about this?" She had no idea how they'd gotten onto this subject, and it was seriously bumming her out. "Eat your coffee cake."

He studied her face for a moment more and then nodded and took a bite. He closed his eyes as he chewed and swallowed. "Wow. I haven't had anything this good in years."

That made her feel all warm inside, just how she shouldn't be feeling, and she chided herself. There was no use getting happy about nurturing Paul. They didn't have a romantic relationship and they wouldn't. In addition to her odds of getting cancer again, she'd promised Wendy she wouldn't tell Paul the truth about Davey. Keeping a secret like that nixed any chance of them getting together. Because breaking her promise and telling Paul the truth might very well destroy Davey's life.

Bad odds all around.

He'd finished his coffee cake, and he pushed his plate away and sighed. "Thank you. You didn't have to bake for me, but I have to admit I'm glad you did."

"You're welcome. Want another piece?"

"I was hoping you'd ask. I'd love one."

Again, that made her happier than it should have, and she scolded herself as she sliced another piece for him, then decided to bring the pan over.

"Thanks," he said. Then he met her eyes, held them. "Just because you have a chance of getting sick, that doesn't mean you can take any risks you want to take."

She so didn't want to discuss this. "It's not a big deal."

"It *is* a big deal. Because people care about you. *I* care."

Whoa. That admission, the intensity with which he said it, took her breath away. She couldn't speak, couldn't look away from him.

His eyes flickered down to her lips, a miniscule movement so quick she wasn't sure she'd seen it.

He sat back, looked away, cleared his throat. "Anyway," he said, "you have to be safe for your daughter."

"You're right." She stabbed at her coffee cake, then looked at him and forced a smile. "Don't you even want to know what I found out, during my oh-so-risky night with Imogene?"

A smile tugged at the corner of his mouth. "Yeah. I guess I do."

She pushed her plate away. "So she's Mary's stepdaughter. She feels guilty about something that happened in the past. And she needs money."

"No surprise there." He frowned. "From how she looked last night, I'd say she needs the money for drugs."

"Yeah. I thought so, too."

"Which is why I want you to stop your so-called investigation of her. It's not safe."

"It's not safe for Mary," Amber protested. "I hate to think of this woman trying to scam her. And I *do* get the impression that's what she's trying to do, from some hints she dropped last night."

"I'm sorry to hear that, and I'm not surprised, but that's not your responsibility. Your brother-in-law's aware of the situation and so am I. You leave it alone." He leaned forward. "Promise me."

"Consider me warned," she said, which wasn't a promise. But it was all she was willing to say at this point.

He studied her face for a moment, sighed and nodded. "Should we get to work?"

So they did, discussing the parameters of the respite house for crime victims. "Should the counseling aspect be just the victims themselves? Or families of victims, too?"

His lips tightened and then he cleared his throat. "Families will need it, too."

"I'll talk to Mary about that." She hesitated, and then her curiosity got the better of her. "That idea of crime victims and their families. Is it personal? Related to the shooting?"

He looked away, then met her eyes and frowned. "Yeah. It is."

She propped her elbows on the table. "I'm a good listener." She took a sip of coffee and tried not to seem overly interested, even though everything about this cryptic man *did* interest her.

Weak sunlight sent rays through the kitchen window, illuminating motes of dust. She wanted him to go at his own pace, but it looked like he was stalling. And he seemed so troubled that she figured he needed to talk about it. "Were... were there kids killed?"

He shook his head. "Thank God, no. Injured, though, pretty badly in a couple of cases. And there was a teacher..." He broke off.

She waited, her stomach cramping because she was pretty sure she knew what he was about to say.

He cleared his throat, a harsh sound. "She was an older teacher, and she was leading her class toward the gym when the gunman opened fire. She stood right at the door, ushering the students in, reassuring them, hurrying them."

Amber didn't want to picture the scene, but she couldn't help it. "Wow. That took some guts."

He nodded. Swallowed hard and looked out the window.

"I'd called for backup and was getting some other kids into their classroom, and he…" He cleared his throat again. "He focused on her. Got angry. Angrier."

Amber closed her eyes and shook her head, then looked at him again. "She died?"

"I was running toward him, yelling to distract him. Couldn't get a good shot because of the other kids and teachers. I could have…" He slapped the heel of his hand on the table, jostling the plates and mugs. "I've relived it hundreds, thousands of times. Thought of ways I could have reacted differently, things I could have said or done…" Finally, he met her eyes. "No point in that, though. What's done is done."

"Oh, Paul." She looked at the muscle jumping in his cheek, and her heart ached for him. The man was well and truly haunted.

She wanted to be the person to comfort him. She wanted to make him forget his pain. He'd probably saved lives, many of them, but it was the one he couldn't save that kept coming back to him, of course. She stood and slipped around the table to sit beside him, leaned her head against his shoulder and wrapped her arms around his brawnier one.

They sat there like that as the pines moved in the wind outside the windows, as Sarge panted and flopped down, as the sound of music from the playlist on her phone pressed on, quietly, the hip-hop she'd been listening to.

Finally, he stirred and flexed his arm, and she lifted her face and glanced up to find him looking at her. "We're quite a pair, aren't we?"

She nodded. "Life stinks sometimes."

He nodded, his gaze never leaving hers, and the mood between them shifted from sympathy to something warmer.

He reached out a hand and tucked a lock of hair behind her ear.

She closed her eyes. It felt so good to be touched in that gentle way.

His hand stayed, cupping her cheek, and she sucked in a breath. He was going to kiss her, which was all kinds of wrong, but she didn't think she could turn away.

His phone buzzed, and the disappointment on his face was gratifying. "I've got to get that, in case it's about Davey."

"Sure. Do it." She pulled back and sucked in a big breath, trying to slow down the pounding of her heart.

He picked up his phone and looked, then took the call. *The school*, he mouthed to her.

He listened, his face getting stormier. "No, they're not authorized to pick him up. Right. I'm the only one."

He listened more. "Let me talk to them," he said.

A moment later, he said: "Ferguson. Why are you at the school? We don't have an agreement for you to see Davey today."

He listened, propping his forehead on his hand, staring down at the floor. "Davey needs to be in a routine, and he needs to be with me. We've discussed this."

He listened again. "No, I'm not giving verbal or any other kind of agreement. You need to check with me before seeing him."

Amber could hear sort of shrill voices in the background. Then Paul looked at the phone, turned it over. "They hung up."

"Davey's grandparents?" she asked gently.

He nodded. "They've got some notion they can barge in on his life and his routines whenever they want to. Even that they should have some custody rights. And it's not happening."

"That was sneaky, showing up at the school."

He nodded, his face grim. "I'm worried about what they might do."

"Understandable."

Paul made a call to the school director and explained the situation. He listened for a few minutes and then ended the call. "Davey's safe and occupied, and his grandparents left. She doesn't think I should come in and bring him home."

"That's probably smart," Amber said. "Kids need routines."

"They do." And as they got back to work, now with no trace of romance in the air between them, Amber focused on one thought: Davey *had* to stay with Paul, not his grandparents. Which meant she couldn't upset the applecart by revealing the truth about Davey's conception. And that was a roadblock for any thought of romance between them.

WEDNESDAY EVENING AS sunset turned the sky purple and pink and gold, Mary stood outside the lobby of the Chesapeake Motor Lodge, talking to Ria Martin, the motel's owner. She'd known Ria for years, ever since she'd first moved to Pleasant Shores, because Ria was her employee Julie's daughter. She'd become a good friend.

"I can't tell you how much I appreciate this," Mary said to Ria. "But you have to enforce the rules with her."

"I'm good at that, I have teenagers," Ria said, her voice wry. "Don't worry, Mary. Your stepdaughter is welcome here."

"Thank you." Imogene, it turned out, had been sleeping on the beach and living out of her car, and she'd gotten a warning from the Pleasant Shores Police Department. So Mary had offered to meet her at Ria's motel and get her a room for the week.

If Mary were a better person, she'd have offered Imogene

her guest room. But the thought of facing her stepdaughter every single day gave her hives.

"I can't believe it's December." Ria lifted her face to the gentle breeze. "Today's been sweater weather. It can stay like this as far as I'm concerned."

"Me, too." But Mary loved the changing seasons of the Chesapeake, its unpredictable weather, so different from LA.

They heard Imogene's car before they saw it spewing dark fumes as it sputtered to a stop in front of them. "This is it?" Imogene asked as she climbed out and looked at the motel, her lip curling just a little. "It's kind of...old."

Older than your car? Mary wanted to say it, but didn't.

After all, Imogene wasn't wrong. The motel had been a part of the community for more than fifty years, and hadn't ever had a decor update that Mary had heard about.

"Around here, we call it retro," Mary said. "Imogene, I'd like for you to meet Ria Martin. She's the owner and manager, and she's found a room for you to stay in for the week."

Imogene raised an eyebrow and opened her mouth, but Ria smiled and held out a hand. "It's a pleasure to meet you, Imogene. The Lodge is a pretty humble place, but we keep it clean and everyone is friendly. And anyone who's a friend of Mary's is a friend of mine."

"Pleased to meet you," Imogene muttered as she shook Ria's hand. Even she, apparently, couldn't withstand Ria's friendliness.

Ria winked at Mary. "Come on," she said to Imogene. "I'll show you the room and you can get settled."

"Thank you for doing this on short notice," Mary said as they followed Ria to a room near the office. Ria opened the door with a key on a classic motel tag, bright blue plastic, imprinted with the motel's name.

Inside, wood-paneled walls, an aqua carpet and accent

chairs upholstered in gold vinyl brought the 1960s to life again, with colorful abstract wall art adding a hippie vibe. "Wow," Mary said, "I don't think I've ever seen one of these rooms before."

"We thought we might update the decor," Ria said, "but our guests seem to love the Elvis-era feel, so for now, we're keeping it this way."

"Are you now." Imogene plunked a suitcase down and looked around, eyebrows raised.

"Yes," Ria said, still smiling. "The great thing about this room is the view of the Chesapeake." She opened the curtains to reveal the bay. "We get the most gorgeous sunsets in the world here."

"Real pretty," Imogene said reluctantly, and then her expression turned thoughtful. "Who knows, I might just stay awhile."

A weight descended onto Mary's shoulders with her words. She was definitely going to have to manage Imogene's expectations about how long she was willing to pay for her room.

"I'll leave you to get settled. Stop in at the office if you need anything." Ria patted Mary's arm on the way out, and then Mary and Imogene were alone together.

"I can help you carry in the rest of your things," Mary offered.

"It's not like I have much, but thanks." Imogene led the way to her beater car and handed Mary another banged-up suitcase, then pulled a couple of grocery bags out of the front seat.

As they trudged back to the room, Mary thought of Imogene's father. He'd been a successful engineer, frighteningly smart, with the kindest heart she'd ever known. He'd doted on Imogene, even when she'd made fun of his heavyset build and lack of hair. He'd thought her beautiful and had been sure she'd grow up to be a success at whatever she did.

How it would have hurt him to see what she'd become. For Ben's sake, she wanted to put in at least some effort to help Imogene.

Mary sat while Imogene shoved clothes haphazardly into drawers. "Tell me how you've been doing and what your plans are."

"That depends on you." Imogene scowled as she carried a makeup case into the bathroom.

Mary drew in a breath and let it out slowly, seeking calm. "Look," she said, "I'll pay for your room for a week, but you need a plan to get back on your feet."

Imogene came back out and plopped down on the bed. "I have no money. I can't make a plan."

"You inherited the same amount I did," Mary said gently. "You must have invested some of it. I know your father's friend Barry advised you about that."

"*That* guy." Imogene snorted. "All he wanted to do was make sure I didn't get one cent ahead of my twenty-first birthday, and then to dole it out in tiny bits afterward."

"Not many people would call that amount of money tiny," Mary said. "And your father had it distributed in stages because he cared for you."

"He would have changed it if he'd known your ex was going to murder him."

Imogene's words stabbed Mary right in the gut. Ben's car, with Mary's beautiful, perfect daughter in a car seat inside, had been run off the road right in front of their house, but by the time she and Imogene had reached it, the person who'd done it had been gone—leaving Mary's life devastated in a way that could never heal.

It had been labeled a hit-and-run, and no perpetrator had

ever been caught, but Mary had known who was behind it. And Ben's ex-wife, who'd been furious she hadn't been included in the will, had researched Mary's background and figured it out. She'd gone to the police and put pressure on Mary to implicate her first husband.

Which was fine. Mary had been so broken by what had happened to Ben and her daughter that she'd fully cooperated with the police, even knowing her first husband's mob connections could send a snitch to an early grave.

But he'd been too skillful, and there had been no trail to follow, no evidence to find.

Of course, Imogene's mother had told Imogene about the whole situation, had whipped her up into a frenzy of hatred against Mary. News had leaked out in the neighborhood, too, and Mary's friends hadn't been able to look her in the eye. It hadn't been Mary who'd driven the car, but she'd still been blamed: for marrying Ben and thus getting him involved in her problems, for letting her first husband know her location, for having been fool enough to marry her first husband at all. She'd moved away within six months.

Imogene flopped back on the bed and stared up at the ceiling. "Anyway, I had to pay off some of my bills with the money you gave me before. I'm flat broke."

"Have you been using?" If Imogene could be blunt, so could Mary.

"What business is it of yours?"

That answer told Mary what she wanted to know. "It's my business," she said, "because if you're using, any money I give you is likely to go to the same place your dad's money went."

Imogene rolled to her side, sat up and glared. "You think you're so perfect," she said. "What if your new friends find out what you're really like?"

Mary's heart accelerated into a too-rapid rhythm. *She has nothing on you. It wasn't your fault.* Counselors over the years had tried to get her to believe that.

But she'd maintained contact with her first husband, against Ben's wishes. That was what had given him access to their location and their habits.

Despite the many years that had passed, her heart still burned with guilt. And she didn't want to contaminate her Pleasant Shores life with the old pain.

She could give Imogene money, a lot, and she'd go away for a while. But as long as Imogene knew she had more, she'd be back.

"I need a smoke." Imogene pulled out a pack of cigarettes and a lighter. "Is this place nonsmoking?"

"I'm sure it is, but there are chairs outside where it's probably okay."

Imogene stomped out of the room and Mary followed her, watching as she lit up, then looking up and down the parking lot. It wasn't full, but there were a healthy number of cars. The motel was doing well, and that made Mary happy for Ria. She needed to focus on good things, her friends' successes for example, not on things in the past she couldn't change.

Her phone buzzed, and she accepted the call, walking away from Imogene.

"Mary, it's Heather. Your offer was accepted!"

It took Mary a minute to switch gears. "I'm sorry, could you say that again?"

"You got the house!"

"Oh, that's great news!"

"We rushed everything through, like you wanted, or at least, Kirk has started the process. You'll need to come in and sign some things, and we'll get the closing scheduled as early as next week."

"Terrific. Thank you so much. I'll be in tomorrow."

Mary's heart lightened with the thought. No matter what Imogene's problems, she was moving on to do something good.

"What's got *you* so happy?" Imogene said from close behind her. It brought back memories. Imogene had always been one to sneak up on you.

"Just some good news," she said, her stomach twisting. The last thing she wanted was for Imogene to find out about this purchase.

CHAPTER ELEVEN

THE NEXT SATURDAY MORNING, Paul sat on his porch, relaxing for what seemed like the first time in days. Davey was playing at another kid's house, a new friend from school, and he'd been excited to go. That was great because Davey had been having trouble sleeping and had been a little cranky the last few days. The child therapist thought he might be starting to reexperience some trauma from his mother's death or from Paul's difficulties after the shooting.

Paul felt deeply ashamed that his own issues—his PTSD and what he'd said and done directly after the school shooting—had hurt his son, but the therapist assured him that kids were resilient. Today was an example of that. Davey had seemed like any carefree kid when he'd gone running into his friend's house.

From the direction of Amber's cottage, he heard a door slam and automatically leaned forward to look in that direction. When he realized what he was doing, he forced himself to sit back and turn his eyes away.

The other day, they'd shared a lot about the past. Paul had told Amber a little about the shooting, something he rarely talked about outside of a therapist's office. It was all part of his healing process, and was prompted by the counselor. But the fact that he'd chosen Amber to confide in was no coincidence.

He liked her. Cared about her. Wanted to know her, and for her to know him.

As for Amber, she had talked about her cancer experience and her fears. She let herself be vulnerable with him and it had made a difference, made him feel closer.

Truth to tell, he'd almost kissed her. And he had had the impression that she wouldn't have minded.

But that couldn't happen. Davey couldn't be allowed to get close to a woman with Amber's health problems. Paul felt like a bad person for that, and if it had just been him, he would have definitely been willing to get close, to see where it went, whatever the risk.

But his job now was to take care of Davey, protect him. That was the main focus of his life. And for Davey's sake, that meant keeping Amber at some kind of a distance.

Amber jogged by without pausing to wave to him, which disappointed him. He could see that she was wearing earbuds, and from what he knew of her, she was probably rocking out to some music he'd always considered way too young for him.

The truth was, Amber was too young for him. If not in years, then in outlook.

He leaned back, hands linked behind his head, looking up at the incredibly blue sky. The air was brisk, but they were still in the middle of a warm spell, more like fall than winter. The waters of the Chesapeake kept the climate here more temperate than in other places Paul had lived.

He could definitely get used to it. He'd never considered actually living here, leaving city life behind, but he liked Pleasant Shores. If Davey settled in well...

But staying here meant staying in close proximity to Amber. The thought of that heated his heart, but also set off warning alarms inside him. He didn't know if he could stay near Amber long-term without pursuing the relationship.

He daydreamed awhile, until an SUV pulled up in front of his cottage and stopped with a jerk and a squeak of brakes. Paul was immediately on his feet, adrenaline flowing, reaching for a gun he didn't carry anymore.

But it was just the mother of the child Davey had had a playdate with. Concerned in a different way, and he headed down the porch steps as she got out of the car quickly, opened the back door and helped Davey climb out. She grabbed his booster seat and marched up the walk, holding Davey's hand.

Paul met them halfway. "What's up?" he asked, kneeling to meet Davey. His eyes skimmed over his son, who seemed physically fine, though his lower lip stuck out a little and his face was streaked with tears.

"Hi, Paul," the mother said. "We needed to have Davey come home a little early."

Half an hour after a playdate started was *really* early. He opened his arms to Davey, who ran into them and buried his face in Paul's chest.

"Did something go wrong?" he asked the mother quietly.

Instead of answering, she pulled something out of her pocket and held it toward Paul. When he saw it, his heart gave a great thump and every muscle in his body tensed as he reached for the weapon. Black, plastic, it was an M1911 replica that, other than a slight difference in size, looked like the real thing. Like most cops, he hated this kind of toy. "What on earth is that?" he asked.

Davey grabbed at it, and Paul held it out of reach. "No way, kiddo. You know you're not allowed to play with guns."

"I was wondering where he got it," the mother said, frowning. "It's way too realistic of a toy gun, especially for such a young child. Davey had it in his backpack, and he got Justin interested in playing with it. It has rubber bullets, too." She reached into her pocket again and pulled out a case of brightly colored bullets. "They weren't able to figure out how to load it, and nobody got hurt. Maybe I'm a wimp, but I'm just not comfortable with this type of toy, and Davey got really upset when I took it away."

This didn't make sense. Paul wiped sweaty hands on his jeans. The last thing he wanted was to see a toy gun in his child's hands. He'd even vetoed squirt guns, so far. "I apologize. I don't know where he got it, but he certainly won't be playing with it anymore." He felt Davey tense and suck in his breath for what was sure to be a wail. "I'll talk to Davey and get to the bottom of this."

"Great, I thought you'd probably want to do that. No judgment here, but I do need to get back to Justin. He hates being left alone in the car." She turned and hurried down the walk, almost colliding with Amber, who was jogging her slow jog. Amber stopped and greeted the woman, and the two exchanged a few seemingly friendly words. Then Justin's mother got into the car and drove away.

Davey grabbed for the gun again. "It's mine!"

Amber continued on toward her house, but after a few steps she paused, turned and walked slowly up the pathway to Paul's porch. "Is everything okay? Any way I can help?" Her eyes widened, and Paul realized she was looking at the gun he was holding out of Davey's reach.

"It's a toy," Paul said. "A toy Davey had without my knowledge, and I'm not sure where he got it. It upset his friend and his friend's mom." He nodded toward the departing car.

"Oh, wow," she said. "How would Davey have gotten a

toy without your knowing about it? Do you think he got it at school or something?"

"Are you kidding? They have a total nonviolence policy, and I'm behind that." He stroked Davey's head. "Look at me, son. Where did you get your toy gun?"

Davey jerked his face away, staring at the ground. "Can't say," he mumbled.

Paul stared blankly at Davey. "Did someone give it to you?" His heart pounded. Was someone stalking Davey?

Amber paused her music and knelt down to Davey's level. "Even if someone tells you to keep a secret, buddy, you never have to do that. You're always allowed to tell your father. You won't get in trouble."

Davey looked up at her and then looked at Paul, his brow furrowed.

Paul nodded. "Miss Amber is right. You won't get in trouble for telling me a secret."

"But Grammy and Grandpa said not to tell you," Davey said. "They said you would be mad."

They were right. Fiery anger built in Paul's chest, but with an effort, he kept his voice steady. "I'm not mad at you. Did Grammy and Grandpa give you the gun?"

"Yeah. And it's *mine*." He grabbed for it again.

Paul kept a hold on it. "No way, pal."

Davey lifted his chin. "You have a gun."

Paul shook his head. "Not anymore. Guns are very, very dangerous." He was glad he could say it, glad he'd given his weapon to Trey for safekeeping. The thought of Davey mixing up this gun with a real one, playing with it, shooting it...ugly terror rose like lava in his gut. He'd been careful, used good rules of gun safety, but he also knew that the best efforts didn't always keep kids safe.

"I'm going to call Grammy and Grandpa and talk to

them," he said. "You did just right, telling me. Let's go inside and get you a snack."

Davey shook his head. "I don't wanna go inside."

Amber touched Paul's arm. "He could come dig me more holes," she suggested, "while you call." She was speaking in a low voice, obviously trying not to let Davey hear in case Paul didn't want him to come.

"Thank you. That would be a help." He didn't want to be close with Amber, or rather, he knew he shouldn't, but he needed to find out what was going on right away. This constituted an emergency. "I'll try to reach them now and pick him up in a few minutes."

"No problem. Come on, Davey, let's you and me and Sarge go get some treats and dig some holes."

"'Kay." Davey grasped the hand she'd extended, and they walked off toward Amber's home.

Paul watched them and thought, again, about how good Amber was with Davey. He'd love to go over there right now with them, sit on the porch with Amber, chill out and talk through what had just happened.

But first, he had to deal with Ferguson and Georgiana. What was going on with them? They'd attempted to pick Davey up at school without Paul's permission and they'd threatened to sue for custody. Now it turned out they'd given Davey an even more inappropriate toy than the jeep. If they were anyone else but Wendy's parents, he'd cut off their access to Davey without a second thought.

But not only was Davey their only connection to the daughter they'd lost, they were important to Davey. They would help keep Wendy alive in Davey's heart, and that mattered. A lot.

He needed to get them to come to a counseling session with him. To try and figure out why they were acting this way, and get them to see that they were only hurting their beloved grandson.

Once he'd called them, he'd figure out what to do next about Amber.

AMBER SAT ON her front steps, shivering in an oversize sweatshirt. Sarge was at her feet and Davey knelt just on the other side of the big dog. "Those are some good holes, Davey," she said to the little boy vigorously digging in her flower beds.

"Thanks." Davey's tongue stuck out a little from the corner of his mouth as he carefully planted the last tulip bulb from the bag. "Any more?"

"Nope, that's all I have, but you're welcome to dig more holes." It seemed like the boy could use more of a physical outlet. She remembered from Hannah's childhood that the more time a kid spent outdoors and active, the better their mood and appetite and sleep.

Davey dug for a short while longer and then threw down the trowel. "I'm hungry," he said. "I'm gonna go home for lunch."

Amber glanced over toward Paul's house. "Come on inside my place. Daddy will be over soon, but I'm sure he won't mind if you have lunch with me first." When Davey opened his mouth to complain, she said, "I make really good grilled cheese sandwiches."

Davey's face brightened. "Okay," he said.

They walked inside, Sarge trailing behind them, and Amber set butter melting in her cast-iron skillet. Then she got Davey to wash his hands and dug up a box of crayons someone had left here. She sat him down to color until lunch was ready.

She was no expert on how to handle kids with problems, except to let them play and feed them well. Hannah had been a dream child, and her mom and Erica had been nothing but supportive. She didn't envy Paul the task of working things out between a troubled kid and his difficult grandparents.

She dipped slices of wheat bread in the melted butter and built sandwiches in the pan. Maybe Paul would be hungry when he came to get Davey.

Exactly what she *shouldn't* be expecting, let alone hoping for.

Sarge gave a low, casual bark as footsteps sounded on the back deck.

"Hey, are you up for a couple of visitors?" It wasn't Paul; it was Erica, baby Hunter on her hip, opening the back door and coming in. That was their habit here in Pleasant Shores, and Amber loved being able to walk into her sister's house and for her sister to do the same here. They'd lived together, Hannah, too, when they'd first moved to Pleasant Shores, and now, their houses seemed like big extensions of the same dwelling, even though Erica and Trey and Hunter lived a block away.

Amber greeted Erica and gave her a one-armed hug, then kissed Hunter's cheek with a loud smack that made the baby laugh. "Davey is visiting me and I'm making grilled cheese. Want some?"

"You know I would never turn down your grilled cheese sandwiches." Erica smiled at Davey. "Hi, buddy."

"Hi." Davey didn't look up, but kept coloring, still with the same intense focus.

"This is cozy," Erica said. "Where's Paul?"

"He'll be over in a few." Amber sliced cheese for more sandwiches as the first set sizzled away in the pan.

"He's calling Grammy and Grandpa because they got me a gun," Davey volunteered. "He's mad."

"I see." Erica glanced at Amber and then walked over

to sit beside Davey. "Looks like you're coloring some great pictures." She leaned closer. "What is that, a dog?"

"Yeah, a police dog," Davey said. "Here's the officer, and this is his gun, but I'm not allowed to have one." He frowned. "Daddy used to have one, but now he doesn't."

Erica glanced at Amber again. "I don't much like guns," she said to Davey. "They can be dangerous."

"I like them!"

Amber came to the table, plates in hand. "Lots of kids do, and that's okay," she said to Davey. "But Daddy makes the rules about what you can play with." She set sandwiches in front of Erica and Davey. Then she returned to the counter, added tomato slices and fresh basil to two more sandwiches, and set them cooking.

From the table, Erica groaned with pleasure. "I don't know how you make something so ordinary taste exotic."

"Everybody's good at something, I guess," Amber joked. But she liked this, feeding people, taking care of them. She missed it now that Hannah was in college.

"I think we had grilled cheese every night for a month when Mom was working that night shift job. Remember?"

"I sure do. That was mainly what was in the refrigerator. White bread, and that awful processed cheese we loved so much. I think we had cans of tomato soup, too." She looked at Davey. "Want me to heat up some soup for you, kiddo?"

Davey shook his head. "'Nother sandwich," he said through a mouthful.

"Sure thing."

A knock sounded at the door, and Sarge lifted his head and gave a half-hearted woof. "I bet that's your daddy," Amber said, and went into the living room. She sucked in her stomach, ran her fingers through her hair and opened the door.

There was Paul, handsome and haunted. She swallowed against her suddenly dry throat. "Come in. You look like you could use some lunch."

"That bad?" He was trying to joke, but there was no humor in his eyes. The conversation with Davey's grandparents must not have gone well.

"Do you want to talk about it? My sister's here," she added so he would know not to share anything confidential.

He shook his head. "No, thanks. I've burdened you enough already."

"Not a burden." She led the way to the kitchen and put the sandwich she'd intended for herself onto a plate, cut it in half and handed it to Paul. "Have a seat. Eat up."

"Hey," Paul said to Erica, and she responded in kind. Then he wrapped his arms around Davey from behind and blew into his neck, making a raspberry sound that made Davey laugh.

"Every time I come over here, I get a meal out of you," Paul said to Amber. "It's starting to seem unfair."

"Are you going to turn it down?" She nodded at the golden grilled cheese she'd handed him.

"No way." He sat and ate the sandwich in just a few bites while Davey showed him the drawing he had made.

Hunter babbled and ate the Cheerios Erica put on the table for him, and the adults talked casually about events and people around town, and it was cozy and warm, like family.

Amber loved it. She was supposed to be such an adventurer, always portrayed herself that way to other people, but in truth, she had a big homebody side. Although she liked excitement and travel, she was happiest when she was taking care of people.

All too soon, Paul stood. "Come on, Davey my man," he said. "We need to take Sarge back home. We're heading to the park this afternoon, but first, we both need a little rest."

"Okay, Daddy." Davey sounded surprisingly amiable.

Father and son thanked Amber, and then the pair of them, with Sarge at their side, walked back toward their cottage.

Amber stood at the window watching them. Paul kept a hand on Davey's shoulder and tilted his head so he could hear what the little boy was saying. When they got to the house, Davey grabbed a small rubber football, one that looked like it was meant for the dog. He threw it, and Paul jumped up and caught it while Sarge barked.

Amber smiled. Paul was upset, but he was still able to be a good dad.

"You've got it bad, don't you?" Erica sounded amused.

"Shut up," Amber said. "Can't I admire the view without you making a big deal of it?"

"Sure you can." Erica came to stand beside her. "It's a very nice view."

"I really like Davey." It was a dodge, but it was also true. Davey was a sweet kid, and motherless, and it brought out Amber's protective side.

"Paul seems like a good guy." Erica returned to the table, where she used a napkin to wipe off Hunter's mouth. "But he's sort of screwed up, right?"

"Well...yeah, he is." Amber sighed. "Through no fault of his own, he's had a lot of bad things happen to him, and they've affected him."

"Uh-huh." Erica watched her and just listened, one of the things Amber loved most about her sister. "And what does that mean to you?"

Amber thought. "It means he's complicated, *and* he has a precious little boy who's had a complicated life, as well. And there are all kinds of reasons why I should keep that in mind and stay away from him."

CHAPTER TWELVE

MARY ALWAYS DID good business during the By Golly, Be Jolly Christmas Shopping Night, traditionally held the first Monday in December. Tonight was no exception, so she was glad she'd gotten all five of her employees to come work part of the evening. That way, everyone could fit in a break to enjoy the festivities and do a little shopping of their own.

She stepped outside herself, felt how brisk the air was and went back inside to grab her cape and hat before heading down the street. All the little trees in front of the shops were lit up with white lights. Down where Main Street dead-ended into Beach Street, a group of carolers sang. At the other end of the block was the big train display, so popular with the kids.

She wanted to take in the peace, think about the reason for the season, enjoy all the friends and acquaintances who greeted her. But she just wasn't feeling it. Was it the plans for Victory Cottage, or was it Imogene? Either way, her anxiety about the past had amplified until it was a constant ache in her stomach.

"Mary!" Amber came over and greeted her, her nephew, Hunter, on one hip. She wore a bright red cap, and her color was high. She looked healthy and happy. "How's business tonight? Come get a hot mulled cider with us!"

"I'd love that, dear." So many people were in family groups during the holidays and at events like this. Mary rarely felt bad about being single and basically childless, but if she were going to feel that way, it would be on a night like tonight. So it was nice to have a friend to walk around with.

"There's Drew and Ria." Amber gestured toward a small group coming out of the clothing store, the man holding a white cane in one hand and his wife's arm in the other. Drew had lost his vision in a police accident. When he'd come to the Healing Heroes cottage to help one of his daughters through a hard time, he'd ended up reconciling with his ex-wife. That made Mary happy.

"Sophia will want to see Hunter if she looks over this way."

"Why...oh." Of course, since Sophia, Drew and Ria's older daughter, was Hunter's biological mother. "Is that hard on you and Erica?"

Amber shook her head. "No, I think it's nice. Good for everyone. Especially this little peanut." She kissed the top of his bald head, making him chortle.

"I think I see Paul and Davey down by the trains," Mary said. "Should we hurry up and try to catch them?"

"No," Amber said quickly. "We shouldn't."

Mary looked sideways at Amber as they walked along. The attraction between her and Paul was so obvious that it shimmered in the air between them every time they were together. "What's the barrier?" she asked, knowing she was being blunt. But Amber was always blunt with her.

"It's complicated." Amber looked down the block toward Paul and Davey then, and the longing in her eyes was so intense it made Mary's heart hurt. "But there *are* barriers, big ones. So the less time I spend near those two, the better." She bounced Hunter. "I need to focus on this guy, anyway. I'm aiming to be Aunt of the Year."

"There's something to be said for that," Mary said.

"Enjoy the child and then give him back to his parents when he gets fussy. And don't forget to buy him lots of books."

"From Lighthouse Lit, of course." Amber smiled. "I'm on it. I stopped in last week and got a whole stack of board books."

"Perfect. We have such cute ones." Mary smiled to picture the bright new selections she'd unpacked a couple of weeks ago, in time for Christmas shoppers.

"Hey, I never thought to ask, but do you have any kids?" Amber asked the question casually, shifting Hunter in her arms, continuing the slow strolling pace they'd gotten into.

Mary looked up at the darkening sky. No matter how many times she heard it, that question always threw her. She bit her lip.

Amber looked sideways at her, eyebrows raised, and then some sort of understanding crossed her face. Obviously, she'd noticed Mary's too-long pause. "Hey." Amber bumped her arm lightly. "I'm sorry if I was out of line. I don't mean to be nosy."

"Not a problem."

"It's okay if you don't want to talk about it, I totally understand. I should know better. People are always asking me invasive questions about my health and my surgeries and my prognosis. In fact, I've figured out the perfect answer to that kind of question. Do you want to hear it?"

"Sure." Mary was grateful that Amber was talking on, giving her a chance to compose herself.

"Just say, '*What* did you ask me?' as if you didn't hear the question. Then they have to ask again. And you say '*What* did you ask me?' again. Makes people stop and listen to themselves, and they usually stifle it at that point." Amber's face twisted into a wry smile. "Except Primrose Miller. She's in a category of her own."

Mary smiled. Primrose prided herself on knowing everything about everyone.

"Go ahead, practice it on me," Amber invited.

"No. You aren't being rude asking such a normal question. My criteria for that is, does the person asking care about me or not. And I think you do."

"I do. I'm glad we're getting to be better friends."

"Me, too." And Mary was lonely and having the odd inclination to share. "I *had* a daughter," she started. Then her throat tightened and she couldn't say anything more.

Amber put an arm around her. "I'm so sorry." They were walking slowly now, a little out of the mainstream of the crowd. "What was her name?"

"Margaret, but we called her..." She sucked in air. "We called her Daisy. And I don't think I can talk about it."

"Of course," Amber said instantly, and gave her shoulders a squeeze. Then she pointed toward the trains. "Uh-oh."

"What's wrong?"

"Here's a change of subject for you. I just noticed that Davey's grandparents joined the fun."

Glad for the distraction, Mary looked down the road and saw an older couple standing behind Paul and Davey, the woman weighed down with bags. "I should get her into my shop. She looks like a big spender."

"Yes, she is." Amber's gaze was fixed on the little group. "And Paul just got really tense. I think things are a little shaky between them."

"Davey seems happy, though." Mary could see the child bouncing excitedly and trying to look into the bags the woman carried. "Doesn't take much to get kids on your side, at Christmas."

A memory of Daisy, waving her arms excitedly as she

stared at the newly lit Christmas tree, formed in Mary's mind, a clearer image than she'd had in years. A hard, aching lump formed in her throat. What was wrong with her, letting herself remember? She knew better.

"Let's walk the other way," Amber said. "I definitely don't want to get in the middle of that."

So they turned around and headed back toward the bay end of the block, and Mary spotted Imogene on the edge of the crowd. She was walking alone, smoking a cigarette and looking at the lights, and Mary felt a surprise pang of sympathy for her. Did Imogene have anyone with whom to spend the holidays, or had she pushed everyone away?

"Just the woman I wanted to see!" Kirk's loud voice rang out behind them. "Have I got news for you!"

"What news?" Mary asked Kirk, and then smiled when she saw that he was walking alongside Trey and Erica and their two dogs. "Merry Christmas shopping," she said to the couple, and gave Erica a quick hug. She reached down to pet Ziggy, who was wearing a large blue cone around his neck, the kind that kept dogs from bothering their wounds after surgery. "Oh, dear. How is his recovery going?"

Erica lifted Hunter out of Amber's arms and handed him to Trey. "He's doing fine, other than wanting to lick his incision. That's why he's wearing the cone of shame."

Mary reached inside the cone to scratch the big dog's ears, and he leaned against her leg. It was a sweet weight, and he was just the right height that she could pet him without even bending down. His fur was soft and fluffy, just as Baby's had been. "I'm sorry, big boy," she crooned. "Poor thing."

A grin tugged at Trey's mouth. "He got what was coming to him, for getting rambunctious in the wrong neighborhood."

"I was waiting to get him neutered until he was older, since he's so big," Erica explained. "It can be better for their bones and tendons and all that. But then we found out some news." She frowned down at the dog, who panted back up at her.

"He's been getting out and getting frisky." Kirk sounded delighted. "That's my big news. The upshot is, there's a whole litter of little Ziggys."

"Oh, no." Mary couldn't help laughing. Ziggy's antics were notorious. "Who's the lucky mama?"

"It's Goody's dog, Cupcake," Erica said. "The black-and-white poodle mix?"

"And Goody's furious," Amber contributed. "Her dog is smaller, and younger, and she didn't intend for her to have a litter yet, especially not with a, quote, mutt like Ziggy. But nature took its course."

"How does she know Ziggy's the father?" Mary remembered a couple of times when the poodle had escaped, and Goody had enlisted everyone in her shop to help find her.

"DNA testing," Trey said, and now he wasn't able to restrain his laughter. "She made us get Ziggy tested, and she tested the pups as soon as they were born, and she got the results last week."

Mary was still petting Ziggy. "I can't believe what they can do with genetic testing these days."

"So anyway," Kirk said, sounding excited, "Goody wants to get rid of the puppies because she thinks they're mutts. I thought you might want one, Mary."

Mary pulled her hand away from Ziggy and stared blankly at Kirk. "Are you kidding? I thought we settled this." Then she couldn't resist rubbing Ziggy's ears some more. "I'm almost seventy. I can't have a dog of this size."

"Well, but they won't be that size," Kirk explained reasonably. "Not quite. Goody's dog only weighs, what, fifty pounds?"

"Something like that." Erica nodded. "So the pups should end up no more than sixty-five pounds. I did promise Goody I'd help her find homes for the pups. Also explained to her that she can charge a lot for a poodle mix, that nobody but a breed purist thinks of them as mutts. They don't shed, and they're so cute." She leaned down and kissed Ziggy's head. "Just like you, huh? Cute, but bad."

"Well, it's impossible for me. I'll just have to keep loving Ziggy as a friend." She scratched the big dog's ears some more and he panted up at her with eyes that seemed full of warmth and sympathy.

"Uh-oh," Amber said, her voice changing as she looked down the block. "I'm gonna scoot." She gave everyone a quick wave and hurried off.

Erica looked at Trey. "We'd better go, too. Keep her company, and it's time for Hunter to get to bed. Ziggy, too." And the little group departed.

Mary automatically looked where Paul, Davey and the grandparents had been, and sure enough, Paul was walking toward her, slowly. Davey and his grandparents headed into the new toy store.

Wondering whether Paul had seen Amber flee, Mary watched him approach and greeted him warmly. "I hope you're having a good night. And I hope you'll bring that grandmother of Davey's into my store. I have a lot of pricey new picture books that need to find a home."

"If there's something shiny and new to be bought, Georgiana will find it," Paul said. "And I'd rather have her buy books for Davey, and support your store, than anything else."

"Thank you, dear." Mary smiled at him.

"Everyone didn't happen to leave you alone here because I was coming, did they?"

Mary studied him. "And by everyone, you mean Amber?"

Paul nodded. "Yeah. As soon as I came in your direction, she left."

"She didn't tell me she was leaving because of you," Mary said, which was technically true. "I think they had to put Hunter to bed. And Ziggy, the goldendoodle, he's just had surgery and needs to rest."

"No big deal." They stood watching the crowd and chatting for a few minutes, and then Mary saw Imogene again. Now she was talking to a man Mary knew vaguely, a fisherman who'd been in town for a few months.

"Is she bothering you?" Paul asked.

"Who, Imogene?" Mary considered the question. "She does have her issues, but it's nothing I can't handle."

"Amber says she doesn't treat you well."

Mary watched her stepdaughter laugh at something the fisherman said. Then they both turned and headed down toward Beach Street, most likely with the destination of the Gusty Gull.

"She doesn't treat me well, it's true," Mary said. "She suffered a trauma a long time ago, and I think she's still bitter about it." She had to wonder at herself, sharing so much information with Paul, and with Amber before. They were both easy to talk to, and it seemed like she wanted to talk.

It was a tendency she'd have to watch in herself.

"Lots of people turn to substance abuse after a trauma," Paul said. "I found that out in my PTSD support group. Or rather, confirmed it there. I'd seen it happen on the streets a lot of times."

Mary turned quickly to look at Paul. "She definitely

has a drug problem," she said, "but I don't think she could have PTSD, could she? That's for veterans, or people like you, police officers."

Paul shook his head. "No, they think now that sometimes civilians have it. Like if they experienced an assault, or lost loved ones suddenly. Especially if there was violence involved."

His words sent a flood of images into Mary's head. Brakes screeching. The loud crunching of metal. Imogene screaming. Both of them running outside to the street in front of their house, to the smoking remains of Ben's car.

She could barely breathe. "I need to get back to the bookstore," she managed to say.

"Are you all right?" Paul looked at her, his forehead wrinkling, and put a hand on her arm.

She shook it off. "Yes, just busy! Nice talking to you!" It was an art, getting people to leave you alone, shutting them out. An art she'd perfected.

If they lost loved ones suddenly... If there was violence involved...

Maybe PTSD would explain why Imogene's issues were so big and unending.

Maybe it would even explain something about Mary herself.

PAUL WASN'T SURPRISED that the first hour of working with Amber, the Tuesday morning after the town's big shopping event, was kind of awkward. He had expected that. He had withdrawn from her that day she'd kept Davey for him while he called Davey's grandparents, and then she'd seemed to run away from him last night.

He wasn't sure why she'd backed away from him, but he was crystal clear on why he'd backed away from her.

He was trying to save himself—and especially Davey—from the attraction sparking between them every time they spoke.

But they needed to do this part of their project together, so he'd suggested working together at his place, making a case by email. They needed to grow up and do their job for the sake of Mary and the crime victims she wanted to help. Trying to work remotely, in their separate homes, would take twice as long and be half as effective.

Pretty quickly they got into a groove. Amber did most of the writing, while he provided a lot of the content about victims as well as law enforcement expertise. They both worked on the technical stuff because they were not only drafting materials to send to various agencies, but they were also working on a public facing website for the program.

They understood each other, had a similar quick pace of work and matching visions for the program. Soon, the awkwardness faded away and they both delved deep into the project.

After several hours of hunching over the computer together, Amber stood and stretched. "I need to move," she said. "I think I'll take a walk down the shore." She hesitated and looked at him.

He looked back at her, opened his mouth and then paused.

"Want to come?" she asked.

"Can I come?" he asked at the same time.

They both laughed, and there was another one of those sparky moments. But Paul ignored it, and soon they were walking down the road in front of the bay. This time, they didn't go toward town, but toward the docks, where Paul hadn't yet spent much time.

Short wooden piers jutted out into the water, some with

boats adjacent, and most with small shacks linking them to the land. Crab traps were stacked beside some of the shacks, and that smell of fish and saltwater was everywhere, sharp but not unpleasant.

It was another unusually warm day for December, or at least, it was unusual to Paul. Apparently, it happened fairly often on the Eastern Shore, where the waters of the bay and the nearby ocean moderated temperatures.

Paul was happy. His heart pounded a little faster than usual, and he looked at Amber a little too often, but it was under control. He was just enjoying a walk on a beautiful day with a beautiful woman.

"Hey, Bisky, Sunny," Amber called.

Two women who had to be mother and daughter turned and waved from where they were doing something over a tin water tub. Then both of them walked toward Paul and Amber, the mother removing rubber gloves and tossing them into a basket by their shed.

Amber hugged the tall one, who pretty much dwarfed her, and then she hugged the teenager, too. Then she stepped back and gestured to Paul. "Bisky, Sunny, I'd like for you to meet Paul Thompson."

Sunny waved a greeting, but Bisky, the mother, grasped his hand in her own large, calloused one. "Heard about you," she said. "You're the one who's staying at Healing Heroes, with the little boy."

"That's right," he said, wondering how she had heard of him. Surely his story wasn't that interesting.

Amber must have noticed his confusion. "Small town," she said, "and gossip spreads especially fast at the docks."

Bisky put an arm around Amber. "We like this girl. Be nice to her."

Paul raised an eyebrow. Bisky seemed to be assuming

that he and Amber were a couple, and he felt no inclination to correct her mistake. "I was planning on that."

Amber, though, went pink. "And I'll be nice to him and to you and to everybody. Come on, Paul, let's leave these ladies to their work."

Obviously, Amber hadn't liked it that Bisky made the assumption they were together. Too bad. He almost wanted to ask her about it. Not that they *were* together, nor ever could be, but he didn't mind if people thought they were.

As they wandered on down the road, Amber seemed intent on changing the subject. "Did Davey have fun at last night's event?"

"What's not to like when your grandparents treat every day like Christmas?" He had tried to rein Georgiana in, but it was hard with Davey jumping up and down beside them, obviously enthralled with all the toys in the shops.

"Yeah, how's that going?" She glanced at him and then looked out over the bay. "Did you have that gun-control-for-four-year-olds discussion with them?"

Her relaxed attitude made him comfortable talking about it. "Yes. It was Ferguson's idea to get the gun, and he's realized the error of his ways."

"Seems like a pretty significant error. How could he be that out of touch?"

Paul grimaced. "Wendy's parents don't exactly mingle with the common herd. He's into skeet shooting, target practice, things like that, and he always wanted a son to share that with. He didn't have one, so Davey is it for him."

"I guess." Amber frowned. "Plus, he's from a different generation. Everyone used to be more comfortable with guns before mass shootings." And then she clapped her hand to her mouth. "I'm sorry. You probably don't even like hearing those mentioned."

Her words *had* made his stomach jump, but he didn't plunge into the memories. Progress. "It's okay. Anyway, Ferguson apologized and they begged to come and spend some time with Davey. The shopping event seemed to be the right thing, and it went well."

"Good."

They'd passed the end of the docks and were coming to a tip of the land with the bay on three sides, a tiny peninsula. At the end was a bench, and Amber gestured toward it. "Would you mind sitting down for a few minutes?" She wrinkled her nose. "I get tired easily. The jogging helps, but I'm still only good for short distances."

"Of course I don't mind." Automatically, Paul took her arm as they walked toward the bench. "I'm sorry, I should have been more thoughtful."

"No, don't apologize! I love it that you don't always think about my medical history. Most people do."

They sat down, close together, the bright sunshine making diamonds on the water. The breeze here was brisk, and Amber shivered a little, so he put his jacket around her shoulders.

He left his arm there rather than pulling it back.

She looked over at him and raised an eyebrow.

This time, he didn't look away. "You're a great person, you know that?"

She laughed and waved a hand and scooted a little away from him. "No, don't say it!"

"Don't say what?" She definitely kept him guessing, and he was charmed by it.

"Don't tell me I'm a great person, and I'll make somebody a great wife/girlfriend/partner one day. Somebody *else*." She rolled her eyes. "Believe me, I've heard that speech a time or two already."

Paul stared at her, puzzled. "That surprises me. I would think men would jump at the chance to be with you."

"Thanks for making me feel better." She gave him a brilliant smile, dazzling him, making it hard to breathe. "I've only heard it from the few nice guys I've dated. They never like my type."

"Do you like nice guys?" he blurted out.

She tilted her head to one side, holding his gaze. "Some of them," she said in a flirtatious voice.

"Why don't they like you? Is it the tattoos?" He dared to reach a finger out and trace a rose on her arm.

She looked up at him through long lashes. "More like what the tattoos represent. I'm not the kind of girl mothers tend to approve of." She laughed a little, then shrugged. "Now that I'm a mother myself, of a girl of dating age, I get it. When Hannah told me she liked a boy on the basketball team who's huge and muscular and looks twenty-five at least, I freaked out."

"Understandable. I'm sure I'll be protective of Davey when the time comes." But now he was studying her tattoos more closely. The rose he'd touched had two smaller roses twisted around it. "What's that one for?"

"The big rose is my mom. She loved roses. Erica and I do, too, so the small roses are us."

She'd used the past tense and he remembered what Trey had told him, that their mother had died young. "When did you lose your mom?"

"Three years ago." She looked down, digging the toe of her sneaker into the sandy soil. "Cancer. It runs in our family," she said.

"I'm sorry."

She shook her head like a dog shaking off water. "Here's

my biker tattoo," she said, pushing up her sleeve to show him a motorcycle topped by two wings.

"Pretty," he said, and tried not to picture her in the arms of some burly biker.

Maybe she read his mind, because she explained. "By the time the tattoo had healed, I'd figured out the biker was a jerk. But by then it was too late. Already had the tattoo." She laughed and shook her head. "I made a lot of dumb decisions when I was younger."

"What's your latest tattoo?"

She raised an eyebrow. "You mean my latest on a public part of my body?"

Paul sucked in a breath, picturing all the private places she might have a tattoo. And she knew it. He opened his mouth to scold her, or to say *something*, but she put up a hand. "Sorry. My last tattoo was actually this one." She held out her elbow, and he saw a horse, running free, tattooed over what looked like a scar.

He touched it, ran his finger along it, and the feel of her skin set a fire that burned its way to his heart. "How'd you get the scar?"

"Riding horses when I didn't know how. That was when I dated the cowboy."

His eyes narrowed. How many men had she dated? And what exactly did dating mean to her?

Again, she seemed to read his mind. "It wasn't serious," she said. She lifted her hair from her temple and showed him another scar that ran along her hairline. "This was the same accident. I got thrown from a horse. He wasn't very sympathetic, so I got myself some medical care in the nearest town and got out of there."

"Jerk." Paul traced that scar, too. It gave him the chance to touch her soft, shiny hair. He'd been wanting to do that.

"Any ill effects from getting tossed onto your head from a horse?"

Her breathing seemed to quicken. "Nothing lasting. I've had a couple of fainting spells over the years, but it's no big deal. Believe me, that's the least of my health worries."

"Good." He let his hand stroke her hair.

She didn't pull away from his touch. He wasn't all that experienced with women, but he could tell from the way she met his eyes and looked away, from the rise and fall of her chest, that she was attracted.

This close, he could smell her perfume, warm and spicy and alluring. He could feel the heat of her body, and no doubt she could feel the heat of his, because he was burning up.

He should make a joke, stand up, get them started back toward town. Get them away from this isolated spot where a great blue heron waded, looking for its lunch, where the pines rustled overhead and the waters gently lapped against the shore.

Normally, Paul did what he knew he should do. As a responsible person, a cop and a dad, he had to. But right now, in this moment, he didn't want to be responsible. He wanted to look into her eyes, and he did.

She looked back at him now, steady and serious, her eyes darkening.

Her gaze flickered to his lips and then back to his eyes. "This is a bad idea for all kinds of reasons," she said, almost in a whisper.

"You're right." He didn't pull away.

Neither did she, and so he moved closer, his eyes steady on hers, looking past their usual mischievous sparkle to the complicated woman revealed in their depths.

She sucked in a breath, let it out, shakily.

He hadn't even touched her, not really, and they were both breathing harder. He let his thumb trace her full lower lip.

She caught his hand in hers, but she didn't push it away; she just held it there, staring at him.

And he was intoxicated. He'd never made any kind of sound like the sound he made as he splayed his fingers through her hair and pulled her close and kissed her.

CHAPTER THIRTEEN

IF SHE'D BEEN ABLE to speak, Amber would have said *wow*.

Whatever she'd thought kissing Paul would be like, it hadn't been this: intense, passionate, one hand tangled in her hair, the other pulling her insistently closer.

And she didn't resist, because she *wanted* to be closer, wanted to be as close as a woman could be to a man, wanted to press against him, taste him, nestle against his strong chest and stay there forever, protected and warm.

She'd been chilled before, and tired. Now she was hot, full of restless energy that made her kiss him back and pull him closer.

Somewhere in the back of her mind, warning bells were ringing. There was a reason this wasn't a good idea. They'd both agreed it wasn't a good idea.

She shoved those rational thoughts aside and sighed against his mouth, then buried her face in his neck, inhaling the scent of him. Clean and fresh, with just a trace of musk underneath to hint at the passionate man she had just discovered him to be. Yeah. She could stay right here, breathing him in while he held her in his strong arms, forever.

He stroked her hair, then rested his cheek on the top of her head. "Whoa, Amber. You're something else."

It was probably just as well that the wind kicked up and made her shiver, because it woke her out of the pleasant spell his kiss had put on her. She pulled back a little and looked at him, unable to keep the smile off her face although she knew she must look as shell-shocked as he did.

"You're cold." He tucked his jacket closer around her.

It was tender, it was sweet, it was... "You're not treating me like an invalid, are you?"

He chuckled, low and throaty. "Believe me, you as an invalid is the last thing I'm thinking about right now. Although—" his voice changed "—we should get you inside. I don't want you to get chilled."

"I'm not chilled," she protested, but another whole-body shiver belied her words.

"Come on," he said. "We need to get you inside. Does your friend Bisky have a house down here?"

"We're not asking Bisky to take me in like I'm some kind of..." She trailed off.

"Cancer survivor? Who's still getting her strength back?" He held out a hand and pulled her to her feet, then held his jacket so she could slide her arms into the sleeves.

Grrr. He knew too much. "Come on, I know just where we can go to get warm." She took his hand and tugged him back toward the road.

Five minutes later, they were walking into the watermen's bar against Paul's protests.

"This is no place for a woman." Paul was looking around, obviously taking in the dim lighting, the neon beer signs, the smoky haze that served as a reminder that this place didn't follow the usual nonsmoking laws.

"Have you ever been here? Because I have. Hi, Steve," she called to the bartender. She gave a wave to the couple other customers who were in here and they nodded back. Now she was showing off, because she didn't know those guys well at all. She did know Steve the bartender, but it wasn't as if she was a regular. She'd been in here once or twice with Bisky, that was all.

They sat at one of the booths that lined the wall, and then Paul went up to the bar. He came back with two mugs of coffee, both black. "Steve said you didn't need any creamer or sugar."

"Steve's a good bartender. He remembers."

"He remembers you drink coffee in a bar." Paul slid in across from her and pushed one of the cups her way. "I think you talk a better game than you play. I don't think you've spent much time in here, and if you did, I don't think you were drinking."

"Busted. I just don't enjoy it the way I did when I was younger and wilder."

"That's best with your health issues. You need to take care of yourself."

It was sweet, and it was probably because he remembered Wendy's cancer. That made her feel strange. He'd loved Wendy, been married to her for years, and all of a sudden, Amber felt weirdly jealous. Of a dead woman.

It also made her think about Wendy and the big secret about Davey. The more Amber knew Paul, the harder Wendy's actions were to fathom.

Wendy had seemed so straight and narrow, almost rigid. It was hard to believe she would have cheated on anyone, let alone a man like Paul: kind, a fantastic dad, a great kisser.

But there it was. Wendy had had an affair, and Davey was the result of it.

She looked at Paul, at his kind, open face. Knowing he wasn't Davey's biological father, knowing Wendy had betrayed him, well, he'd be devastated.

And Wendy wasn't around to ask if the secret could be told, anyway.

She took a big gulp of coffee for courage. Then she looked directly into Paul's eyes. "That kiss shouldn't have happened."

He tilted his head to one side, studying her as if he wondered where she was coming from.

"It wouldn't work between us. I'm not up for a quick hookup, although…" She couldn't resist grinning at him. "I think we can both see that a quick hookup would be awesome while it was happening."

"It would be," he said. "But it wouldn't have to be quick."

She sucked in a breath. "Okay, so it would probably be a long, slow, sexy hookup."

His eyes heated, and for a minute, he looked like he was going to come across the table at her.

She swallowed and leaned back, away from his intensity. "But then it would be over, and neither of us would feel good about it. We're just not at a place in life where something casual will work."

"Why does it have to be casual?"

"I have a 40 percent chance of recurrence." Even just saying those words made her stomach cramp, but she pushed past it. This was too important to wimp out about, so she forced herself to go on. "I could die. You've already been through that, and more importantly, Davey has already been through that, and he shouldn't go through it again."

Paul's eyes closed for a moment then he opened them, reached across the table and grasped her hand.

She pulled it away. "Go date other people. Find someone else."

"What if I want you?" He reached for her hand again, and this time, he kept hold of it even when she tried to pull it away. Her hand felt small inside his, delicate.

The temptation was strong to let him take care of her.

To let him put his coat around her, hold her hand, soothe her worries.

He was strong and handsome. Caring and compassionate. The clink of glasses, the low voices of the men at the bar, the country music playing softly, all of it faded until there was nothing but her and Paul and this thing that shouldn't happen, couldn't happen, between them.

She needed to find some resolve, some way to go against her own heart and cut off this sweet and promising connection.

It's for Davey, she told herself. *Davey needs his dad, and who knows how Paul will feel if he finds out the truth.*

"If you get together with me, people will feel sorry for you. They'll think you're a horrible father for doing this to Davey. They'll ask you how I'm doing in that quiet church tone." She heard her own voice getting louder. "They'll say how skinny I am. They'll think there's something wrong with you for hooking up with another cancer victim."

"Amber. Don't get riled up."

"Don't tell me what to do and how to feel!" Now she was being loud and shrewish; she heard it in her own voice and hated it. She stood, looking down at him. "I'm sorry. But see, I'm scarred by this disease and it isn't just physical. You would have a lot to deal with, just like you did with Wendy. Probably more."

He stood, too, and grasped her arm, stroked it. "Hey, hey, calm down. We don't have to figure all this out today."

He was being kind. But everything she had said was true. He would have a lot to deal with, just like he had with Wendy. In fact, he didn't even realize all he'd had to deal with regarding Wendy. He didn't know the truth about her.

And he could never find out. And that meant that, even if their other barriers could be overcome, she could never get together with him. "There's nothing to figure out," she said. "We're not having a relationship, and that's that."

AMBER HAD BEEN RIGHT. He knew she was right. They couldn't have a relationship.

But Paul couldn't forget yesterday's kiss. Running his fingers through her soft hair, pulling her close and feeling how slender she was and yet how strong, finally, finally getting a taste of her lips. One touch and they'd ignited like a forest fire.

He knelt at the edge of Davey's classroom, watching the kids greeting each other and having a few minutes of free play before the official start of class activities. The bright colors, the play areas full of educational toys and the happy voices of the children would lift anyone's spirits.

Paul was glad he had agreed to help out today at the school. Not only was Davey thrilled, but it had given Paul a sure excuse not to work with Amber today.

Another woman came rushing in with her child, full of apologies for being late, taking off her coat. She was obviously the other parent helping in the classroom today, and when he recognized Laura, the mother who'd found Davey's toy gun and bailed on the playdate, he groaned inside. He'd sent her an email on Sunday after talking to Georgiana and Ferguson, but she hadn't answered.

He wouldn't blame the woman for keeping her child away from him and Davey indefinitely. He might have done the same had their roles been reversed. But Davey had been begging for another playdate with Justin, so he guessed he would have to confront the mom today and find out whether she was holding a grudge against Davey and him.

The teacher was doing some kind of opening exercise now with the whole group, so Paul walked over to the side of the room where Laura was standing. "I don't know if you got my email, but I spoke to Davey's grandparents right after that playdate," he said quietly. "Turns out they're the ones who got him the gun. It's gone, and they understand they are not to buy him any gun-type toys again."

She looked at him blankly for a minute, and then seemed to process what he'd said. "Oh, my email, I haven't checked it. Life has been crazy. I haven't even had time to comb my hair, which you can probably tell."

Paul chuckled. Nice to see another parent struggling in the trenches, the way he did every single day. And he *could* tell she hadn't combed her hair, but she looked fine and he told her so. "I just wanted to apologize for upsetting you and Justin. I don't think I've ever been so shocked as when you pulled out that plastic gun and handed it to me."

"I was shocked to see it, too, and I probably overreacted," Laura said. "Let's set up another playdate soon."

Good. That was that. The teacher called them into service, and they got their assignments helping the children at different stations. Paul was assigned the play kitchen, so he sat on the floor while the kids cooked pretend pizza and vegetables on the little stove. One of the little girls gave him a baby doll to hold, and another fed him plastic corn on the cob. When he exclaimed how good it was, several more kids clustered around him, clamoring to feed him what they'd cooked.

They were probably getting a little too loud and rowdy, but Paul couldn't bring himself to scold them because Davey obviously loved having him here. He plopped himself into Paul's lap, displaced the doll and took charge, making the kids line up to offer Paul their meals.

They were so innocent, so sweet, and he felt protective of all of them. Most of all, Davey. Paul had to protect Davey at all costs. That meant he had to protect himself and keep control of himself, a control that Amber threatened in a way Wendy never had. Paul had never been in so much danger of being swept away as he had yesterday, kissing Amber, and he felt guilty for being so attracted to her.

Kids from the other groups started drifting into the kitchen play area, and finally, Laura brought her group over. "All the kids want to be with the dad," she said. "Moms are a dime a dozen."

Davey had climbed out of Paul's lap and was now hitting the table with a plastic hammer, repairing it, another little boy offering advice at his side. Now he looked up. "I wish I had a mom," Davey said, and then went back to his hammering.

His words twisted a knife in Paul's gut.

Laura sat down on a child-sized chair beside Davey. She studied him and then looked at Paul. "Is his mother…" she asked softly, and trailed off.

"She died of cancer two years ago."

"I'm sorry. That must be so hard to deal with." She ran a hand over Davey's hair, and he leaned into it before turning back to his hammering task.

"We're coping," Paul said, matching her quiet tone.

"Are you dating again?"

The blunt question took him off guard. "No!" He wasn't. Kissing Amber didn't count as dating.

"If you're looking to be set up, I'm good friends with Kayla Harris." She gestured toward Davey's teacher. "She's great, and she's single, and Davey likes her. All the kids do."

Paul pulled his mind away from Amber and let Laura's words sink in. He turned to look at Miss Harris.

She was pretty for sure, and fun. He could ask her out. *I don't want to ask her out.*

But maybe his reaction to Amber was just physical. Its intensity had taken away his sense.

He'd been thinking for a while that he ought to date, that Davey would benefit from having a woman in his life. His son's casual statement just now, that he wished he had a mom, confirmed that notion.

He should do it.

"Do you want me to set something up?" Laura asked.

"No. No, thanks, but I appreciate your giving me the idea." If he was going to ask Davey's teacher out, he'd do it himself rather than having someone help him like they were preschoolers themselves.

He looked over at Laura and saw that Davey had leaned against her again. She was stroking his hair.

Yes, Davey needed a woman in his life. He needed a mom.

Paul would wait until school was over and then speak to Kayla Harris, ask her out. No matter that it felt like a betrayal. Not a betrayal of Wendy, but of Amber.

CHAPTER FOURTEEN

"This is where you live?" Imogene's voice dripped with scorn.

Mary sighed inwardly as she stepped out onto the porch to hold the door open for her stepdaughter. She looked up and down Sunset Lane, trying to see it from Imogene's perspective. The short street, which dead-ended at the school grounds, consisted of single-story homes fairly close together. Each house had a little yard in front, most with small flower gardens, some sporting picket fences.

At this time of year the flowers had died, and the most that you could see was the light brown remains of some standing tall grasses. Mary forced a smile. "It's a little dreary right now, but it's a comfortable place to live."

Yes, there was the challenge of having Kirk James right next door, but he didn't ever intrude by dropping by unannounced. And Primrose Miller, down the block, tended to sit and look out her window, seeking gossip to spread, but that was more of an annoyance than an actual problem. Primrose had health issues that made it hard for her to get out, so reporting on her neighbors was sometimes the most exciting part of her day. Mary always listened politely to Primrose's stories and then mentally discounted three-quarters of what she had heard.

"Pretty crappy location if you ask me. Thought you'd live somewhere like we lived before." When Mary had married Ben, they'd lived with Imogene and Daisy in a big, new home on a street of other big, new homes. Mary hadn't been a fan of the monotonous beige of the houses nor the lack of big trees, but Ben had loved it and she had loved Ben, so it had been fine. A happy home for her and her daughter, who'd loved the big, wooden playset in the backyard and the pink-painted bedroom they'd decorated in princess style.

The memories squeezed at Mary's chest. She breathed deeply, trying to focus on the present moment.

Imogene walked into the front room without wiping her muddy feet. Mary opened her mouth to call her on it and then snapped it shut again. This was a visit designed to build bridges, not walls. She wouldn't have criticized another guest for the lapse so she shouldn't criticize Imogene.

Letting Imogene know where she lived had been scary, but Mary was hoping this visit would break through Imogene's anger and help both of them to heal.

If what Paul had said at the Christmas shopping event was correct, if PTSD was a bigger thing than just soldiers and cops, then maybe Imogene had it. Maybe they both did. Maybe the unpleasant, sometimes downright mean way Imogene acted wasn't her fault, and maybe there was help available.

Mary gestured to the three big boxes of decorations set up in the living room. "After dinner, I was hoping you'd help me decorate." When Imogene didn't respond with interest, Mary walked over to the box of lights and pulled out a couple of strands. "I always debate between white and colored lights, so I ended up having both. What do you prefer?"

Imogene flopped down on the couch. "Doesn't matter to me."

Mary's stomach tightened but she pressed forward.

She was always trying to make restitution, help others, but maybe God wanted her to do that closer to home, with Imogene. Helping others wasn't always an easy thing to do, but it was the right thing.

"You got any of our old decorations?" Imogene's voice sounded sullen. But at least she'd asked a question.

Mary handed Imogene the oldest of the boxes. "A few ornaments. You're welcome to look through and see what you remember. Take anything you'd like." She'd gotten rid of all the holiday decorations related to her daughter, because seeing the little handprint ornament, or the angel with Daisy's face pasted on, was just too painful. But she'd kept a few of Ben's decorations that hadn't seemed so personal, hadn't hurt so badly.

"You trying to soften me up, being all sweet and family oriented?" Imogene flipped roughly through the box of ornaments and then shoved them away as she spoke, not looking at Mary.

Mary braced herself, hearing the tension in Imogene's voice and knowing it was likely to rise into a full-out display of histrionics. Maybe, not likely but maybe, she could tamp that down. "You were upset about Thanksgiving, about not being involved with any family activities, so I thought you might like to get involved with some Christmas things. Besides, I want to talk to you."

"You think I have extra time to sit and shoot the breeze with you?"

It seemed to Mary that Imogene had nothing but time. "Come eat first."

Imogene followed her into the kitchen and watched, leaning against the counter, while Mary took the steaming pot of oyster stew off the stove and poured it into a pretty tureen. The table was already set, and she pulled a skillet of cornbread from the oven she'd turned off right before Imogene arrived. "I remember how you always loved cornbread, so I made some," she said brightly. "It goes perfectly with the local specialty of oyster stew."

"I just can't believe you live in such a little place with all the money you have." Imogene looked around the modest kitchen, her lip curling. "You don't even have a dishwasher."

Weariness pressed in as memories of trying to reach the teenage Imogene rose in her, along with the heavy sadness that had punctuated that time in her life. "Well, dear, I live alone. It doesn't make a whole lot of sense to use a dishwasher. Some of the houses up and down the street have them, but I never got around to the purchase." She considered handing Imogene the tureen of soup to carry in, decided against it and handed her a plate of cornbread instead. If Imogene dropped it, whether accidentally or on purpose, there'd be less to clean up.

They sat down, and Mary decided to forgo her usual praycr. It would do nothing but annoy Imogene. She ladled soup into her stepdaughter's bowl and handed it to her, then passed her the cornbread and butter.

"Got any wine?" For the first time, Imogene's voice was a little humble. "I could really use a glass."

Mary didn't like to lie, but this time she felt it was the lesser of two evils. "I don't tend to keep alcohol in the house."

"You're kidding me." Imogene stared at her, looking disgusted. Then she ate a couple spoonfuls of oyster stew and made a face.

Mary did deep breathing while she served herself. Imogene really hadn't changed a whole lot since her teen years when Mary had met her.

Some people just never grew up, apparently. After she'd

taken a couple of bites of stew, and Imogene had eaten a large piece of cornbread, Mary figured she might as well break the silence. "Have you ever heard of PTSD?"

Imogene glared. "I wasn't raised under a rock."

The windows rattled, and outside, pine branches whipped and swayed. Mary forced herself to take a bite of cornbread, chewed it, took a sip of water. "Have you ever thought that the incident we witnessed could have caused you to have it? That maybe that's been part of your problem all these years?"

Imogene shoved away her dishes, sloshing stew out of her nearly full bowl. "I don't have a problem. Why would you say I have a problem?"

Being gentle was getting Mary nowhere. "Well, let's see. You're almost fifty years old and you're broke and begging money from your stepmother, who you can't stand." Mary pushed her own dish away and met Imogene's eyes with a steady gaze. "If that's not a problem, I don't know what is."

"Is that what you invited me here for, to insult me?" Imogene stood quickly, her leg bumping against the table, causing more soup to slosh out of their bowls. "Look at you. You live here alone, a pathetic old lady in a crappy house with no friends. Here I'm trying to help you, and you're acting hateful."

Mary raised her chin. "You're trying to help me?"

"That's right! I'm trying to show you what you can do to make up for the horrible accident you caused. You can help the only thing you have that's close to a family, me, but you're too selfish to do it."

Mary was no stranger to beating up on herself, but she could also recognize a line of baloney when she heard it. "Look, if you ever want to talk about PTSD in a civil way,

I'm here. I'll work with you to find help, counseling, support. It's out there."

"Shut up, you hear me?" Imogene's voice rose to a shrill cry. "Just shut up!" Her fists clenched.

The doorbell rang, and Mary slid out of her chair and almost ran to open it. Only now that someone had come over did she realize that she was actually afraid of Imogene, of what the younger woman might do to her in a rage. She was even glad to see Kirk on the other side of the door, and she opened it immediately and invited him in.

"What's *he* doing here?" Imogene said. Her voice had modulated from the earlier shrillness, but only by a few degrees, and her face was an open sneer. And while Mary could tolerate that type of behavior toward herself, was used to it, she couldn't stand seeing a friend treated that way. "Kirk is a guest in my home," Mary said. "Watch your tone."

"I heard yelling and wanted to check on you." Kirk looked from Mary to Imogene. "Everything okay here?"

"Yes, everything's okay." Imogene had gone back to sounding like a teenager, and rolling her eyes like one, too. "She's fine. Your *girlfriend's* fine. I was just leaving." Imogene kicked at the box of ornaments as she walked by it. Then she took an inordinate amount of time finding her coat and getting into it.

Kirk looked at Imogene, shrugged and turned back toward Mary. "There's another reason I stopped by. Let's go see Goody's puppies. We need to put a down payment on one because apparently, they're going fast."

Mary welcomed the change of subject. It gave her a chance to settle her chaotic emotions, even if Kirk was being his usual pushy self. "Is Goody still mad about the whole situation?"

"Not so much," Kirk said with a chuckle, "now that she's realized how much of a gold mine these poodle mixes are."

At the door now, Imogene turned to face them, her face tightening. "You can afford an expensive dog but you can't help me financially?" She called Mary a bad name under her breath, but audible to both of them.

"Have some respect," Kirk scolded.

"Shut up! Just shut up, old man!" Imogene glared at Kirk and then at Mary. "Don't even try to be nice to me. Cooking me one lousy meal doesn't make up for anything you did." She stepped through the door and then leaned back in. "I'll be in touch, and it won't be pretty, unless you give me what we talked about."

Weariness pressed in on Mary. She lifted the window curtain and peered out to make sure Imogene was gone and then sank down on the couch. "Oh, my, what a mistake," she said. "I thought I could make a connection, but I was wrong."

"Why do you even want to connect with that woman?" Kirk sat down on the edge of the couch and then stood again, his face red. "I get that she's your stepdaughter, but she's extremely disrespectful. What does she have on you?"

Mary's throat tightened to the point where she couldn't talk. She just waved a hand and shook her head, then stood and started putting ornaments back into the box.

When she came upon the old star Ben had liked to put atop the Christmas tree, she went still and held it in her hand. It was as if that kind man had come back to her. He would never have endorsed Imogene's behavior.

But without Mary's coming into his life, he might very well be alive now, providing Imogene with the guidance she so desperately needed, guidance she hadn't gotten from her self-centered mother.

Mary should never have invited Imogene over, but the guilty young stepmother inside her still yearned to make things right with Ben's angry, grieving daughter.

She should have known better. Even before the disaster, Imogene had tried to embarrass her in front of her friends and discredit her in front of Ben. In her eyes, Mary had stolen the attention of her only decent parent, her father, sweet Ben.

Thinking of him, thinking of her hopes and dreams of forming a strong, protective family for herself and her daughter and Ben and Imogene, Mary's heart ached.

"I'm glad you came by," she said to Kirk. "Thank you. But I can't go see the puppies right now. I need a little alone time to pull myself together, if you don't mind."

Kirk came to stand beside her, took her hand and squeezed it. "I respect that," he said, "and I'm always happy to help you, whatever the issue. Remember that."

As he left, Mary looked after him, biting her lip. He'd help her now, but if he found out what had happened, he'd be singing a different tune.

ON SATURDAY NIGHT, Amber put an arm around Erica and squeezed her shoulders. "Thanks for coming. I needed a sisters' night out."

"Are you kidding? I wouldn't miss Crabby Christmas for anything! And there's no one I'd rather be here with than you."

"Not even your handsome husband?" Amber teased.

"Not even him," Erica said firmly. "Because I wouldn't be able to relax and enjoy cocktail hour if he and Hunter were here."

"Cheers." Amber tapped her mocktail against Erica's glass and then leaned back on her bar stool to survey the scene. DiGiorno's Restaurant was lit with tiny white lights and candles on each table. Big windows looked out on the bay, and the remains of a spectacular sunset lit the sky pink and orange. The room was loud with people talking and laughing and glasses clinking.

Crabby Christmas was an annual event that started with an adult cocktail hour and then continued with various family activities. Most people in town participated in at least some of the festivities. Amber spotted Kirk James and his father, Drew and Ria Martin, and even Goody, who was rarely seen outside her own restaurant.

Bisky Castleman was serving as an emcee, resplendent in a gem-encrusted red dress that was a departure from her usual worker's attire. Her hair was pulled back as usual, but it looked softer when accentuated with big sparkling earrings, and she wore makeup that emphasized her eyes and high cheekbones. Amber wasn't the only one who noticed the transformation, judging from the admiring way several local men watched her.

"You know, Bisky is actually gorgeous," she said.

"Right? I never noticed that about her before. She usually hides her looks."

"She has a spectacular figure, now that it's not covered up in fishing clothes." Bisky was tall and always looked fit, but in the dress she was wearing, her tiny waist, well-endowed chest and long legs were displayed to advantage.

Bisky waved to them and then grabbed her microphone. "Okay, everyone, start making your way over to Goody's. I hear Santa's arrived, and there's hot chocolate and cookies for all the nice little boys and girls. And even some of you rascals," she added, winking at Kirk's father.

A couple of the watermen, also looking different in their dressed-up clothes, catcalled Bisky, and old Mr. James blew her a kiss, prompting her to go over to him and give him a big hug. Amid a lot of laughter, people started toward Goody's.

Amber and Erica followed the crowd past the stores with Christmas-decorated windows. The streetlamps glistened with garland. Across the street on the bay side, tiny white lights wound around the railing.

A hum of excited voices and the smell of Christmas baked sweets drifted out from Goody's. As she walked in behind Erica, Amber spotted Paul, who was hard to miss because Davey was on his shoulders. Her breath caught.

He was laughing, lifting Davey down to go inside, obviously enjoying his son's excitement about Santa. She couldn't take her eyes off him. Couldn't stop herself from thinking about what it had felt like to kiss him.

She'd been trying to forget that kiss for the past four days, to no avail. Involuntarily, she took a step toward him.

"Wait." Erica gripped her arm, holding her back.

She turned to her sister, puzzled because Erica had seemed to be in favor of her having at least a friendship with Paul.

Erica's eyes squinted a little, the same worried expression she'd had when they were kids and Amber was about to make some kind of mistake. "I think he might be with someone."

"What?" Amber looked back in Paul's direction. The crowd parted enough for her to see Davey let go of Paul's hand...and grab the hand of Miss Harris, his teacher, on his other side.

At the same moment, Paul put his hand on Kayla Harris's back to steer her through the crowd and toward the line of kids waiting for Santa.

Amber felt like all the air had been sucked out of her lungs. Her throat got tight, filled with an impossibly big lump.

Miraculously, the table beside them was empty. Amber sat.

Erica grabbed the chair across from her and leaned forward. "Did you see that? What's going on? I thought…" She trailed off, studying Amber's face, frowning.

Yeah, Amber had thought, too. She'd thought that kissing her the way Paul had kissed her meant that he felt something for her, actually felt a lot, wanted to date her.

But how much more perfect for him to be with Kayla Harris, who was pretty and sweet and healthy. Probably, she didn't have the kind of checkered past Amber had. Davey's grandparents wouldn't have anything against her. And Davey obviously already loved her.

It *was* perfect, and Amber…wasn't. She stared down at the table, picked at a dried speck of ice cream that whoever had wiped the tables off had missed. Around them, the festive crowd sounds seemed discordant.

"Well, that jerk," Erica said after a minute. "I thought he was a nice guy, but I don't like this at all."

"She seems lonely," Amber said. She was articulating clearly, as if she were on the radio. As if she had no feelings whatsoever about the matter. "Kayla, I mean. She and her mom have had a hard row to hoe, from what I've heard."

"Everybody has problems," Erica said, her voice impatient. "Paul acted like he cared about you. Are you just going to let this go?"

Amber closed her eyes for just a moment, then opened them and met her sister's gaze. "I told him he should date someone else. I told him I could have a recurrence." She just hadn't expected him to take her advice quite so quickly.

Erica slapped a hand down on the table, the sound making a few surrounding people look their way. "He could be hit by a car! He could get sick! In fact, he already is sick. He's got enough PTSD that he can't own a gun. It's not like he's such a prize." She glared over in Paul's direction. "Idiot."

Through the pain that was squeezing her gut, Amber felt the corner of her mouth lift. Oh, how she loved her loyal sister. Erica understood Amber's health issues more than anyone else, because she carried the same genetic mutation that Amber did, had some of the same susceptibility to illness that Amber had.

Erica propped the side of her head on her fist. "I knew— I know—that I'm at more risk than the general population. And yet I got married." She spoke like she was feeling her way. "And I'm glad I did, despite the possibilities of something bad happening to me. Trey and I are good together. We're good for Hunter, too, even though there are times I worry about what the future will hold for him and for Trey, if I get sick."

Amber nodded slowly. "You were right to get married, and you and Trey are a great couple. But this is a different situation. Paul has Davey, and Davey already lost a mom to cancer. He can't risk losing another one, and I think Paul understands that. Paul has to put Davey first."

"But what about you, your feelings?"

Amber stared at the table. Images of Paul's hand at the small of Kayla's back, of Davey grabbing Kayla's hand, kept flashing before her eyes.

"You okay?"

Amber forced herself to meet her sister's eyes. She even tried on a smile, but it wouldn't stay on her face. "I'm fine. I'll be fine. Hannah's getting home tomorrow for Christmas break, and I'll concentrate on her, and forget about him." Of course, it wouldn't be that easy, but she didn't want Erica fussing over her. Erica was definitely a fusser.

"What's Hannah got to do with it?" Erica scooted her chair closer to the table to make way for the increasing crowd. "I think she'd be glad if you fell in love."

"Well...maybe." Hannah *had* said she wanted Amber to date someone, but that was probably related to her worries about her mother's health.

Erica frowned at a man who'd jostled her chair, and then her face softened when she saw the struggling little girl in his arms, who kept shouting, "Wanna see Santa! Wanna see Santa!"

"Sorry," the man said as he sidled past their table. "Shh, honey. We'll see Santa, but we have to wait in line."

The noise around them was getting louder now—other excited kids, Christmas music, even a few dogs barking. Goody didn't normally allow dogs in her shop, but it seemed like she was relaxing the rule at Christmas.

"Hannah would probably be a little jealous at first," Erica said, speaking up over the crowd, "but I bet in the end, she'd be fine with you having a relationship. She's such a thoughtful kid. And she wants the best for you."

"Yeah, and she worries about me." Amber leaned closer to her sister so she could be heard. "She did the whole, 'I'm gonna go to community college here so I can take care of you' thing at Thanksgiving."

"Hannah?"

"I know, right?" Hannah was the last kid who'd want to stay local and limit her ambitions, at least in any ordinary situation. But having a mom who'd been terribly sick, not once but twice, wasn't exactly ordinary.

Erica frowned. "She might feel more like she could go on with her own life if she knew you had a partner and she didn't need to look after you. But whether or not you're seeing someone, you know I've always got your back, and Hannah should know it, too."

"That's what I told her."

Erica cupped a hand around her ear and shook her head, and Amber smiled and shrugged and waved a hand. No point in trying to have a serious conversation now, with the crowd growing by the minute.

But she couldn't stop the thoughts swirling in her head. If Amber were in a relationship, maybe Erica was right and it would be a relief to Hannah. Only because Hannah would feel reassured that Amber would have someone to take care of her.

But Amber couldn't impose that on Paul. He had enough on his plate. And besides, he'd taken her advice to heart and was dating someone else.

Trying not to be obvious, Amber looked around to see if Paul and Davey and Kayla were still here, but from this sitting position, she couldn't see them.

She ought to be glad about it. Paul and Davey needed a woman in their lives. And oh, how she ached to have it be her, but there was no way.

Erica scooted her chair around so she was right next to Amber and practically shouted into her ear. "What if you were a hundred percent healed now, sure you wouldn't have a recurrence? What would you do about this thing with Paul?"

Wouldn't that be a dream come true, to have what she'd long ago stopped taking for granted—normal health? "It still wouldn't work."

"Why not?"

Amber hesitated. "Can you keep a secret?" she asked finally. She'd promised not to tell, but telling Erica wasn't really telling. Erica was the most trustworthy person on the planet.

Erica nodded. "You know I can."

Amber leaned closer and spoke into Erica's ear. "Davey's not really Paul's son. Wendy told me, shortly before she died."

"What?" Erica's mouth fell open and she stared at Amber. "He has no idea?" she asked finally.

"None."

"You've got to tell him!" Erica's expression was shocked, but the conviction in her voice left no room for doubt.

"I can't," Amber said. "What if it pushed him away from Davey, and Davey had to go live with those awful grandparents?"

"But what if there's a genetic issue? We of all people know how important that is."

That was something Amber had avoided thinking about. "You're right, but...I promised Wendy I wouldn't tell. Anyway, I don't even know who the father is. What good would it do to tell?"

Erica's forehead wrinkled and her mouth twisted to one side. "Right, sure. So you're going to keep quiet and leave him to someone else. To Miss Harris the schoolteacher."

"Exactly." Amber leaned back and crossed her arms.

"Come on, then." Erica stood and took Amber's hand and tugged at it. "If you're doing so fine, let's go say hi to him and Davey."

"I'm not *that* fine!" Amber protested. "But I do want to get out of here. It's a little close." In fact, she felt almost dizzy from all the emotion as well as the crowd.

"This way." Erica dragged her toward the exit, which was near Santa.

"Miss Amber!" Davey's voice rang out, sweet and high above the noise. "I'm gonna see Santa!"

Could she pretend she hadn't heard him?

No, she couldn't. Slowly, she turned, focused on the child's sweet face, and walked over to the line of people. "That'll be really fun," she said to Davey. She didn't look at Paul.

"I know!" Davey bounced up and down.

"Hi, Amber." Paul's voice sounded strained. "Do you know Kayla?"

She met his eyes then, and the communication that flashed between them was intense, and nonverbal, and she knew exactly what it meant.

You told me to date other people and that's what I'm doing.
Fine. I'm not arguing with you.
But that kiss...

"We've met." Kayla's voice sounded funny. Wry, almost.

"Nice to see you," Amber lied, and then she couldn't look at either adult anymore. Thank heavens for Davey. She knelt to his level. "What are you going to ask for from Santa?"

"A 'lectric train!" Davey half yelled. "A really, really big one!"

Amber lifted an eyebrow and looked up at Paul. "Is that Davey's idea, or yours?"

"Busted," he said, a grin starting to form on his face. Then he looked from Amber to Kayla and the grin faded.

Amber couldn't stand it anymore. Her heart ached and her throat felt tight and there was no way she was going to stay here and cry. She stood. "I'm sure Davey will love a train," she forced out. "Nice talking to you." She turned to Erica, who'd been watching the whole exchange. "Come on, I need some air."

And some space. And some recovery time because seeing Paul with another woman felt kind of like being hit by a really big train.

CHAPTER FIFTEEN

"So, HOW LONG HAVE you been crazy about Amber Rowe?"

Kayla's question took Paul by surprise and he looked at her blankly. It was dark, and Davey and a couple of his friends were leaning on the low railing that fronted the bay, watching the boat parade. Kayla and Paul sat on a bench behind them.

It was chilly enough that he could see his breath. The small, jolly crowd was decked out in bright Christmas sweaters and scarves, and a street band played "Deck the Halls." Smoke from a bonfire scented the air.

And his date had noticed that he was more interested in someone else than her. Nice. He looked at her closely, trying to read whether she was upset. "It's obvious?"

Kayla raised her eyebrows and tilted her head to one side. "Uh, yeah. Very."

"I'm really sorry." He shook his head. "I guess I shouldn't have asked you out when…" He couldn't finish. *When I'm half in love with someone I can't have?*

"It's fine." She shrugged philosophically, lifting both hands, palms up. "I have bad luck with men. And I shouldn't necessarily date a parent, either."

"I feel like a jerk." He really did like Kayla. She was a great person, a wonderful teacher, pretty and kind. She'd be a great girlfriend. In fact, he couldn't figure out why she was single.

The only problem for Paul was, she wasn't Amber.

Kayla leaned back against the bench, studying him. "Why aren't you dating her? Pretty sure she's crazy about you, too, from the way she reacted to seeing us together."

Paul opened his mouth to answer when everything exploded around them. Flashing lights and the sound of gunfire, and he leaped off the bench to get to Davey.

"Paul! What's wrong?"

Take a breath, he told himself as he clung to the railing by Davey for dear life. *Figure out what's really going on.* The words from his support group tried to hammer their way into his head.

Maybe it *wasn't* gunfire. Because he could look around and see that really, people were staying put, not running. They talked and laughed and pointed up at the beautiful fireworks in the sky.

He was just having an attack. His heart raced out of control and he was breathing hard and in his head, he could see people running and hear kids screaming and smell something sulfur-like.

Kayla stood beside him, rubbing his arm. "Paul! Paul, are you okay?"

He shook the hand off his arm, trying to catch his breath, trying to keep control. So far, Davey hadn't noticed his panic. He tried not to touch his son, not wanting to scare him.

"Paul. It's Kayla. Breathe. Take a deep breath. Let it out slowly."

He tried to do what Kayla told him. It was what his counselor said, too. But the popping and explosions and flashes kept on.

"Let's go," Kayla said. "Come on, Davey. We're going home."

"Davey." Now he couldn't help reaching for his son. He

felt his scrawny shoulders, looked at his upset face. He was okay. Davey was okay.

Kayla tugged at his arm with one hand and squeezed Davey's shoulder with the other. "Let's go. No, honey, we can't stay until the end, but when we get back to your house, I have a surprise for you. Come on. Let's race-walk to the car." Kayla's voice was soothing, and then they were walking away.

"I want fireworks!" Davey's voice was a high whine.

"I know, buddy." Paul had to normalize himself for Davey, but he could barely speak amidst the booms and pops and flashes, could barely keep himself from grabbing Davey and running for cover.

By the time they reached Kayla's car, he'd started to come down. Which, unfortunately, meant that he was shaking, but he felt he needed to assert his manhood and keep this from being the absolute worst date the poor woman had ever had. "I can drive Davey and myself home," he said.

"No, you can't. Get in." She opened the back door for Davey. "See, I even have a booster seat for just this type of occasion."

With Davey in the car, Paul had no choice but to get in, too. Truthfully, he was glad to have a little help right now.

Behind them, people were still oohing and aahing over the fireworks, but the street around them was quiet and deserted. Kayla played classical music on the radio as she drove the five minutes to Paul's cottage.

"I'm sorry." He kept his voice low so Davey wouldn't hear. "I had a rough therapy session yesterday and I was warned it might kick some things up." He'd also had it recommended that he go to a retreat this weekend for police and military PTSD sufferers, but he'd declined. His therapist didn't understand what it was like to be a single dad.

He couldn't easily get childcare he trusted for his son, not for a whole weekend.

But Paul wasn't exactly a contender for Father of the Year now. Maybe his therapist had understood him better than he'd realized.

Kayla pulled into his driveway and turned off the car. "No need to apologize for something that's not your fault," she said. "Let me help you get Davey to bed."

"You said you had a s'prise." Davey's voice was sulky and sleepy both.

"I do." She reached into the glove box and pulled out a toy from a kids' fast-food meal. "You can have it when you get into bed."

"Okay." Davey didn't thank her, but neither did he inform her that he already had two of the same toy, which seemed like admirable restraint in an almost five-year-old.

Paul drew in a deep breath and let it out. Thinking about your kid's manners seemed so normal. He was returning to normal.

Paul carried Davey inside and upstairs and tucked him in, and Davey was asleep within two minutes. When he came back downstairs, Kayla was sitting on the couch.

"Thanks, you didn't have to wait," he said. "Do you want something to drink?"

"I'll take a bottle of water, a pillow and a spare toothbrush." She was kicking off her shoes.

"You don't have to stay. I'm fine now."

"I'm staying," she said. "What if you have a nightmare or something?"

"No. I'm fine. I'll stay awake."

She held out a hand. "Toothbrush, please. I'm sleeping on your couch tonight. And don't worry, I don't have designs on your virtue."

That made him snort. He really did like Kayla. And given his experience tonight, she was probably right: it was best if she stayed.

So he got her a bottle of water and an extra toothbrush. Offered to make up his own bed for her, and when she refused, got her a pillow and a couple of blankets.

Then he went into his bedroom and made two phone calls. The first was to Ferguson, a night owl who right away said he and Georgiana could come tomorrow to care for Davey. The second was to his counselor. He got voice mail and asked if he could jump in on the second day of the retreat.

Tonight had taught him that, for real and for sure, he couldn't go it alone.

SUNDAY MORNING, AMBER dragged her suitcase out of the closet, tossed it on her bed and opened it. She grabbed shirts and shoes and threw them in haphazardly.

And tried not to cry.

Stupid, stupid, stupid.

Why had she expected anything different from Paul? He was a guy. And she was… Well, she was a girl who was fun for the short-term, but easily forgotten.

You should have known. You've been here before.

Except she hadn't, not with someone she cared about the way she cared about Paul. Somehow, he and his son had wiggled their way into her heart.

It had been bad enough to see Paul and Davey with Kayla last night. When they'd laughed together, when Davey had swung between them, clasping both their hands, she'd died a little inside.

But the heart was absurdly optimistic. She'd allowed herself to hope, when Paul and Kayla left early, that things hadn't gone well. Not very nice, wishing a bad time on other people, but hey, she was only human.

When she'd gotten home and seen Kayla's car—a strange car, anyway, and she assumed it was Kayla's—outside of Paul's house, her optimism had fled and her heart just hurt.

When she'd gotten up this morning and seen that the car was still there, her heart had turned to stone.

Kayla had spent the night with Paul. Less than a week after kissing Amber in such an extraordinary way that she couldn't stop thinking about it, he'd slept with someone else.

She threw jeans and socks and underwear into the suitcase, trying to find comfort in the familiar action of packing up. There. That was probably enough clothes for a couple of weeks, so she went into the bathroom and pulled out her travel case, always packed with shampoo and toiletries and a little makeup, always ready to go.

She threw it into her suitcase, then went back to the bathroom for her pill bottles. She had started to forget who she was. Had started to forget she was the girl who was always ready to travel, footloose. Fun and relaxed and uncommitted.

She was *not* the girl who got together with the reliable, gorgeous homebody of a single dad and his adorable son.

Hannah wouldn't be happy at the idea of packing up and going on a trip the moment she got home from college. She wanted to relax and bake Christmas cookies and see Erica and Trey and Hunter.

But Amber hoped that, as they drove south, Hannah would be converted to the idea that a Christmas trip to a warmer climate was just what they needed. A new bikini and a couple of beach reads, and Hannah would be fine with the unconventional holiday. It would make for great social media posts.

Her eyes narrowed. Maybe she'd post some pictures herself, show that she was having a great time without Paul. No bikini for her, but she still looked pretty good in a pair of cutoff shorts and a tank top. Hopefully, Paul followed her on social media and would feel at least a moment's regret for what he was missing.

Would Paul be sad? Would Davey miss her? Well, Davey might. He was a sweet little boy and he'd liked her.

Paul, well…she'd overestimated him. She'd thought that his intense kisses and words of caring meant something. She should have known better, but Paul had seemed different from the casual boyfriends of her past. He'd seemed like the type who wouldn't say things he didn't mean.

So much for her great perceptiveness about people's characters. Paul was just like any other man, only worse because he presented as good and honorable.

In reality, he was quick to forget. He hadn't meant it when he'd gotten all passionate kissing her. Or at least, the passionate side didn't mean anything.

Stepping to the window, she looked out at the bay covered with whitecaps from the breezy day. Normally, the sight of it brought her comfort, serenity.

Now she felt as stormy as the roiling clouds coming in from the east.

Something red caught her eye, and she squinted to see Davey's little jeep driving off down the beach. She looked for Paul, who always stuck pretty close to Davey when he was playing with the toy vehicle. But she didn't see him. Meanwhile, Davey was cruising. It wasn't exactly fast, but it was as fast as an adult's brisk walking. He could get out of sight quickly at that pace.

Where was Paul? Had he tired himself out so much last night, with Kayla, that he couldn't even take care of his kid?

It would serve him right if... No.

No matter what Paul had done to hurt Amber's feelings, Davey needed to stay happy and safe. She hurried down the stairs and out onto her own back steps and craned her neck, looking in the direction Davey had been going. She was relieved to see he hadn't gotten much farther away and was now driving the jeep in circles. She heard a bark, and realized he must have Sarge in the jeep with him. Against the rules Paul had set for the child, but it made Amber feel better. With the bloodhound at his side, nothing very bad would happen to Davey.

Still, he shouldn't be supervised just by a dog. Should she run after him?

No. There were a few people on the beach, and surely they would keep an eye on a little kid. She would just watch. She couldn't stay attached to Davey nor allow him to continue being attached to her. He couldn't be the victim in the mess that was her and Paul's bumbling failed start of a relationship.

Actually, Davey was the winner because he would be much better off with his teacher. Kayla, kind and pretty and healthy.

She looked over at Paul's silent house and then scanned the beach again. There was still no sign of Paul, so reluctantly, she pulled out her phone and called him.

It went directly to voice mail.

Great, so he *was* exhausted from his night with the lovely Kayla. "Paul, it's Amber. I noticed Davey is driving his jeep down the beach and wanted to make sure you knew about it. It's about 10 a.m." She paused, unable to think of how to end the call. "See ya," she mumbled finally, and touched the end button.

There, that was enough to do, right? She had fulfilled her obligation.

She looked down to where Davey had been. He'd stopped doing circles and was headed down the beach again, away from home.

Amber heaved a sigh, grabbed a paper towel, wet it and wiped beneath her eyes to make sure there were no mascara stains.

Then she marched over to Paul's house and pounded on the door.

To her surprise, Georgiana answered, looking uncharacteristically dirty and sweaty. Ferguson was right behind her.

Neither of them looked friendly, but that was no surprise.

"Davey just drove off down the beach in his jeep," she said.

"No, he didn't. He's playing on the deck." Georgiana started to close the door.

"You might want to check."

Ferguson opened the door a little bit more. "Thanks," he said curtly, and then the door closed in her face.

Well, okay, then. "You're welcome," she muttered. She walked slowly back to her cottage and sank down on the steps, waiting to see what would happen. She didn't want to run after Davey, didn't want to maintain an attachment that was doomed to end quickly, but she would do it if his safety was at risk.

In fact, it was a little strange that Ferguson and Georgiana were babysitting him. She'd thought Paul said he wasn't going to allow that to happen much anymore, if at all. But whatever. She didn't understand Paul nearly as well as she had thought she did.

The back door of Paul's cottage opened. "Davey! Get back here!" Ferguson's deep, loud voice rang out, and then the man jogged down the steps and along the narrow beach toward Davey. All that golfing and tennis must have kept him in good shape, because he moved fairly briskly. He soon caught up with the little car and it stopped. He leaned in, obviously lecturing, and then Sarge jumped out. Soon the jeep was moving back in the direction of Paul's cottage, Ferguson and Sarge walking alongside it.

Relieved, Amber turned to go inside when there was a shout from Georgiana. The woman beckoned to Amber as if she were a servant.

Amber contemplated ignoring her and going inside, but curiosity tugged at her. She blew out a disgusted breath and walked over to the front porch of Paul's house where Georgiana stood. "What?"

"Wendy said…she said a lot of crazy things at the…at the end. It wasn't like her." Georgiana's chin was trembling. She cleared her throat. "Whatever she might have said to you…well, we're on it."

Amber tilted her head to one side and stared at the older woman. "What are you talking about?"

"If she said anything strange to you about Davey." Georgiana seemed to force out the words. "Just keep it to yourself. It's not your business."

Amber opened her mouth to ask a question, and then the pieces clicked into place and she gasped. "Are you talking about…"

Georgiana turned and went inside, her narrow shoulders slumping. Almost as an afterthought, she reached back and closed the door, once again, in Amber's face.

Amber stared at it, and then, slowly, she turned and walked the short distance back to her place.

They knew. Ferguson and Georgiana knew that Davey wasn't Paul's child. And they hadn't told him, either.

The question was, what would they do with the knowledge?

CHAPTER SIXTEEN

AFTER MASS SUNDAY MORNING, Mary sat in the pew as people got up to leave, greeting each other, shaking the priest's hand. At first she was just giving people the opportunity to clear out, because she didn't have any place in particular to go. But then, even when the crowd thinned out, she found herself still sitting, feeling limp and tired. She drew in the mixed scents of candles and incense and tried to muster up the energy to make her way home.

"May I walk you out, pretty lady?"

She turned and there was Kirk, sidling in beside her, holding out a hand. Most of her close friends were Protestant, if they went to church at all. Kirk was one of the few other Catholics in her group.

She didn't really want to be around him. Didn't want to be around people, generally, when she felt this out of sorts. But that was rude of her. She was in church. She smiled and let him help her out of her seat, and they greeted the priest and walked out together.

The wind was cool, and Mary wrapped her coat more tightly around her. Despite the weather, Mary had walked to church, and it looked like Kirk had, as well.

Kirk helped her adjust her coat. One thing you could say about him, he had excellent, old-fashioned manners. "Can I ask why you don't take Communion?"

Mary's face warmed. "It's a private decision."

Without seeming to hear what she had said, Kirk started mansplaining. "You know, you don't have to go to confession beforehand every single time, like when we were kids. Most people don't, these days."

Did he think she hadn't noticed that? Most weeks, she was the only person who remained in the pew while the rest of the congregation filed up front to partake of the bread and cup. "You're right," she said, hoping to placate him and in that way, get him off the subject. "Most people do go to Communion."

"I go, and you can just imagine all the sins I've committed."

"I can," she said dryly.

She'd stopped going, of course, when Ben and her daughter were killed. She'd talked to several priests since then, spent time on her knees. She'd gone to confession, prayed the Act of Contrition, done her Hail Marys. But none of it had helped her heart. She still felt too guilty and too wrong to partake of the elements, too angry at God for taking away her child.

"Is it anything to do with that stepdaughter of yours?" Kirk asked as they walked slowly toward Sunset Lane.

She frowned sideways at him and didn't answer. He was too outspoken and too blustery, but he was also too astute. She didn't want to talk to him about Imogene, but it was probably inevitable.

The sun peeked out through the clouds, making the day feel warmer. "Maybe it'll turn into a nice day," she said, trying to change the subject.

"Would you want to walk a little more?" he asked promptly.

Mary opened her mouth to turn him down, like she always did, but going home to her empty house didn't hold a lot of appeal. "Okay, I guess."

He put a hand on her lower back to guide her around the corner and toward downtown, but thankfully, after that he dropped it, and he didn't try to hold her hand as he had several times in the past. They talked about the house she was buying, how the planned closing date was pretty close to the Christmas holiday, which wasn't necessarily wise, but it was probably going to work out.

She really was grateful to have him on her side in this real estate transaction. His years of experience and persistent attitude were invaluable in getting the deal done. And she really, really wanted to get the deal done. Church and prayer hadn't helped her guilt much, but doing things for other people did. If she could get the new project off the ground, she knew she'd be that much closer to making amends.

"Come this way," Kirk said after they'd walked a block down Beach Street. He led the way down a short side street. Then they were at Goody's house, which stood directly behind her restaurant, and he stopped. "I need to speak to Goody for a minute."

"Do you want me to wait out here?"

"No. It's too cold, and Goody won't mind."

As he hurried her up Goody's front walkway, smiling a little, again with a hand on her back, suspicion rose in her. What did he have up his sleeve?

He knocked on Goody's door, and there was the sound of Goody's dog barking, and then Goody opened the door. She looked right past Mary to Kirk. "There's only one left, and you're not going to like her."

The puppies! He'd brought her here to look at the puppies Ziggy had fathered. "Kirk!" Mary scolded. "You know I'm not interested in a puppy right now."

"Oh, I know. But since we're here, let's just look." Kirk said it like the salesman he was.

Maybe it was because they'd just come from church, or maybe it was her blue mood, but Mary couldn't seem to muster the energy to fight off Kirk's determination. They followed Goody into a back bedroom, where an area was penned off. A small, fluffy chocolate-and-white puppy sat alone in a corner of the pen.

"That's what's left?" Kirk frowned. "I was hoping for one of the white ones."

"You and everyone else. Those two were snapped up right away. And then the spotted ones went, the ones with the cute black markings around their eyes." Goody frowned at the remaining puppy.

Mary sat on the floor to see the little pup who huddled at the back of the pen, a pink collar identifying her as a female. Her face was chocolate colored with a white spot on one side. The rest of her body was white, except for a large brown spot toward her tail. Her uneven coloring, plus the way she cringed back from attention, made it clear why she hadn't been a favorite of Goody's puppy buyers.

"You can't complain," Kirk said to Goody. "Old Ziggy made you a lot of money in the end."

"That's true," Goody admitted. "And they were nice pups, friendly as could be, most of them." She reached down and lifted the chocolate-and-white pup out of the pen. As soon as she set it down on the floor, it darted away from her, right into Mary's lap.

The dog would no doubt get huge, given the size of the father. Right now, though, she was almost exactly the size Baby had been.

"Cupcake is done," Goody said. "She doesn't want to nurse anymore. It's ten weeks now and the others have all been sold, so she's ignoring this little girl. If I can't find someone to buy her soon, I may have to sell her to a pet store."

"Oh, no." Mary stroked the little dog. "She needs peace and quiet and love, not a bunch of loud people poking at her and knocking on glass to scare her."

Goody shrugged. "You're not wrong," she said, "but I have a business to run. Honestly, I've had enough of puppies for now, too. I didn't sign up for this."

The little dog peered at Mary, and there seemed to be a plea in those brown eyes.

Mary looked up at Goody, then at Kirk, who had a hint of a smile on his face, the trickster. And then she ran a gentle hand over the puppy's soft fur. "I'll take her."

PAUL ARRIVED HOME Sunday night feeling one hundred percent better about life, ready to resume the mantle of fatherhood. He unlocked the door of the cottage and looked around the empty front room, then checked his watch. Ferguson and Georgiana must be upstairs giving Davey a bath. It was almost time for bed. "Davey boy! I'm home!"

Except for a welcoming bark from Sarge, the house was dark and silent.

He frowned and walked through, trotting upstairs and then back down, flipping on lights. "Davey, buddy! Where are you?"

In the kitchen he found a note in Georgiana's perfect handwriting. "Took Davey for ice cream! Back soon!"

That was nice, right? But he felt a little uneasy. Georgiana wasn't an exclamation point type of person.

He walked through the house, scanning everything. A juice box lay on its side on the coffee table dribbling juice, and there were toys scattered across the family room floor. The front closet, where he kept a box of Wendy's things he'd planned to go through, was open. And the lid on the box was askew.

That wasn't like Ferguson and Georgiana. They were almost obsessively neat.

None of it necessarily meant anything. His in-laws knew about the box, and it would be just like them to start going through it without him. Putting the kindest interpretation on it, maybe they had wanted to show Davey something from his mother's past.

As for the mess, he knew exactly how that could happen. Probably, Davey had gotten cranky and refused to put away his toys, and they had whisked him out rather than letting him have a tantrum and a scene. Paul had been there. He understood.

There was nothing to worry about. At the workshop today, the presenter had reiterated that feeling scared or nervous, feeling that sense of impending doom, didn't necessarily mean anything about the real world. It was a function of the PTSD brain.

He drew in a couple of deep breaths, said a quick prayer, then relaxed his shoulders. He should take advantage of having a little time to relax.

He glanced over toward Amber's house, something he did fairly often. He had gotten the message from her about Davey going off in his jeep and had been briefly worried, but she'd called back and left a second message that everything was fine. He'd gotten both of them at the same time, one after another, when he'd finished his morning workshop session.

What had she seen? This was the perfect chance to talk to her, before Davey got home.

He was halfway to her place before he told himself the truth: he just really wanted to see her.

And he wasn't going to second-guess himself. He jogged up her steps and knocked on the door.

When she opened it, his hope of a friendly greeting died a quick death. Her jaw was clenched square and she wasn't smiling. Her hair was pulled back under a scarf and she wasn't wearing makeup. Her eyes were actually a little red.

His heart lurched. "Is everything okay? Hannah?"

"She's fine. Out with friends. And it depends on what you mean by everything." She didn't invite him in. Instead, she crossed her arms over her chest. Shutting him out.

"I, um, wanted to talk to you about those messages, find out more about what you saw."

She let out an obvious sigh. "I told you everything I know," she said.

"Please? Can we talk a few minutes?"

Another sigh. "Come in," she said, and unlatched the door for him. "Where's Davey?"

"Ferguson and Georgiana took him to Goody's," he said.

She led the way into the front room and sat down on the edge of a chair. Not on the couch where they could be friendly.

Oh, well. A short visit was better than none. "Can you tell me what you saw, what worried you?"

"I'm sure everything's fine," she said. "I saw Davey driving the toy jeep down the beach and got worried because there was no adult with him, so after I called you I went over and told Ferguson and Georgiana. Ferguson came out and ran down and caught up with Davey. No harm done."

Paul frowned. "They didn't know Davey had driven off?"

"No, and they didn't want to believe me, not until they

checked for themselves and saw that he was gone. But that's no big surprise. They don't like me."

He hated that he couldn't contradict her bald statement. "They have issues."

"No doubt."

And then there was a little awkward silence between them. She raised an eyebrow as if daring him to say something. Or maybe she just wanted him to leave.

"Listen," he said, "speaking of what you saw...can we talk a little bit about what you saw last night?"

She lifted her eyebrows and her chin at the same time. "Really?"

He cleared his throat. "I asked Kayla out and I shouldn't have."

Amber waved a hand as if to shoo away his words. "No need to explain anything to me. I don't have a claim on you."

"I know. In fact, you told me I should try to be with someone else, and I thought you were probably right, but you weren't. I shouldn't have listened."

"Considering that she spent the night, seems like things must have gone pretty well." There were patches of red on her cheeks and her voice was a little high, almost shrill, which wasn't like her.

So that was it. She'd seen Kayla's car. "She did spend the night, but not for the reason you're thinking." He sucked in a breath and then told her about the PTSD attack, and how Kayla had stayed on the couch to make sure Davey was okay.

She gave him an icy smile. "That's a creative story to explain having another woman at your house. I've never heard that one before. Well done."

He plowed ahead, ignoring her tone. "My counselor had recommended that I attend a weekend retreat, but I didn't listen. After the fireworks threw me into a panic attack, I called him to see if I could get in on the last day, and he agreed. Then I called Ferguson and Georgiana to see if they could take care of Davey. That's why they were here today."

"Uh-huh." Her expression had softened a little, but it still wasn't exactly warm.

"The workshop was good. Very helpful, and I'm feeling better." He leaned forward a little bit. "Were you upset?"

The lights in her living room cast long, soft shadows. She hadn't drawn the curtain, and the rising moon created a little path of light, visible through the bay window. From the kitchen, music played. Not her usual lively hip-hop, but what sounded like something you'd hear in the background at a spa.

She studied his face as if to discern whether he was sincere. Finally, she spoke. "Yeah, actually, I was a little upset." Then she looked away.

"Why were you upset?" Now he slid forward to where he was sitting on the ottoman in front of her chair. They were knee to knee.

She didn't back away as he'd feared she would; instead, she met his gaze steadily. "You know why."

He reached out and cupped the side of her face with his hand, letting his thumb run along her cheek, tucking a strand of hair behind her ear. "I don't want someone else. I want you."

"But we're doomed," she said. "That hasn't changed."

Now that he was touching her, he couldn't seem to take his hand away. "Maybe it doesn't make sense, but can we at least explore it a little?"

She bit her lip and studied his face.

He leaned closer. "Please?"

After another moment of looking into his eyes, she gave the tiniest of nods.

It felt like permission, and he moved forward and brushed his lips against hers. They were so full, so soft, he wanted to get lost in kissing her, touching her. His hands of their own accord threaded into her hair to pull her closer. And he did, for just a moment, kissing her harder.

But they had a lot to talk about and figure out. He'd hurt her, and he couldn't take advantage of her vulnerability to get physical. Besides, he had responsibilities. Reluctantly, he let her go, keeping one hand on her, sliding it down her arm to clasp her hand in his.

"Davey will be getting home any minute," he said. "I should go back."

She nodded quickly, glanced at her phone sitting on the table beside her. "Go. In fact, Goody's closed a while back."

"Then they're probably home now, wondering where I am." But the uneasiness he'd felt before returned, a prickling on his neck. He squeezed her hand once and let it go, stood and moved to her window to look out.

His in-laws' car wasn't in front of his place. "I wonder if they took him somewhere else after?" He pulled out his phone and called them, but the call didn't go through. Not a good time for the shore's spotty reception to be a problem.

"Maybe Goody would know. She knows most things that go on in town. I have her number."

He held out his phone and punched in the numbers she showed him. Quickly, he explained the situation and asked Goody if she knew where Ferguson and Georgiana might have taken Davey after the ice cream visit.

"How would I know?" she asked, sounding annoyed. "Business was terrible tonight. They never came in."

"Oh. Thanks." He ended the call and relayed what she had said to Amber. "I think something's wrong."

CHAPTER SEVENTEEN

As THEY DROVE through the night, heading up the coast toward Davey's grandparents' home, Amber studied Paul's hands on the steering wheel. He was focused, but not gripping it tightly. Concerned, but not freaking out. She could see the cop in him.

She could see the passionate man in him, too. *Could we explore it a little?* he'd asked.

We could have fun together. This could be the adventure I'm looking for.

But no. Her past was too much of a checkerboard, her future too iffy. Despite the fact that Paul had disavowed his interest in Kayla, the fact remained that another woman would be better for Paul than Amber was.

From the back seat, Sarge whined a little, and Amber half turned and reached back a hand to rub the big bloodhound's head. "He knows we're heading to Davey, doesn't he?"

For the first time during the drive, a smile flashed across Paul's face. "I think he does. He's pretty protective, and he and Davey have a real bond." He glanced down at his phone.

"They're still not answering?"

Paul shook his head. "No, and I'm not calling them anymore. From what John said, I'm 90 percent sure they have Davey, and I don't want to warn them and make them run." John, Amber had learned, was a neighbor of Davey's grandparents, and he'd been good friends with Paul, Wendy and Davey. Paul had called and found out that Davey was at the house with Ferguson and Georgiana or at least, John had seen him there earlier that day.

Why Ferguson and Georgiana would take Davey from Paul's place and run was anyone's guess. "Would they hurt him?"

Paul shook his head. "If I thought they would, I would have called the police right away. But they love him and he loves them. It's just that they don't know how to work with me, and they started acting really weird these last couple of weeks."

Amber felt her hands start to sweat. She was pretty sure she knew why Ferguson and Georgiana were acting weird. They had found out the truth about Wendy, about the fact that she had had an affair. They'd found out that Paul wasn't Davey's father.

"Just a few minutes now," Paul said. He pressed his lips together, his eyes narrowing a little, his jaw square. He seemed to be gathering his focus and energy for the confrontation ahead.

Amber didn't bother him. She just took deep breaths and tried to be a calming presence.

They drove into a community of large, modern homes, the sort of place only the very wealthy could afford, and that made Amber curious. Paul was so down-to-earth, but clearly, Wendy had been from a much higher income bracket than he, or than most people.

Paul pulled into the driveway just as Ferguson and Georgiana were getting out of the car. Ferguson opened the back door and Davey jumped out. When he saw Paul, he ran to him. "Daddy!"

Paul held open his arms and Davey rushed into them. Father and son embraced, and Paul's eyes closed as he slowly rocked his son from side to side. Only then was it obvious to Amber how worried Paul had been.

Georgiana watched them, and suddenly, her face twisted and she began to cry.

Paul frowned at her, as if he couldn't decide between yelling at her and comforting her. Amber got Paul's attention and gestured toward Ferguson, who was taking a couple of discount-store bags from the trunk of the car. She hoped he'd understand that she was trying to help, sending him toward the more rational member of the couple to provide real answers.

Amber, meanwhile, went over to the sobbing Georgiana and put a tentative hand on the older woman's arm. "Is there anything I can do?"

Georgiana twisted away. "No!"

Amber lifted her hands, palms out. "Okay, that's fine. Just trying to help." She glanced over toward Paul, but he was now talking to Ferguson in a low voice. He'd put Davey down, and Davey was rolling a ball for Sarge, who rushed to grab it and bring it back to his young master in a display of energy Amber had never seen in him before.

Sarge must have been worried about Davey, too.

Georgiana cleared her throat. "I guess you know the truth about Davey's father," she said, her voice low and choked.

Amber felt like a deer in headlights. She didn't want to collaborate with this woman, didn't want to be on her side against Paul. But Georgiana was right: she did know the truth, or some of it, the part Wendy had told her in confidence.

"We took Davey to…to his real father. He's a wealthy man, from our community. We were thinking he might want to help us raise Davey in the way…well, anyway. It didn't work." Her shoulders heaved. "It turns out he knew about Davey all along. He wants nothing to do with him."

Amber stared, her jaw dropping. How could anyone look at their own son without wanting to know him, be involved? "That's awful!"

Georgiana nodded. "He's married with a child and another on the way. He doesn't want his family to find out about Davey."

"Wow." Amber shook her head back and forth, slowly. She couldn't fathom it, and from Georgiana's reaction, she couldn't, either. It was one thing they agreed on.

"He says Davey isn't his problem." Georgiana put her face into her hands and then looked up at Amber. "So it's best that we just let things stay the way they are."

"Stay the way… Don't you think Paul deserves to know?" Amber felt almost dizzy with all the information, all the secrets swirling around.

"If he knew, he'd reject Davey, and then what?" Georgiana's voice was low and urgent. "We love the child, of course, and for a time we thought we wanted custody, but today has made us realize we're not equipped to care for him. He's getting bigger, more energetic. We'll be so old by the time he's a teenager."

Amber blew out a sigh. She had no idea what to do.

Paul was walking toward them now, Ferguson in his wake. Davey lay relaxed against Paul's shoulder. "I'd like to hear your side. What happened?" he asked Georgiana.

Ferguson hurried after him. "We were truly just taking him out to get ice cream, but on the way there, we changed our minds and brought him here."

"That's right." Georgiana jumped in too readily, and it seemed like this was a story they'd rehearsed. "We knew we were neglectful, letting Davey drive off down the beach, and that woman saw." She nodded at Amber. "I thought you probably wouldn't allow us to see him anymore."

Paul tilted his head to one side. "You know that wasn't a real logical thing to do, right?"

Ferguson opened his mouth as if to protest and then closed it again. "You're right."

Paul frowned, looking at the ground, obviously thinking.

It was something Amber admired about him: he was deliberate and careful. He couldn't be rushed into a rash decision.

Finally, he lifted his head and looked steadily at Georgiana, then at Ferguson. "I want the two of you to get some counseling before you see Davey again," he said.

Ferguson opened his mouth as if to protest, then closed it and nodded. "I'm not much for counseling, but it's probably smart. We made a mistake, Paul."

"Yes, you did."

"We need to get Davey home," Amber said, because her head was spinning. And then a feeling of warmth and nausea came over her. Light-headed, she sat down abruptly. Everything around her turned gray, and that was all she remembered.

CHAPTER EIGHTEEN

MINUTES AFTER PAUL squealed into the hospital parking lot, as he was explaining Amber's symptoms to the medics who were transferring her to a stretcher, Erica came rushing over to them. "I'm her sister," she said breathlessly, and ran alongside as they rolled Amber inside.

Paul had called Mary while driving and she had gotten word out to the people who needed to know. Now, of course, Erica was allowed to go back into the treatment area with Amber. Paul watched her go, his heart pounding, and then lifted a drowsy Davey out of his car seat and carried him into the waiting area.

He'd never experienced anything quite like this with Wendy. Her symptoms had come on gradually, which meant that there was always plenty of time to get medical help. As bad as her last days had been, there had never been a real emergency.

But no two cancer cases were alike. His mind raced, thinking of all the things that might have caused her to pass out. Pressure on a vital organ. Internal bleeding. A metastasis to her heart or lungs.

Before he could spiral into horrible possibilities, he forced his attention back to the here and now. He had his son to care for, and he had to be here to help Amber in whatever way she needed. There would be plenty of time to worry and panic and grieve once they'd learned what was wrong.

Paul was getting Davey a snack from the vending machine when Mary and Hannah arrived. They all hugged, and Mary kept an arm around Hannah. "Tell us what happened, and then I'm sure Hannah can go back to see her mom."

Mary was smart, trying to put off Hannah's visit to her mom's hospital room as long as possible. If there were something serious going on, it would be just as well if Hannah wasn't there to witness the worst of it. Legally, she was an adult, but she was only eighteen. She looked awfully young as she stood, eyes wet, biting her lips.

"We were talking to Davey's grandparents," Paul explained. "Just standing in the driveway of their country house. All of a sudden, Amber sat down on the ground and then she passed out."

"She fell over on her side, like this!" Davey sat down and toppled over to the side just as Amber had done.

"*That's* what happened? Did she hit her head?" Hannah stopped fidgeting. She even pulled out her phone and checked it before looking back at Paul.

"No, she didn't hit her head," Paul said.

"Daddy ran over and caught her, like this!" Davey ran halfway down the row of chairs and then slid on his knees the rest of the way. Which, indeed, was how Paul had caught Amber. He had the torn patches on the knees of his jeans to prove it.

"It's probably just the fainting thing from her accident," Hannah said. She wiped a smear of mascara from underneath her eye, using her phone's camera as a mirror.

"It's happened before?" Paul remembered now, that

Amber had mentioned a horse-riding accident. Maybe she'd even said something about fainting spells.

Hannah nodded. "A couple of times, and it scares me to death every time. You always worry that it's related to her cancer, but it isn't."

Relief coursed over Paul. "Maybe I overreacted." Nothing would make him happier. The sight of Amber unconscious on the ground had aged him ten years.

"You were right to bring her here," Mary said. "Hannah, why don't you go try to see your mom. I bet they'll let you in if you just ask them in your sweet way. Paul and I will take Davey to the playroom." She gestured toward the other side of the lobby, where Paul now saw there was a glassed-in play area for kids.

"Good idea, since he's wide-awake now." It was way past Davey's bedtime, and he'd sleep for hours once he'd settled, but right now he was overexcited. Some physical play would do him good.

They took some water out to Sarge, who was sleeping in the back seat of Paul's car, and then came back in and headed for the children's area, and Paul grabbed antiseptic wipes from the dispenser by the door. He started wiping down the toys he thought would be the most appealing to Davey. But it was a losing battle because Davey moved from toy to toy at lightning speed. The poor kid was exhausted and upset, and Paul couldn't blame him. Paul was exhausted and upset, too. He tossed the handful of wipes into the trash.

Mary sat down on a bench that ran along the wall and smiled at him. "Try as you will, you can't control germs, any more than you can control life. You've had quite the day, haven't you?"

Mary didn't know the half of it. After the fireworks episode last night, and waking up with a woman he barely knew sleeping in his house, he had gone to the PTSD workshop. He had come home to find his child missing, had had a major confrontation with his in-laws and now this scare with Amber.

He watched Davey run a truck across the room and back, making engine noises. Of course, it was a truck he hadn't wiped down. "It's true, I can't control much. But I still have to do my best to protect my son."

Something that looked like pain flashed across Mary's face and then was gone. "You absolutely do have to protect your son. That's your biggest priority."

He sat beside her. "The trouble is," he said, keeping his voice low enough that Davey couldn't hear them, "protecting my son means keeping him from getting attached to someone who's got health problems that could take her away from him."

"Amber."

He nodded. "When she passed out today, and I had to rush her here, he was upset. He already cares for her, a lot."

"Yes, well, emotions are tough to tamp down," Mary said. They sat and watched Davey play for a few minutes more. He was climbing up a slide and sliding down it, but he was moving slower each time. He kept rubbing his eyes.

"Want a distraction?" Mary asked, her eyes twinkling.

"Sure. I could use one."

Mary pulled out her phone. "Look at my new family member," she said, and showed him a picture of a cute brown-and-white puppy with a drooping head and sad eyes.

Just looking at it made him smile, and he remembered how often he'd heard, in counseling sessions and workshops, about the healing power of animals. He nodded as

Mary showed him another picture, this one of the puppy lying on its back. "Cute, but, man, you're going to be busy."

Mary nodded, rolling her eyes. "It was a spur-of-the-moment decision."

"You probably need to get home to your dog." He felt bad that he hadn't considered that Mary might have other things going on in her life.

"I'll go home soon," she said. "But I blame Kirk James for talking me into it, and so it only seems right that he's got puppy duty now."

"Definitely seems fair. Hey, Davey, come see Miss Mary's new puppy," he called, and Davey ran over to them.

Mary showed him the picture.

Davey smiled. "Maybe he can come play with Sarge sometime," he said.

Mary nodded promptly. "She's a girl, and yes. When she's a little bigger, she'll need someone to teach her the rules of being a dog."

Davey leaned against Paul's leg while Mary thumbed through more pictures of the puppy, and he yawned hugely.

Mary smiled down at Davey. "Speaking of Sarge, you and your dad should probably get home and put him to bed."

"Good idea," Paul said.

Mary stood. "I'm going to stop in and see if I can see Amber, and then I'll be heading home to my pup, too."

Paul knew she was right, and that he should go home. Had to go home because he had to tend to Sarge and get Davey settled down. But he hated to leave without seeing Amber. The sight of her passed out, pale and unresponsive, had done a number on him.

"I got something for Miss Amber." Davey reached into the pocket of his jeans and pulled out a crusty brown lump. He held it out to Mary.

To her credit, she accepted it immediately. "What's this?"

"It's magical," Davey explained. "It goes deep in the dark ground and turns into a real live flower."

"A bulb," Mary and Paul said at the same time.

"Is that from when you helped Miss Amber plant them?" Paul wondered whether it had gone through the washing machine a few times, or whether this pair of jeans had really not been washed for a month.

Davey nodded, and then two lines appeared between his eyebrows, a sign that he was thinking hard. "Mommy went into the ground and she didn't come up 'live. If Miss Amber goes into the ground, give her this so she can come out 'live."

Mary let out a sound that was half sigh, half an "oh" of understanding. She glanced at Paul as her fingers closed around the brown lump. "Of course, I'll give this to Miss Amber. You know, honey, she's going to be fine."

"Okay," Davey said, nodding politely. But the lines between his brows remained.

Paul stood, picked up Davey and thanked Mary for all she had done. His voice remained steady through the whole thing, and he carried Davey easily. He didn't fall apart, because he was a dad, and dads couldn't fall apart. On the outside at least.

Inside was a different story. Paul was a wreck.

He should never have let Davey get so attached that he would put Amber into the same category as his mother.

Paul had failed to protect his son.

AT ELEVEN O'CLOCK Monday morning, Mary opened her front door and hurried down to greet Amber and her daughter, Hannah. After spending the night in observation in the hospital, Amber had been released, and she'd called to see if she could visit the new puppy on the way home while Hannah picked up a prescription for her. Mary had gotten the feeling Amber wanted a few minutes away from her overprotective daughter.

Mary helped Amber up the steps, Hannah holding her other arm. They walked her into the front room and got her seated on the couch.

"You don't have to treat me like an invalid." Amber sounded exasperated.

"Humor us," Mary said. "And meet Coco," she added. She picked the little puppy up out of the pen she'd improvised.

Both Amber and Hannah squealed and raved over how cute the dog was. "Can I hold her?" Hannah asked.

But Coco quavered, obviously terrified.

"We'd better keep our distance," Amber said. "Let her get used to her new home for a little while."

"I don't know what happened to scare her," Mary said, "but she seems to have a very timid personality. Or maybe it's just the change from Goody's place."

Amber raised an eyebrow. "So you picked out the needy one, did you?"

"She was the only one left!" Mary protested. "Besides, Goody was ready to sell her to a pet store. When I saw how skittish she was, I knew that wouldn't do."

Hannah reached out a finger and ran it over the puppy's soft coat. "Okay, I'm going to run over to the drugstore and pick up your meds. When I come back, Mom, we're going home and you're going to bed."

Amber rolled her eyes. "You see what I'm dealing with here," she said to Mary. "It took all my persuasive powers to be allowed to visit you for twenty minutes."

"Well, I'm glad you did," Mary said as Hannah disappeared out the door. She stroked the puppy in her lap. "So how are you doing today?"

"Not real happy." Amber propped an elbow on the arm of the couch and rested her head on her hand. "Every time I get sick in a 'normal' way, people think I'm dying. It's a bit of a weight to carry. No more than I deserve, I suppose, but I hate it."

"So everything's fine? They're not worried about the fainting?"

Amber shook her head. "Nope, not worried. It's from a horseback-riding accident I was in. Unrelated to the cancer."

That still sounded a little scary, but Mary got what Amber meant. "People automatically assume that you're having a recurrence, I guess. Probably including you."

Amber nodded. "Whenever I get sick, I worry. Goes with the territory."

"I'm sure." Mary studied the younger woman. "You said something else. What do you mean, it's no more than you deserve?"

Amber kicked off her shoes and pulled her feet up under herself. "I didn't make very good choices as a younger woman. Didn't really take care of myself. I didn't think it mattered."

The puppy wiggled in Mary's lap, and she set it down to walk around the floor in its cute, clumsy way. "I hear that. I definitely have regrets about the past. They can be hard to shake."

"Yeah. So now, I kind of wish—I really wish—that I had good health and could move forward in a new direction."

"Like a direction of getting close to a certain man and boy?"

Amber's mouth twisted to one side. "I guess it's obvious."

Mary saw the puppy start to squat. "Oh no you don't!" She jumped up and grabbed it, then hurried toward the back door. "Emergency potty run," she called over her shoulder. She was trying to take the puppy out every half hour or so to help her get house-trained. Last night, she'd barely slept between the puppy's crying, and taking her outside, and googling for information on raising puppies.

Outside, she was rewarded by the puppy doing its business in the grass. "Whee, success!" she crowed to Amber, who had followed her.

"She's going to be a great dog. I'm happy for you."

"I'm happy, too," Mary said. She waved a hand toward Kirk's house. "Kirk was right, after all. But where were we when we got interrupted?"

Amber lifted her hands, palms up. "I was complaining, feeling sorry for myself. No big deal."

The poor woman was berating herself over something that clearly wasn't her fault. "You know, Amber, sometimes we blame ourselves for things because it's the only way we can feel like we have any control. At least, that's what a fairly wise therapist said to me one time." She knelt to pick up a stick, showed it to the puppy and then tossed it a few feet away.

The puppy ran after it and pounced, and they both laughed.

"Anyway," Mary continued, "you're not at fault for your cancer at all, nor for your fainting spells. And blaming yourself isn't going to have an impact on your health. At least, not a positive one."

Amber tilted her head to one side, her expression skeptical. "You could be right."

"Give it some thought." Mary felt a twist of hypocrisy because she knew that she was doing the same thing: blaming herself for something she hadn't been able, really, to stop from happening. Now she was trying to find peace and self-forgiveness through her actions, through her charitable activities. It helped, but didn't make her feel completely cleansed.

"There's another problem," Amber said. "I'm keeping a pretty big secret from Paul. Not something I did, but something I promised not to tell. Even if my health wasn't a barrier, that would be."

"Don't keep secrets," Mary said automatically. "They're toxic." She picked up the puppy to walk inside and saw a car pull up to her house. The driver-side door opened and Mary suppressed a sigh. "Oh, no."

Amber had started back toward the house, but now she turned toward Mary. "What's wrong?"

Mary just nodded at Imogene, now headed up the sidewalk toward the front door. She hadn't yet spotted Mary and Amber.

"You don't want to see her?" Amber kept her voice low.

"Not in the least, but I have no choice."

Amber nudged Mary toward the side of the yard that wasn't visible from the front. "Take the puppy in and don't answer the door," she said. "I'll go out and say I was bringing you food because you're sick."

"She's not going to believe that."

"Then I'll improvise. I can weave a good story when I need to." Amber grinned. "Go on. I can't get her out of your hair permanently, but I can give you respite for today. It'll make me feel useful."

Mary scooped up the puppy. "All right. Thank you." She would probably pay the price for avoiding Imogene, but she just wanted a day to enjoy her puppy and relax by herself. She gave Amber a quick hug, buried her face in the puppy's fur and sneaked inside.

CHAPTER NINETEEN

STAY HOME, GET extra rest, don't drive. Yada yada yada.

The same afternoon she'd gotten home from the hospital, Amber rolled out dough for gingerbread boys, mentally picturing elaborate ways to decorate them. She felt restless. She'd already driven Hannah crazy enough that she'd gone off to spend the day with some friends. Which was good; Amber didn't want Hannah staying home worrying about her.

Trouble was, she didn't want to stay home herself. She needed to be doing something so she could stop thinking about Paul and Davey and what they might be doing, how things had gone after she'd passed out at Davey's grandparents' house.

The knock on the door came as a welcome surprise, and Amber felt pathetically eager as she hurried to get it.

When she opened the door, she couldn't help clapping her hands. There was Davey, and behind him, Paul, barely visible behind a bunch of rolls of Christmas wrapping paper and several bags. Beside them, Sarge gave a friendly woof of greeting.

"We came to help you wrap gifts!" Davey said. "Because you're sick."

"I know it's intrusive, and early for wrapping. We can leave if you're not feeling up to this. But we were getting ready to wrap the presents we've bought so far, and I wondered if you needed help with yours."

"And Daddy doesn't do it right," Davey contributed.

Amber laughed and stepped back from the door so they could all come in. "I would love to have the company," she said. "And I *am* good at wrapping presents. So it might be me helping you, rather than the reverse."

Paul smiled, a lazy smile that warmed her to her toes. "My dream come true."

"Are you making cookies?" Davey was sniffing the air.

"I sure am, but I don't know if I can get them all decorated by myself. Do you like to decorate cookies?"

Davey looked up at Paul.

"When you were little, you loved it. Remember that picture of you with icing all over your face?"

"I was a baby," Davey said.

Which meant they decorated cookies together as a family, Davey and Wendy and maybe Paul, as well. Amber rolled that notion around in her mind for a minute and decided it didn't bother her. She'd felt traces of jealousy about Wendy here and there, but it seemed to be gone now. "It's nice you did that with your mom," she said.

"Mommy loved me." Davey said it matter-of-factly as he marched through the living room and into the kitchen as if he owned the place.

Amber glanced at Paul and saw him swallowing hard. Of course, he'd have good memories of Christmases with his family before Wendy had gotten sick. She walked beside him, following Davey, and rubbed a hand across his back to show she felt for him.

He put an arm around her and they walked that way for a few steps, following Davey. And Amber flashed on the future she'd never let herself dream of. Cookies baking in the kitchen, and a little boy to wrap presents with, and a wonderful, kind, handsome man at her side.

Her eyes filled with unexpected tears. And *what* was that all about? She stepped away from Paul as they entered the kitchen, checked the cookies in the oven and pulled them out just in time.

She set the pan on a trivet beside the stove and managed, via a lot of rapid blinking and by sipping water, to get her emotions under control. "I guess you heard we got the house for the new program," she said, keeping her voice businesslike. "I'm really glad. I think it'll cheer Mary up, and she needs that right now."

"Did the funding come through?"

"The funding isn't a problem with Mary," Amber said, "but it was more getting the inspection and closing done this close to Christmas. It's working, though, thanks to Kirk James."

Davey was unpacking the bag of wrapping paper and ribbons, strewing things everywhere.

Paul moved to assist him. "Let's put the rolls all in a row over here," he suggested, pulling out one of the chairs. "And we can leave the ribbons in the bag, or you can line them up along the edge of the table."

"I'll line 'em up!" Davey started doing just that.

Paul raised his eyebrows and smiled at Amber. "Sorry to take over your kitchen like this. But I'm glad to hear that Mary is getting the house for the new program. What's our next step?"

"It's up to us to make sure the program is planned well enough to apply for some grant funding in the spring," Amber said. "Mary is providing the initial funds, but lately, she's been really keen on having everything set up so that even if she's not able to keep funding the whole thing, the program will continue."

"It's definitely needed," Paul said. "I'm sure we can get the state groups to contribute or at least endorse it."

"Come *on*, Daddy." Davey tugged at Paul's arm. "We got to decorate and wrap and stuff!"

"Okay, sure, sorry." Paul grinned at Amber and it took her breath away. He was incredibly handsome. And he cared about Mary as well as his son. He'd even been kind enough to come here to help her out, almost certainly realizing that she'd be bored and lonely on a day like this.

She sat down at the table and started looking through the wrapping paper they'd brought. "Why are you going all black and white and brown?"

"It's classy?" He shrugged. "Wendy's family always went for these colors for their wrappings. And it does look nice under the tree."

"Not questioning that." Amber was sure it looked like *House Beautiful*. "In fact, I bet they use white lights rather than multicolored ones, right?"

"Yes, they do," Paul said. "Davey and I do, too." He glanced at her and then away, and it seemed like he was expecting her to make fun of their drab ways.

She had always been a multicolored lights person herself, admittedly verging on the tacky. But that wasn't important. "I think it's nice that you keep some of Wendy's traditions alive," she said quietly.

She thought about the woman she'd met so briefly. She had definitely seemed tense and anxious to Amber. And she'd been really troubled, because she'd done something on impulse that she couldn't figure out how to fix except by lying. From everything Amber knew about Wendy, everything she'd heard as well, it seemed that Wendy was normally a very moral person. The fact that she had strayed from Paul, that the results of her affair were alive and in front of her every day in her son's beautiful face, must have been terribly hard for her.

But the hardest thing, harder even than that, was the fact that she'd gotten so sick so young. Amber had had a taste of the fear a mother felt at the thought of possibly not being there for her child. She'd worried about Hannah constantly from the moment she'd gotten her diagnosis almost ten years ago. She worried about Hannah still.

But for Wendy, it had to have been so much worse. Wendy had been the mother of a younger child, more vulnerable, and what's more, she had known that he wasn't biologically Paul's child. How that must have terrified her, the thought that Paul would find out and abandon Davey.

And from what Georgiana had said, the biological father wasn't willing to take responsibility. Wendy had probably known that about him, or at least guessed it.

In a terribly difficult situation, in a traumatized state of mind, Wendy had made the best decision she knew how to make.

Amber got a sudden impulse. "Do you have any pictures of how Wendy and her parents decorated and wrapped their gifts?" she asked Paul.

"Do I…" He frowned. "Actually, I do. We always took a lot of pictures on Christmas." He scrolled through his phone and soon came upon several examples of Christmas morning pictures, with the gifts wrapped in tastefully matching shades of black and white and tan, with matching bows. "It looks like you did a different color of bows each year," she said.

"Yeah, that's right." He opened one of the shopping bags he brought, and inside was a jumble of various colors of bows. "I didn't go that far, though. These are left over from other years."

"Tell you what. Let's use the neutral wrapping paper and we'll choose a color family for this year. It looks like you might have enough blues and purples and greens to do all your packages. If not, I can probably dig up some bows in those colors myself."

"Thanks." He let his hand rest briefly on hers, and she heard what he wasn't saying. Appreciation for her willingness to carry on Wendy's traditions in this area, for Davey's sake.

"When are we going to decorate cookies?" Davey asked. Clearly, he'd gotten bored with the gift-wrapping discussion.

"Just give me five minutes, buddy," Amber said. "What color frosting do you think would look best on the gingerbread boys?"

"All the colors!" Davey waved his hands wide. "'Specially blue. That's my favorite."

"Well, okay, then." Amber pulled up the white frosting she'd made before, quickly divided it into smaller bowls and found her food coloring. She hummed as she stirred it in, creating a rainbow of frosting colors, with Davey kneeling on a chair beside her, giving advice. All the while, she kept putting in new trays of gingerbread men to bake, assembly line fashion.

Quickly, she got both Davey and Paul set up with frosting and gingerbread boys. "You decorate these however you want to," she said. "I trust your judgment."

"That might be a mistake," Paul said, but he gamely scooped up a lump of pink frosting and spread it over one of the cookies. Davey watched, then did the same with blue frosting.

Amber found some colored sugar and other decorations

that she and Hannah had used to make cookies in years past, and she pulled out a bunch of them for the boys to use. Sarge ran around devouring bits of cookie and frosting that fell to the floor.

"We're decorating cookies in school," Davey said, his tongue poking out the corner of his mouth as he concentrated on his work. "Miss Kayla said I was good at it. Now I'll be even better."

"Miss Kayla is smart," Amber commented, letting her gaze flicker to Paul's. She was pretty sure she didn't have anything to worry about in terms of Kayla, from what Paul had said before, but she couldn't restrain a slight feeling of jealousy.

"She's very understanding," Paul said, raising his eyebrows at Amber. "She can read between the lines. I'll have to tell you about that sometime."

"She's a good reader," Davey agreed. He squirted a huge glob of yellow frosting onto the head of a gingerbread boy.

Amber had to laugh at the double conversation that was going on, and Paul's lips twitched, as well.

She loved sharing a joke with him. Loved sharing holiday preparations and memories with him. The air was full of the smell of cookies, along with the pine scent of the little Christmas tree she'd bought. Christmas carols hummed away on the radio.

If only this could go on. Maybe it *could* go on. But not if secrets stood between them.

Certainty came to her: if she wanted to get closer to Paul and Davey, she needed to tell Paul the truth, and sooner rather than later.

"THANKS FOR COMING." Mary opened the door to Imogene, who looked almost dressed up in jeans and a flowered, smock-type top, her hair combed. "Meet my new baby, Coco."

Mary picked up Coco, who was walking toward the door with a mixture of interest and fear. Mary's initial assessment had been exactly right: Coco was on the timid side.

"Cute." Imogene glanced at the dog and then walked into the middle of the living room and looked around. "So, is this a social visit or..."

Actually, this was Mary's last effort. If it didn't work, she was going to withdraw support from Imogene and, if anything happened, file a harassment claim against her. Something about her conversations with Kirk and Amber, and then taking the step forward to adopt a new puppy, had given her courage. She didn't like feeling cowed and dependent on Imogene.

But she'd decided to give their relationship one last chance, and to really go for it, be honest and open, try to connect as adults.

She snuggled Coco close for a minute and then put the dog down so she could focus on her stepdaughter. "Listen, we've been so at odds since you arrived in town, and I realized I don't quite understand why. I haven't taken the time to listen to you. I was hoping we could chat, and you could tell me what made you so angry at me."

Imogene stared at her, eyebrows rising high. "Don't act like you don't know."

"I know that something terrible happened to both of us. I don't know why it made you so angry at me."

Imogene stared at her, mouth hanging open a little, and then spoke. "You killed my father."

The words were a claw digging at Mary's chest, but she was glad to have it out in the open. "No, Imogene. A bad man killed your father."

"Yeah, your ex-husband."

"Yes, I know." Mary closed her eyes for a moment, then opened them again. The puppy leaned against her leg and she reached down to scratch it. "I know. That's what I believe, too, though he was never convicted. Believe me, I wish I'd never married your dad to bring that into his life."

"Me, too." Imogene started pacing restlessly around the room, picking up knickknacks and pillows and putting them down. "You never did anything for me except take my dad's attention away. And get him killed. My life sucked after that."

"I'm sorry about that." Mary should probably have offered to take Imogene after Ben had been killed. Imogene's biological mother was not a nice woman, which was why Ben had had full custody of his daughter. But Mary had been so flattened with grief about her own daughter, and about Ben, that she'd been unable to fathom how to nurture an angry, grieving fifteen-year-old who already hated her.

Imogene finally sat down, flopped back against the back of the sofa and ran her hands through her hair. "You knew what your ex was like and you let him know where you were. Where we were. You had an affair with him, and you invited him to come and take out Dad to get his money."

Mary blew out a breath. She'd gotten bits and pieces of that story over the years, but had never heard the whole thing put together. "If that's what you think, then I don't blame you for hating me. But, Imogene, it's not true."

"My mom explained it all to me," Imogene said, her eyebrows drawing together. "She figured it out, and she told me how it was."

Mary shook her head back and forth, slowly, holding Imogene's gaze. "I loved your father very much. I would never have done anything to intentionally harm him."

"You say that now, but why would you have married my dad if not for his money? He was ugly and awkward."

"He was pure goodness." Even picturing him now, Mary could almost see the sweetness coming from his eyes, feel the kindness of his hands holding her. He'd offered protection and a refuge when she needed it, but it wasn't just that. She'd never known a man as good as Ben, before or since.

"He was a schmuck, at least that's what my mom said. She said there was nothing good about him except his money."

Mary pressed her lips together to keep herself from shouting at Imogene. After all, Imogene was just repeating what she'd heard. Most likely, there was a part of Imogene that wanted to respect her father, that remembered him with love. However tainted by her mother's harsh views, Imogene had at one time made a sandcastle with her father. They'd played catch, and he'd even let her paint his toenails pink. She knew all that from family pictures she'd looked through after marrying Ben.

The trick now was to counter what Imogene's mother had said without totally offending Imogene. Mary knew that Imogene's mother had been a beautiful woman who in fact had married Ben for his money and then had had multiple affairs. No wonder she'd accused Mary of the same. Pure projection.

So Mary started with a question. "Did your mom ever bend the truth or lie to you?"

"Are you calling her a liar?"

Mary sighed. "Not completely. I just had a very different perception of your father than she did. It's possible she was wrong."

"You're calling her a liar," Imogene said flatly.

This line of discussion was going nowhere. "I have some

old pictures I thought maybe you'd want to go through. If there are some you want, you're welcome to take them." Imogene didn't immediately say no, so Mary went to the dining room table and pulled two old-fashioned photo albums off it. She carried them over and handed them to Imogene.

Imogene grabbed the top one and flipped the pages, ripping one, and Mary had to clench her fist to keep from grabbing the books back. But that wasn't the point. She was trying to build a bridge. She sat down beside her stepdaughter and watched as images of her younger self, her daughter, Ben and, yes, Imogene, played before her eyes.

Seeing Daisy at three, four and then five choked Mary up. Daisy had been such a sweet child; all her teachers, all the other mothers had commented on it. She'd been the first to run over and help another child who'd fallen on the playground. She had cried when Mary hit a fly with a flyswatter or stepped on a spider. And she'd adored her new big sister, even though Imogene hadn't returned the warmth at all.

Seeing her younger self made her shake her head. She'd thought she knew difficulty and pain then, but she'd barely scratched the surface of those emotions.

Savor what you've got, she wanted to cry out to her younger self.

Imogene ran a finger over the picture of her father standing beside Mary. "You were so pretty," she said.

It was the closest thing to a compliment that Mary had ever heard from Imogene. Maybe they were getting somewhere. "So were you," Mary said, and it was true. Imogene had been a beautiful teenager.

Beautiful, but unpleasant and thoughtless, like most fifteen-year-old girls. Had Imogene been more that way than most? Mary couldn't be sure. It might be that she'd been too damaged by her childhood with her mother and her issues, or it might be that the loss of her father and the aftermath of that was what had pushed her into a basically ruined life.

They came to a photo of Ben holding Daisy. "He liked your daughter better than me!" Imogene's voice was tortured.

"No, honey, he didn't. He loved you the best, of course. You were his pride and joy."

"Then why'd he take her with him that day?" The words burst out as if straight from Imogene's troubled heart.

Mary's heart twisted. Here it was, the core of Imogene's anger and grief. She reached a hand toward Imogene, but the younger woman recoiled before contact was made.

Understandable. They'd have to talk it out, then, not hug it out.

And Mary had thought about Imogene's question time and time again. God forgive her, but she'd wished Ben had chosen Imogene over Daisy, as he usually did. Wished it had been Imogene in the accident, which was terribly, terribly wrong, another source of guilt. "He didn't take Daisy with him because he liked her better, not at all," Mary said truthfully. "I was supposed to bond with you that day. Your father thought it might help our relationship." Which had certainly been rocky. A young stepmother with a small child of her own was the worst-case scenario for a teenage girl who had her doting father wrapped around her little finger.

She studied Imogene thoughtfully. Her earlier suspicion turned into certainty. Imogene hadn't ever changed from that sullen fifteen-year-old. It was as if she'd been frozen at that stage, by all the trauma.

They flipped a couple of pages ahead, and there was

a picture of Mary and Ben on their wedding day. It took Mary's breath away because she remembered the love. Love she'd never experienced before or since.

"I miss him," Imogene said, her voice choked.

"I do, too, and I'm so sorry about what happened. I never meant it to turn out the way it did, no one would, but I'm just so sorry." She paused, then added, "To this day, I'll never understand why he came back home so quickly. If he hadn't, if he'd continued on to the park like they'd planned, I wonder if he might have…if they both might have…been safe. I wondered if maybe I was supposed to be the target, not your dad."

Imogene's face turned red. She grabbed the photo, ripped it in half and threw it to the ground. "I hate you for what you did!"

Mary hated herself, too, had for years. She leaned forward and picked up the pieces, putting them on the end table beside her, smoothing them out. "I can understand that."

Imogene thrust the album aside and rested her face in her hands. After a minute, Mary dared to put an arm around her.

To her shock, Imogene leaned into her, crying. Mary stroked her hair. Despite everything Imogene had done, Mary still felt the younger woman's pain as if it were her own. How terrible to lose your beloved father at such a young age, when you were still dependent on him but unable to show it.

Suddenly, Imogene jerked away and shoved at Mary. "Don't be so understanding!"

Coco had been sleeping at their feet, but the jerky movements woke her and she snapped at Imogene's ankle.

Imogene kicked out, and the little dog flew several feet

and landed, yelping. Mary rushed to pick her up, running her hands over the pup's body, her heart pounding.

Coco cried a few more little bleats and then settled into Mary's arms, nibbling at her, too.

Mary sank down into an armchair beside her, cradling the dog.

"You love that dog more than me, just like you loved your baby more than me." Imogene came toward them, reaching toward Coco, eyes fierce and angry.

Mary stood and turned so that Coco was shielded by her body. "Stop," she said. "Hurting an animal is just wrong."

"Hurting an animal is just wrong," Imogene said in a mocking, shrill voice, exactly the way she'd sounded at fifteen.

And Mary realized, finally, that all of her efforts were futile. Maybe someone else could help Imogene. She certainly needed help, a lot of it.

But if Imogene was sick enough to threaten a puppy, she was too sick for Mary to even nudge onto the road toward healing. "You need to go," she said. "Now."

"Scared of me, old lady?" Imogene taunted, looming over her.

Actually...yes. Mary *was* afraid. Imogene's eyes looked like those of a villain in a horror movie.

But showing fear was the wrong thing to do. Mary had learned that from her abusive first husband. So she narrowed her eyes and, still holding the puppy close to her body, she moved past Imogene. She walked to the front door, opened it and stepped out onto the porch.

At a time like this, she was glad Kirk James and his father lived next door, was glad of Primrose Miller's habit of watching everything that went on in the neighborhood. If

Imogene attacked her physically, someone would at least call the police.

She held open the door. "You need to leave," she said.

Imogene came toward her, stepped out the door and hesitated, too close.

Mary braced herself and turned the puppy farther away from Imogene's reach.

Kirk James's ninetysomething father came out on the porch next door, a cell phone in his hand. He didn't speak; he just stood watching them.

Imogene made a disgusted noise, spat on Mary's porch and stomped down the stairs and off down the street.

And Mary collapsed onto her porch chair, waved thanks to old Mr. James and cuddled her dog close to her chest.

For better or worse, she was done trying to connect with Imogene.

CHAPTER TWENTY

PAUL LOOKED AROUND Mary's store, at the little circle of parents and children listening to Mary read a Christmas picture book to them, and felt incredibly grateful to be here, among these people, in this small town that was starting to feel like home.

When Davey climbed out of Paul's lap and into Amber's, snuggling against her, he felt even happier. Especially about the loving way Amber cuddled him close.

It was a Christmas event with cocoa and puppets and a free book for every child. Paul had invited Amber after they'd wrapped presents together two nights ago. Now she looked over at him, caught him studying her and Davey, and smiled. What was she thinking?

Even Trey and Erica were there with Hunter. *He's way too young*, Erica had told Paul beforehand, *but we love stuff like this. I can't wait till I can read to him more.* She was cuddling Hunter in one of Mary's comfy chairs right behind where Paul and Amber sat with the others on the floor. Trey stood beside Erica's chair, his back to the wall.

Stop being a cop, Amber mouthed to him, making Paul smile.

A text came in on Paul's phone from an unknown number, and he ignored it. But when another from the same number popped up, he opened the message.

This is awkward, but I need to talk to you. I'm a friend of Wendy's, and I'm in downtown Pleasant Shores, hoping to see you for a few minutes.

The mention of Wendy made him curious enough that he responded with his location, and the person texted back that they would be there in five minutes. So after listening to a little more of the story Mary was reading, Paul whispered to Amber that he was leaving for a minute and headed outside.

He was in a great mood. Such a wonderful, warmhearted community, so good for Davey. He'd like to stay here. And he'd like to be here with Amber, and so would Davey.

There was a lot to think about.

Outside the store, a man in the kind of designer outdoor clothing favored by Wendy's parents lifted a hand. "Andrew McMartin," he said, holding out a hand. "You're Paul Thompson?"

"Yes." Paul got a strange, nervous vibe from the man. "You wanted to connect because of having known Wendy?"

Andrew nodded. He sucked in a breath and looked off down the block, then met Paul's eyes. "This is embarrassing, but let me just dive in. I was with your wife, and, well, you should know that your son is technically mine."

"What?" Paul stared at the other man, trying to process the nonsensical words. "What are you talking about?"

"I would never try to claim custody. But look. If you need to make some kind of financial arrangement…"

"What?" Why was this person talking about money? What was he saying? "What do you mean you were with Wendy?"

The guy looked at him like he was dense. "We had an affair," he said.

Paul shook his head. "You couldn't have." Wendy had been committed to him one hundred percent. This guy must be some kind of nut who'd managed to find Paul's number. Why, Paul couldn't fathom.

Or maybe he was an ex of Wendy's, or a delusional co-worker. Paul wasn't sure whether to try to get him to leave or to get his contact information just so he could keep track of him, make sure his hallucination didn't lead him to do something stupid.

The man talked on, and Paul tuned back in. "Big mistake," he was saying, "and we both knew that almost right away. We were only together a few times."

This man, this Andrew, spoke logically, calmly. Not like a deranged person, even though his words were impossible to believe.

"I didn't want to tell you. What was the point? But after this past weekend, I figured I should." He paused, seeming to wait for Paul to say something, and then went on, rubbing the back of his neck as he spoke. "Again, man, I'm not saying I want custody or anything. In fact, I'd like to keep this quiet."

A sick feeling rose in Paul's stomach. Was it possible that he was telling the truth?

"When I saw him this weekend, I panicked. Figured I'd better come and talk to you, make sure we were on the same page."

This weekend… Paul was starting to understand, but he couldn't find words. Couldn't figure out how to feel. "Did you say you're Davey's biological father?"

Andrew nodded his head yes as he peered through the store window. "Is that him in there? With the skinny gal?"

Paul nodded slowly. He noticed his own breathing had

sped up. His heart pounded, too, but it wasn't like a panic attack. This was something else.

Andrew shoved his hands in his pockets, still looking into the store where Davey sat leaning against Amber. "Wow. Cute." He shook his head a little. "That's that author, right? The pretty one." He shook his head. "I never did understand why Wendy chose her to confide in."

Once again, the man was saying something that didn't compute. "What do you mean?"

"I guess Wendy felt guilty. She was the guilty type, you know? She sent me an email right toward the end, telling me she'd let that woman know about the affair and about Davey, but she hadn't told anyone else." He frowned. "Wendy thought that author lady could keep it to herself. Guess she was wrong. Women sure do like to gossip."

Paul reached out a hand and turned the intruder to face him.

Fear rose in the man's eyes and he lifted his hands and started to back away.

All of a sudden, Paul's fist connected with the guy's cheekbone and sent him flying.

He felt like he was dreaming as he watched—what was his name? Paul kept forgetting—scramble to his knees and put a hand to his face.

Paul was going to wake up soon. He'd feel the sun on his face and hear Davey in the next room and realize he'd overslept.

The door of the bookstore opened and Trey came out. "What's going on here?"

Andrew was getting awkwardly to his feet.

So it wasn't a dream. "I just got some surprising news." The voice was coming out of Paul's mouth, but it seemed to belong to someone else.

Trey and Paul watched as Andrew brushed himself off and hurried down the street, glancing back as if afraid he would be followed.

"Will he press charges?" Trey asked.

Paul shook his head and rubbed his knuckles. They didn't hurt—adrenaline—but they were red and starting to swell. "Doubt it. The slime." He looked in through the window at Davey, who'd climbed all the way into Amber's lap now, looking half-asleep.

The idea that Davey wasn't his son was impossible to process. Paul's whole life was centered around protecting Davey, and he felt no diminution of the desire to do that. No way, no *way* was this jerk Andrew going to have any contact whatsoever with Davey.

Bits and pieces of significance were tapping on his skull now, demanding entry into his brain. Wendy, perfect, angelic Wendy, had had an affair. Was that even possible? Wendy had been so strict with herself in every way. Strict with others, too, but she'd never held them to a higher standard than she had for herself.

But why would this Andrew, the pretentious jerk, have come to him claiming such a thing if it weren't true?

He was still looking into the store, so he saw how Davey shifted in Amber's arms, leaning more against her, his eyes closing.

Amber knew. Andrew had said Amber knew.

That wasn't possible, because Amber would have told him if she knew something that momentous about his family and his life, about Davey. But something must have given Andrew that impression.

Paul didn't trust himself to walk into the store just now. He didn't feel like he could be with ordinary people.

"Would you mind asking Amber to come out here a minute? I need to talk to her."

Trey didn't move toward the store. "Do you have control of yourself?"

Of course, Trey was being protective of his sister-in-law. Rightly so, since Paul had just hit a man. Paul drew in a long, slow breath, relaxed his shoulders and nodded. "I have control. I just want to talk to her out here for a couple of minutes." He kept his voice steady. He was proud of that. "Maybe Erica or you could hold Davey for a few?"

"Okay, but I've got my eye on you." Trey gave him a warning glare and then walked into the store and tapped Amber on the shoulder, whispered something into her ear. She looked over toward Paul, then nodded and handed Davey to Trey, who stood inside the store window where he could see Paul.

Amber came toward him, questions in her eyes.

He watched her come, this woman he'd gotten close with, come to care about, maybe even loved. What was he going to say to her? What could he say?

As Amber walked toward the entrance of the store, she caught the expression on Paul's face and dread wrapped around her heart. His brow was wrinkled, his eyes strained, his mouth a flat line.

Something had happened. Something was wrong. She pushed open the door of the store, shivering as the cool wind hit her. She'd left her coat inside.

Paul was rubbing his knuckles absently, and when she looked at the hand he was rubbing, she saw some discoloration. "What happened? Are you okay?"

He was studying her face as if trying to read hieroglyphics. "You knew."

"Knew about what?"

He glanced down the street. "A man was here who said he had…" He shook his head. "He said you knew. He said Wendy said you were the only person she told."

Oh. Oh, no.

"Is it true?" The muscles in his jaw were working. "That Wendy had an affair? That Davey's not my son?"

She looked into his eyes, his dear eyes, now stormy. Everything was about to change between them and not for the better.

But the truth had to be told. Slowly, she nodded. "It's true." She reached out to touch his arm, wanting contact, wanting to know he didn't hate her.

He jerked away. "How could it be true? And how could you know something like that and not tell me?"

Amber's throat felt so dry that it was hard to get any words out, but she had to explain. "I'm basing it on what Wendy said, but yes. She had an affair and…" Amber swallowed the lump in her throat. "And conceived Davey that way. She made me promise not to tell you."

"But…why?" Paul's voice was plaintive, and Amber's heart ached for him. "Why would she do that? And why would she tell you?"

A gust of cold wind hit Amber, making her wrap her arms around herself. There was no answering the question of why Wendy had done it; that secret had gone to the grave with her. Amber could only attempt to answer the second question. "I don't know why she told me. It just happened that, that last time I visited with her and interviewed her, she obviously had something on her heart that she needed to say. I guess I was just the person who was there when she got that urge to confess."

"To confess."

Amber nodded. "She said she loved you so much, and she knew that it would break you. And she was afraid that you'd stop caring for Davey if you knew, and you're such a great father... Paul, she felt terrible about the whole thing. She couldn't stop crying. And she begged me not to tell you. I didn't know what to do, so I just listened and then did what she said." It wasn't an adequate explanation, but it was the truth.

His arms crossed over his chest. His eyes were cold, colder than the wind.

Clearly, from Paul's reaction now, she'd made the wrong decision.

The days and weeks leading up to this day seemed to flash before her eyes. The night Davey had come to her house, upset. The time Paul had called her to come help him at the preschool. The work they'd done together. Their kiss.

When in there could she have fit in a conversation about the fact that his wife had had an affair and his son wasn't his son?

But she should have found a way. Clearly, she should have found a way. By not telling him, she had ruined any chance of them being together, of him trusting her.

And why should he trust her? He was an honorable man, and she... Well, it was never going to work for a guy like him and a girl like her, anyway.

Only now, as it was withering away, did she realize how strong her hope had grown. How much she'd wanted to be part of Paul and Davey's family.

Davey. She looked back into the bookstore and saw that Davey was now in Erica's arms, while Trey held Hunter. Davey was looking in their direction, his expression worried.

"Paul." This felt like the most urgent part of the whole thing and she had to say it right. And from the looks of things, she had to say it fast, before Paul completely turned off to her. She grabbed his folded forearm, held on when he attempted to fling her off. "Be mad at me," she said, "but don't take it out on Davey. Let's move where he can't see us." She pulled at his arm, hoping to shepherd him away from the plate glass window.

He pushed her hand off his arm, gently enough, but she felt the quivering rage beneath those fingers. "Don't touch me." Paul's face was steel.

"You're the only father he's ever known and you have to stick with him. You *are* his dad."

He stared at her blankly then. "You think I'd abandon Davey? What do you think I am?" He glanced toward Davey, and then he did step out of the child's sight line. That meant he was closer to Amber, facing her down. "Were you ever going to tell me? Or were you just going to let me be the dupe who didn't even know he was raising someone else's kid?"

She felt lower than a piece of mud on someone's shoe. This had to be such a horrible shock to Paul. She tried to imagine what it would feel like if she discovered that Hannah wasn't her biological child, but that was impossible. Her love for Hannah was all tangled up with the fact that she'd borne Hannah from her body. And not to imply that adoptive parents couldn't feel that way, because Amber knew they could, but adoptive parents had known the situation from the beginning. Paul was only now discovering it, discovering his whole set of beliefs about Davey—about Wendy—were wrong. Her heart ached for him.

He rubbed a hand over his face, looking dazed as well as furious.

"Look," she started, "this must be so hard to take in—"

"Don't even try." He cut her off. "How could you dare

to try to comfort me about this? This secret you've been keeping from me while you were acting like you were my friend. Like you were even more than my friend." His voice had risen as he'd spoken until he was practically yelling, and a family, two parents and a child, coming out of the store stared at them, looking shocked. The father picked up his little girl and they hurried away.

She had to get him to calm down, for his sake and for Davey's. "Don't yell. You don't want people to think poorly of you," she said. "These are Davey's friends' parents. Don't say things you'll regret."

He glanced over at the retreating family. There was another family coming out of the store, too. She saw him breathe in deeply, saw him twist his neck as if it hurt.

When he spoke again, it was in a low, steady voice that was somehow worse than the shouting. "I never want to see you again. Get out of my life."

"Oh, Paul..." She drew in a breath and nodded. This wasn't unexpected. This was what she deserved.

"You're not worth caring about." He nearly spat the words.

Mechanically, she went back into the store to get her purse and her jacket, trying to keep hold of herself, trying not to cry.

Davey attached himself to her leg. "Miss Amber, stay with me," he said.

She bit her lip and closed her eyes for a moment, trying to shut out his cuteness. But she couldn't shut out his high-pitched child's voice. "Stay with me," he begged again, with that telltale whine that meant he was getting tired.

She reached down and, as gently as possible, pulled his hand away from her leg.

He grabbed on again, harder.

Her throat tightened into an ache. More firmly now, she loosened his fingers and then held on to his wrists. "Davey, honey. I have to leave."

"No, don't go." He started to cry. It was as if, somewhere in his perceptive young soul, he sensed the finality of this, and his quiet sobs broke her heart. Her own tears overflowing, she waited until Paul came in the door and started walking toward Davey, his eyes determinedly away from hers, and then she left in misery, passing Imogene on her way out.

She'd been through a lot in her thirtysomething years. Most notably, getting diagnosed with cancer, losing her mother and getting diagnosed with a recurrence. Those were horrible days.

But this day, in some ways, was the worst of all. Happiness had been at her fingertips, like a colorful helium balloon.

It hadn't even floated away slowly; it had burst.

Happiness, her chance at it, was gone.

CHAPTER TWENTY-ONE

MARY SCANNED the bookstore and sighed with satisfaction. The event had been successful, as evidenced by the fact that people didn't seem to want to leave. The families milled around, talking to each other, eating more cookies and shopping for books for their kids. And Mary was fine with it. She was feeling great about the store and her work here.

Telling off Imogene had been hard, but worth it. Finally, she'd admitted to herself that there was nothing she, personally, could do to help Imogene fight her demons. She'd texted referrals to a couple of counselors and an online support group. Now it was up to Imogene to follow up.

She felt like she'd shed a huge weight.

From her spot behind the counter, she handed out free books to the families that hadn't gotten them already. Everyone was so enthusiastic and grateful. She listened to the happy voices and sucked in the smell of chocolate and evergreen. Yes, she was getting into the Christmas spirit.

"Hey, everrybody." It was Imogene's voice, coming from the front of the bookstore.

Funny how one word from one person could put a damper on her mood. In the past, she would've rushed over to Imogene and tried to placate her, but she was through with that. Instead, she leaned forward, elbows on the counter, and watched as Imogene lurched around. It was pretty obvious she'd been drinking.

"Hey, listen up," Imogene called out.

Mary's insides twisted. Yes, she'd given up on helping Imogene herself, and yes, she felt good about that. But Imogene still had the power to hurt her.

"You all think Mary is so great," Imogene said in a loud voice that had most people staring at her. "But did you know she's involved with the mob? Where'd you think she got her money?"

Mary's stomach was churning now as her customers stared from her to Imogene and back again. Other conversations had stopped, and Imogene moved to the center of the store, turning slowly around as if she wanted to look at everyone.

Then she spoke. "Did you know she's had people killed?"

The words hung in the air and made Mary's heart lurch. Yes, she blamed herself in many ways for what had happened to her daughter and Ben. But to think that there were people, at least one person, who thought she'd ordered the hit? That was beyond belief.

Everything seemed frozen to her — people's shocked faces, Imogene's sneer, the children's confused questions. The Christmas music blared on, sounding tinny and cheap, and she reached down and shut it off.

"Someone should call the police," a woman said.

Mary felt dizzy. Was one of her customers going to call the police on Mary, even after all this time?

"She shouldn't be allowed to make a scene like that," the woman continued, and Mary realized she meant she might call the police on Imogene. And then there were several of her customers clustered around her.

"It's *her* fault, not mine," Imogene yelled.

"Sit down." Erica urged Mary onto the stool behind the counter.

Trey had approached Imogene. "Ma'am, you need to leave," he said in his best police-authority voice.

"What an awful end to a really nice night," one of the mothers said. "That woman is obviously out of her mind."

The voices couldn't seem to melt the ice inside her. She was humiliated, her privacy broken, her past revealed. She felt raw, scraped open.

Trey was ushering Imogene out, and Imogene was going, though she continued to call out threats and accusations.

Mary looked around, then spoke in a low voice to Erica. "Could you ask everyone to leave? I just want to go home."

"Of course." Erica moved through the little crowd, speaking to everyone. A couple of people were cleaning up the cookies and napkins and plates, and others expressed concern and sympathy, or even just squeezed her hand, before exiting the store. And then everyone was gone and she was alone.

No, not alone. "We're driving you home," Erica said, and she and Trey walked with Mary to their vehicle and drove for the short distance, then deposited her at her house. Erica insisted on walking her inside.

Once Erica left, Mary sank down into a chair, staring straight ahead while memories played across the screen of her mind. Ben's voice, his cheery goodbye that morning. Her daughter's excitement about getting to go somewhere with her stepdaddy, just her alone. The feel of the little arms around her neck, hugging her goodbye.

And then once they'd left, she'd gone back inside and planned her earnest effort to connect with Imogene. She'd bake her favorite coffee cake, ask her about school and friends. It wouldn't make their relationship perfect, not right away, but she'd hoped that by putting something positive into the bank of their relationship, it would continue to improve.

But before she could get started on her plan, a loud crash had sounded outside. They'd both rushed out and discovered Ben's truck, wrapped around a giant tree in their front yard. In the distance, another car engine sound was disappearing.

She'd never forget the sight of twisted metal, of bodies, of blood. Her whole world, and Imogene's as well, shattered.

Mary heard a whining sound, and at first she was so lost in the past that she didn't know where it came from. It sounded again and she realized it was her puppy, Coco. The little dog managed the great leap to the ottoman and then another into Mary's lap. There, she planted her paws on Mary's chest and licked her face.

Her face, that was wet with tears. She cuddled the dog close to her chest and gave herself up to the pain she'd been trying to shut out for years.

Sometime later—she had no idea how long—the phone rang. This late at night, it was either a wrong number or bad news.

She wasn't going to answer, but it stopped and started again, and she warily picked it up and clicked into the call. "Hello?" she croaked out.

"This is the Pleasant Shores Police Department, is this Mary Rhoades? Listen, a vandal broke into your store and destroyed a bunch of the books."

"Excuse me. What did you say?" She couldn't take it in, couldn't take anything in, not tonight.

"No need to come down now. We've got it cordoned off and the rest of your merchandise should be safe tonight, but you'll need to call your insurance company in the morning." He went on, talking about fingerprints and photographs and cleanup.

She agreed to everything and after ending the call, let her head tilt back against the chair.

There was no doubt in her mind as to who the vandal was: Imogene.

It drove home the fact that this was never going to go away. Why had she thought she could start over? She would always have to deal with Imogene and with the past. And it wasn't fair to the citizens of Pleasant Shores to have her here.

She looked down at the puppy. She'd have to move. And moving, with no idea of where she was going... She couldn't put a puppy through that upheaval.

She clutched Coco, her chest heaving with a sob. She didn't want to give the dog up. Didn't want to lose everything, not again.

But fair was fair. She'd hold the puppy for one more night, take it into her bed and tomorrow she would take it to Kirk or Goody, let them find a new home for it.

The puppy's fur was wet. So wet. She tried to dry it off with her sleeve, but the source of the moisture was her own tears. And they weren't drying anytime soon.

On Thursday morning, Paul walked through the door of Mary's vandalized bookstore. Some self-preserving part of him was glad that he had something constructive to do this morning.

He'd gone through the motions of helping Davey get dressed, fixing him breakfast and dropping him off at school, but he was numb inside. Every time he started to feel, or think, the huge realignment his world had made last night threatened to overwhelm him. Better to just stay busy.

"Glad you could come," Trey said. "Mary didn't even come in yet. Too upset. We already took prints and got all the evidence we could, so now we just want to get the place cleaned up to help Mary out."

"Sounds good." Paul hadn't seen any vandalism when he walked in the door, but when he progressed farther into the shop, he realized that books were ripped off the shelves and thrown all around, some defaced with paint, some that looked like they had been stomped. Compared to the cozy and comfortable environment it had been last night, this was a travesty. "Was it her stepdaughter?"

"You know about her? Yeah, we think so. Earl and one of the other guys are looking for her right now." Trey shook his head. "I just don't get how anybody could do this to a bookstore. To any place, really, but books help people. They're a good thing."

"That's why," came a voice from the counter, and Paul looked over to see Drew Martin, a guy he'd met a few times but didn't know well. Drew had been in the Healing Heroes cottage last year. "To some people, anything good is something they should destroy."

Yeah. Paul swallowed. But sometimes things that were good just destroyed themselves. Sometimes, things that seemed good really weren't. An image of Wendy smiling at him and hugging him, singing alongside him in church, tried to press itself into his mind. He shook it away like a dog emerging from a lake would shake off water. "What's the plan here?"

"I just took a bunch of pictures for the insurance people," Trey said. "They said we could clean up, but that we should save the damaged books and store them somewhere safe. Any that are undamaged, put on that display table up front for Mary to go through and organize."

"We'll inventory all of that later," Drew said. "For now, I'm doing phone calls. Insurance, cleaning companies, workers that were to come in today."

Paul started in, helping Trey. Picking up the stacks of destroyed books and loading them into boxes made Paul feel a little sick. "These books could have made kids happy," he said.

"Yeah, I noticed that it's mostly kids' books that are destroyed. Wonder what that's about." Trey put another armload into a box.

"What about the young adult books, for teenagers?" Drew asked.

Paul walked over to that section. He'd noticed Mary had a good collection of those books last night.

Almost every shelf was bare. The floor was ankle-deep in ripped, stomped books. "Destroyed," he told Drew.

Like his own life had been destroyed. He shook off the self-oriented thought, grabbed another box and knelt in the young adult section, loading up the ruined books.

"At one point," Trey said, "Mary mentioned that she hadn't seen the stepdaughter since the girl was a teenager. Wonder if there's a connection with her destroying kids' and teenagers' books?"

"My thought exactly," Drew said.

When his phone vibrated with a text and Paul pulled it out and saw his in-laws' names, he blew out a sigh.

Need to see you today. Where are you?

Great. But this day couldn't get much worse, so he texted his location and they said they would be there in an hour or less.

It hit him then: they were related to Davey by blood.

Paul himself wasn't, if last night's story was to be believed. They'd be shocked to even hear it hinted that their daughter had had an affair.

Paul and Trey continued working through the mess in the bookstore, sorting the books. Paul started hauling boxes to the storeroom in back while Trey dragged in a carpet cleaning machine.

As Paul stacked up the boxes of damaged books, he found himself wishing he could do the same with his own problems. Just load them up and put them away. Have things go back to the way they'd been before last night.

All he'd wanted was to control his life and protect his son. But that had been blown out of the water because his son wasn't his son.

Images of Davey kept flashing before his eyes, but it was as if the focus had shifted. Now he kept noticing ways that he and his son—because Davey still felt like his son, absolutely—he kept noticing ways they were different. Had Davey's freckles come from his biological father? How about his left-handedness?

And then he would start thinking about Wendy. Her affair had happened years ago, before she had ever gotten sick. She'd carried that lie through their marriage without ever telling him. Had she loved the guy? Had she thought about him every time she looked at Davey? Obviously, it had been at the forefront of her mind in the last days. It had bothered her enough that she told Amber.

"You okay, man?" Trey's voice behind him made him realize he'd been standing in the storeroom way too long.

"Yeah. Sure."

Trey just looked at him.

"I found out something," he said, and headed back into the front of the bookstore.

"Something to do with what happened last night?" Trey asked, following him.

Paul nodded. "Sorry to worry you. I'd never hurt Amber."

Drew's face turned in their direction. "Amber's a good person."

"So everybody says," Paul said. "I thought so, too."

Drew's eyebrows lifted.

Trey gave him a sideways glance as he poured something from a plastic bottle into the carpet cleaner. "Whatever she did to make you mad, I can guarantee it wasn't from a bad heart. Amber's definitely unconventional, but like Drew says, she's a good person."

Paul didn't answer.

"Women can sure make you mad," Drew said. "There have been times I've wanted to walk away from Ria. In fact, I did, for a while."

"Coming back was the right thing to do," Trey said. "You have a good family."

Paul didn't want to hear about other people's good families. He walked over to a door that led to a supply closet, now ripped off its hinges. He studied it, wondering if he could at least rig something up for now.

He'd thought he had a good family. Yeah, they'd been stricken by tragedy, but the memory of Wendy, Davey and him had shone bright. Now it was tarnished.

If he was being truthful with himself, he had to admit that he'd started to have fantasies of a new family, with Amber as his wife, as Davey's mom.

That wouldn't be happening. Amber had known the truth and she'd kept it from him, kept him in the dark. Made him feel like an idiot. Acted like he wasn't even worthy of the simple courtesy of being told the truth.

Georgiana hurried into the store, Ferguson right behind her. She waved when she spotted Paul. "We need to talk to you right away."

Paul hoped he could be patient with them. His temper was already frayed.

Ferguson cleared his throat. "Is there somewhere private we could have a conversation?"

"Maybe we can use Mary's office," Paul said, and after getting the okay from the other two guys, they headed through the door behind the cash register, entered Mary's office and closed the door.

Paul leaned against the wall, giving the older couple the two seats. The office was small, with a tiny window that faced an alley and let in some pale winter sunshine. Georgiana sat in the seat obviously meant for a visitor, comfortable wood and padded leather. Ferguson took the chair from behind Mary's desk, rolled it to his wife's side and sat down. No matter their flaws, they were a unit.

Now, unusually, they didn't look smug and sure of themselves. Georgiana kept twisting her hands in her lap, and Ferguson rubbed the back of his neck.

Paul just waited. He couldn't seem to find in himself the social skills to make nice with Wendy's parents. He'd known their values were off-kilter, but he thought they were basically sound, and that they had raised Wendy that way. If anything, her upbringing had made her a little rigid, or so he thought.

Now he found out she'd cheated on him.

"Andrew McMartin came to see us this morning," Ferguson said. "He had a big shiner, and he said he got it from you."

"No more than he deserved." Then Paul realized what they'd said. "Wait a minute. You know McMartin?"

Georgiana nodded. "We've known his family since the children were small. They belonged to our club."

So that was how it was. Paul had figured McMartin to be a wealthy guy, just from his clothes and the way he carried himself and spoke. But to know he and Wendy had known each other all their lives... Yeah. That made a few more pieces click into place, but he didn't like the picture that was emerging.

Ferguson cleared his throat. "He said he'd told you about Davey."

Paul stared at him. "He did. Did he tell you as well or did you already know?"

The two of them glanced at each other, which was all the confirmation Paul needed. His fists clenched reflexively but he forced himself to relax them, drawing in deep breaths and letting them out slowly as his PTSD therapist advised when he was having a panic attack. This wasn't a panic attack. It was more like an anger attack.

His in-laws had known about their daughter's infidelity, had known Davey wasn't even Paul's child, and they never said anything?

"You knew." He spoke carefully, forced his body to stay in a relaxed posture. No matter their flaws, Ferguson and Georgiana were older and they were Davey's grandparents. They didn't deserve violence or even a feeling of physical threat from him.

"It was my fault," Georgiana said. "I had Wendy's old computer, and one day a few weeks ago, when I was really missing her, I found her password and scrolled through her old emails. I just wanted to remember her, but...but that's when I discovered the truth about Davey."

Ferguson took over the story. "That's why we've been

acting so strange lately," he said. "We were so confused. Who had the real rights to take care of Davey?"

"I did," Paul said. "I still do."

The couple glanced at each other. "After the whole…situation over the weekend, with taking Davey to our house, we understand things better." Georgiana ran her fingers through her normally perfect hair, messing it. "We took Davey to Andrew's house—"

"You what?" Paul leaned toward Georgiana, not sure he'd heard her right.

Her husband stepped in. "Andrew never even saw Davey up close, nor vice versa," he said. "Davey stayed in the car. It turns out that Andrew didn't want anything to disrupt his family life, so we just drove back home."

Overwhelmed with all the new information, Paul sat on the edge of the desk, shaking his head. "I don't know what to say."

"Our counselor—we saw a counselor for the first time yesterday—she says we should try to work it out with you, that we shouldn't keep secrets." Georgiana's chin trembled. "I'm sorry, Paul. I don't know why Wendy would do that. She wasn't using good judgment."

That was an understatement Paul didn't even know how to process.

Ferguson took up the story. "From the email Georgiana accessed, we learned a little bit of the story. She thought, for a short while, that she wanted a different life from what she could have with you, but she pretty quickly regretted the notion. By then, it was too late. She was pregnant."

"At first I hoped it wasn't true," Georgiana said. "But that day we took care of Davey, we dug through Wendy's things and found her journal. It…" Her voice quavered. "It confirmed everything."

Paul tried to imagine such a thing. He'd sometimes felt restricted by Wendy's desire for a higher-priced lifestyle than he could provide, but he'd always loved her, always been loyal to her, never thought of straying or of breaking up.

His own faithfulness made him feel like a fool.

He thought back to the time before Davey was conceived. He and Wendy had fought a lot, usually over money. It had led to such a chill between them that he'd been surprised when she had come up pregnant.

Now it all made an ugly kind of sense.

Ferguson leaned forward. "What are your thoughts about keeping Davey in light of what you found out?"

Paul stared at him. Then he looked at Georgiana. She was intent, too. How could they not know his answer? "Of course I'm keeping Davey. He's my son. I'm the only father he's ever known."

Only after the words were out of his mouth did he realize that he was directly quoting Amber, what she had said to him last night.

"That's good of you, Paul." Ferguson sounded relieved. "Of course we would take him if you refused, but we're getting too old to care for a young active boy like Davey. You've been a wonderful father to him, and we would very much like to see that continue uninterrupted."

Georgiana frowned. "Apparently, Wendy told that woman the truth about Davey. We don't know why she told her, but not us."

It took Paul a moment to realize that *that woman* was Amber. For just a moment, he thought of Amber and Wendy laughing together and contrasted it with the tears and tension that had usually accompanied a visit from her parents. He wasn't surprised that Wendy hadn't told them something so shocking. And when he thought about it, thought about how accepting Amber was, he couldn't be surprised that Wendy had told her.

But Amber had been practically a stranger. Wendy must have suffered terribly to let down her usual guard and pour out such a truth to someone she barely knew.

She couldn't tell me, either.

Because Paul was almost as judgmental as her parents. Wendy had made a terrible mistake, and no one close to her had been the type to listen, accept it, help her deal with it.

"Look, I'll need time to think all this through," he said. "Provided we can come up with a safe, comfortable way for it to happen, I'd like for you to stay in Davey's life. He loves you and needs you." He paused and looked from Ferguson to Georgiana. "But make no mistake: I make the decisions about him. He's my son."

CHAPTER TWENTY-TWO

AMBER PUT HER arm around Hannah as they walked out of the doctor's office. "I'm so glad you could come with me to my appointment," she said, giving her daughter a side-arm squeeze.

She still wasn't used to thinking of Hannah as an adult, but there it was. After so many years of taking Hannah to doctors' appointments for her yearly checkups, now Hannah was helping her with hers.

Hannah returned Amber's gesture, sliding an arm around her waist and bouncing a little. "I'm so happy! You're, like, perfect!"

Amber laughed. "Not exactly. You've seen my criss-cross of scars."

Hannah danced away from Amber and lifted her hands, palms up, walking backward. "So you can't wear a bikini anymore. The important thing is that your scans are good. Your blood tests are good. It's all good."

"You're right." When she'd thought something might go forward with Paul, she had let herself worry, a little, what he would think of her body and its imperfections. Now that wasn't an issue.

Her thoughts of Paul seemed to transmit, telepathically, to her daughter. "So, this opens the door for you to get more serious with that hot guy you were interested in." Hannah came back to walk beside her. "What was his name, Paul?"

Amber shrugged and hoped it worked to feign indifference. "Doubtful anything will happen there."

"Why not?"

Even though Hannah was seeming more and more grown-up and independent, there was no way Amber was going to share dating information with her. So she waved a hand. "We just had a little falling-out. I don't think he's right for me, after all."

"Even with that adorable little boy?"

"Yeah, Davey is a cutie, for sure." Amber's throat tightened, thinking of him. She wondered how Paul had explained the fact that she wasn't around anymore. Had he painted her as evil in his explanation to Davey? Did Davey even care?

She still couldn't quite believe that it had happened. Both that he'd found out the truth, and that he had reacted so intensely. But when she thought more about it, of course he reacted intensely.

Paul was an upright, honest person. He knew you couldn't have a good relationship based on lies, and lying was what she had been doing. She was a fool to have thrown away something so good and promising.

But that was what she did, who she was. She wasn't a person who would ever have a good partner like Paul. Didn't deserve him. Didn't deserve Davey.

The familiar feeling of inadequacy and wrongness pressed down on her, but something made her press back. Was she really so undeserving?

Amber didn't deserve Hannah, either, but she'd been blessed with her. She tried to tune back into what her daughter was saying.

"It's so cool that you can travel again. Because..." Hannah trailed off and looked sideways at her.

They were walking along toward the bay now, the wind blowing hard, making Amber's eyes water a little. "What were you about to say?" she asked Hannah. "It's cool I can travel because why?"

"I was going to say… You can come see me when I go abroad! Did I tell you I'm practically signed up for a semester abroad? If you sign off on it, of course, and it's expensive, but…"

"I'm in favor." Amber ignored the lurch in her chest. "I want to hear all about it."

Hannah glanced sideways at her again and seemed to be reassured by the calm, curious expression Amber had pasted on her face. "I'm loving my international business class so much, Mom. And I'm doing really well in French, too. So I'm thinking about a minor in modern languages, and…" Hannah hesitated and studied her face. "Honestly, I didn't think I could do it because of your health, but now it sounds like you can come see me wherever I am, anytime you want to."

Pain tried to wrap around Amber's heart, but she shoved it down. "I'm so glad you're excited about your schoolwork and your future." Her voice croaked a little at the end, but fortunately, Hannah got a phone call and couldn't analyze her reaction.

The thing was, she *was* happy for Hannah. Hannah must have inherited some of her adventurous genes and Amber wouldn't dream of stopping her.

Amber had always known how important it was for parents to have a life of their own, rather than living through their children, and this was why. It was what enabled you to open your hands and let your little bird fly free.

It was time for Amber to think about her own life, and the good news from the doctor just hadn't struck her yet, probably. Probably, she would be thrilled about the opportunity to travel, to take up her book project again, once this gloom about Paul had worn off.

They'd parked right by the Coastal Kids preschool building, and as they approached the car, children's voices rang out from that direction. When Amber saw that a group of children was outside, she paused and squinted, and there was Davey. He was talking to the teacher Kayla. Kayla reached down and gave him a little hug before sending him back to a group of boys playing some kind of a game with the ball.

So Davey was fine. Of course he was fine, and that was good.

It was good he was close to his teacher. Maybe she and Paul would get together now. Kayla was a far better match for him, far better for Davey, as well.

That tight feeling in her chest wouldn't go away, though, it seemed, no matter how much logic she threw at it.

It was just that everything was turning upside down for her. She had wanted an adventurous life, but now she was realizing something: love was the adventure. Love was the challenge.

But you had to merit that love, deserve it, earn it, and the truth was, she didn't. She wanted to be loved for who she was, but who she was, well, it wasn't that great.

She swallowed hard, trying to keep her emotions under control. No way was she going to inflict this mood on her daughter.

But Hannah was talking excitedly into her phone. "Okay, see you in a few!" She clicked off and turned to Amber. "Steff and Hailey are home, and I'm going to go meet them at Goody's." She paused, studying Amber's face. "If that's okay with you."

Amber forced a smile. "Of course, go have fun with your friends. Thanks for coming with me to the doctor." She swallowed. "Love you," she managed to say through a tight throat.

"I love you so much, Mom." Hannah hugged her tight. "You're the best."

Appreciation and gratitude for her daughter brought tears to Amber's eyes. Fortunately, Hannah didn't notice, but spun and half jogged down the street.

And Amber made it to the car before she started to cry.

ON SATURDAY, PAUL took Davey to the Christmas Fair at the Pleasant Shores Community Center. It was the nineteenth, just six days before Christmas, and Paul hadn't finished his shopping. He hoped to remedy that at the fair.

And he hoped to cheer himself up, or at least avoid inflicting his bad mood on Davey.

Sarge loped along beside them. The dog was adjusting surprisingly well to civilian life and seemed to be perfectly content to be a pet. Still, Paul cringed when he thought about what the guys in his old K-9 unit would have to say about taking a police dog to Pet Pictures with Santa.

The community center was a big, wide-open room with tables set up around the edges, featuring local, handmade gifts, candles and Christmas ornaments, and sea glass decorations. The scent of doughnuts and baked goods filled the air, and big urns of coffee and hot chocolate were set up in one corner.

Paul headed for the coffee—he hadn't had time to make any this morning—but Davey tugged at his hand. "Look, Daddy, there's Santa! Can we go see him first?"

"Sure thing." He changed directions and they walked toward the corner where kids and pets were making a lot of noise. Sarge veered toward one of the tables offering little sausage and biscuit snacks, and Paul scolded him and tugged him back to a heel position.

They reached the short line of families and pets waiting for their photographs and then he saw her.

Amber was one of Santa's helpers. Well, of course she was, because that was the kind of thing Amber did. She wore a green elf suit complete with short velvet skirt and green tights, and a red-and-green cap on her head, and she looked... Paul swallowed. Wow, did she look good.

He was automatically stepping toward her, opening his mouth to greet her, and then he remembered. She'd lied to him. She'd known Wendy's secret about Davey.

He looked down at Davey and got that semi-sick feeling in his stomach that had dominated his bodily sensations for the past few days. Ever since he'd learned that Davey wasn't, technically and biologically, his son.

She caught sight of them and her smile, the hope on her face, made him breathless. But he steeled himself against his wildly vacillating feelings, closed his heart and turned his face away.

Davey spotted her, too. "Miss Amber!"

Paul looked again and saw that Amber was talking to another elf, this one white-haired. It was Mary, wearing a similar elf suit in red. Amber gave Davey a fake smile and apologetic little wave, and then she hurried off in the direction of a kids' craft area.

Paul's hand had been out to stop Davey from running to her, but it wasn't necessary. Mary came over and started talking to Davey about whether Sarge would wear a Christmas hat or kerchief. She showed Davey both options and when he'd decided Sarge should wear a kerchief, she let him choose which one he thought would look best with the bloodhound's brown fur.

She completely ignored Paul.

And somehow, Paul felt like the bad guy.

An argument started in his head. He needed to protect Davey from Amber. He also needed to protect himself. Amber had been terribly wrong to conceal what she knew from him.

But somehow, he felt less than honorable holding that against her.

They reached the front of the line, and Davey decided Sarge needed a hat, too, after all. Mary agreed and helped to tie a little elf hat on the poor dog, who gamely accepted it and sat still for several poses: one with Davey, one with all three of them and even one with Mary.

If he hadn't pushed Amber away, there could have been a picture with her. He'd have liked to have that, even after everything that had happened.

But it wasn't to be, and Paul needed to stop thinking about it. He listened while Davey sat on Santa's lap and told him what he wanted for Christmas, making mental notes on a few items he might still have time to purchase. As they walked away, he forced himself to focus on his son, not his regrets. "What do you want to do next? There's a bunch of trains and antique toys over there, and look, Mr. Kirk is showing everyone how they work."

But Davey shook his head. "Want to get a present for Miss Amber," he said, and tugged Paul toward a table full of pastel-knitted decorations and flowery-smelling bean-bag-type items. Davey couldn't read, but he'd unerringly picked the "Gifts for Mom" table. "Can we, Daddy?"

Now, what was Paul supposed to say to that? Was he

supposed to stifle Davey's generosity? "I don't know if that's a good idea," he said, stalling.

"Why not? I love her." Davey smiled up at him, an innocent smile that stabbed at Paul's heart.

Davey, however mistakenly, was more generous than he was.

And yet Amber *wasn't* Davey's mom, nor was there any chance that she'd gain that role by marriage. Not anymore.

"We'll think about that kind of gift later," he hedged. When Davey's face fell, he felt like a jerk.

As Paul steered Davey over toward the toy display, a loud bang made Paul jump.

Trey rushed out from behind the counter and grabbed Paul's shoulder, then yelled, "Cut it out," at Kirk. "Sorry, man, it's just this toy battleship he's been obsessed with," he said to Paul. "It sounds way too realistic. You okay?"

"I'm fine." Paul looked at his concerned face, looked down at Davey, who was also fine, and then realized what Trey was thinking.

A week ago, fireworks had set off a huge panic attack. Today, a loud banging toy hadn't. Maybe he was making some progress.

"Go look at the toys," he told Davey, who ran over to a group of kids clustered around Kirk. "Thanks for worrying about me," he said to Trey, "but that one didn't hit me. I'm not saying I'm over the PTSD, but I'm getting better."

"Good man," Trey said, and went to help someone unload more boxes of Christmas books.

Paul strolled through the aisles of the fair, keeping an eye on Davey, paying attention to what he liked so that he could come back and buy a couple of items later.

As he followed after Davey and kept Sarge at his side, his mind wandered. It was great that he was getting past the panic attacks. The counseling was helping. Being here in Pleasant Shores was helping. It was a good community, full of caring people like Trey, who was looking out for him and understood his issues, and Mary, who'd helped Davey enjoy dressing Sarge up for Santa.

And Amber, his conscience reminded him. She was a good person, too, had been kind to both him and Davey from that first night Davey had run off and ended up at her house.

But she lied!

Yes, to help a dying woman gain peace.

It was true. That was why Amber had kept her silence. Not out of meanness, or self-interest, but because she was keeping a promise.

It was *Paul* who was acting mean and self-interested.

Davey's grandparents had found out the truth weeks ago, apparently, and they, too, had kept the truth from him for a time. Their reaction to Wendy's adultery had been to panic and go behind Paul's back, trying to take Davey from him, even sneaking him to his biological father and basically offering Davey to that self-absorbed rich idiot who didn't know a good kid when he saw one. Paul's fists clenched just thinking about it.

Davey's grandparents had acted like jerks to both Paul and Davey.

Paul had acted like a jerk to Amber.

Amber was the only one who hadn't acted like a jerk.

He thought of her face when she'd seen them come in today, how it had lit up and then fallen. He'd hurt her. He'd told her he never wanted to see her again.

But the truth was, he didn't just want to see her, he wanted to keep seeing her. He was in love with her, and he wanted to marry her.

He stopped still as the realization hit him hard.

He loved her and he wanted to marry her.

Wanted her to be his wife. Wanted her to be Davey's mom.

So she'd made a mistake in how she'd handled Wendy's secret. It wasn't as if Paul had never made a mistake himself.

And yeah, thinking about something long-term with her, the risks were there. She might not be healthy or live to a ripe old age, and that was heartbreaking to even contemplate.

But he thought of Davey, who'd given his heart to Amber in a simple, uncomplicated way without regard for the consequences.

A little child shall lead them.

Unless you become like little children, you will never enter the kingdom of heaven.

Paul wasn't all that well trained in the Bible, but there was a reason those particular verses were sayings most people knew and remembered: they were true and right and worth living by.

If Davey could let the future take care of itself and love Amber now, could Paul do any less?

The only problem was, he'd blown it with Amber. He'd said cruel things, blamed her for something that wasn't her fault, acted judgmental and self-righteous.

If he had any chance with her, he had to do something big.

CHAPTER TWENTY-THREE

IT WASN'T WALKING WEATHER on this late-morning Sunday, but Amber went for a walk, anyway.

When life gets you down, get moving. It had been her philosophy for years. She'd done it when she'd been undergoing treatments in the hospital, sneaking outside to stroll the grounds or hang with the smokers even when she was supposed to be confined to her room.

Before that, she'd dragged Hannah out all the time when she was a baby and toddler. They'd gone to the lake with friends and to the shore with a short-term boyfriend and to Texas, one memorable summer, just the two of them. She hadn't had money to travel far, back in those days, but she'd scrimped in the rest of her life so they wouldn't be stuck at home for long stretches with nothing new and exciting to do.

No doubt that contributed to the wanderlust Hannah felt now, the wanderlust that was taking her further out of Amber's circle and influence. Amber applauded it, and she blamed herself for it, but it was still sad for a mother to see her only chick spread her wings and fly away.

She reached the line of shops on Beach Street and wrapped her coat more tightly around herself. It was a gray day, with temperatures in the forties, but the damp made it feel colder.

Being cold, outside in the windy weather, made her think

of Paul, how he'd wrapped his coat around her and fussed like a mother hen on that unforgettable day when he'd finally kissed her. Then again, everything made her think of Paul.

Seeing Paul and Davey at the Christmas Fair had nearly broken Amber. The open, welcoming happiness in Davey's eyes; the coldness in Paul's.

As she passed Lighthouse Lit, a movement inside caught her eye and she stopped. She'd figured it would be closed until noon, like the other stores.

The sign on the door said Closed, but there was Mary, alone inside, moving a stack of books.

Amber tapped on the glass and pointed at the door.

Mary put down the stack and opened the door. "Hello, dear," she said, her voice quieter than usual.

She didn't look well. Dark circles sagged beneath her eyes, and her normally gorgeous white hair frizzed out beneath a kerchief. She wore faded blue jeans and a T-shirt, not at all her usual attire.

Come to think of it, she hadn't looked her usual self when they'd been elves together, either.

"Are you okay?" Amber asked. "Do you mind if I come in for a few minutes?"

Mary hesitated as if she were about to refuse, but then stepped aside and let Amber walk through the door.

Amber looked around. She'd heard about the vandalism at the bookstore, but everything seemed to be pretty much in its place.

What was different were the signs topping most of the displays: 50% Off! Everything Must Go!

"What's going on?" she asked.

"Help me put this up, dear," Mary said, beckoning her

to the back of the store. She pulled out a banner. "I guess we'll just tape this up across the window."

The banner read Store Closing Sale.

"I'm not helping you put that up," Amber protested. "You can't close down. Why would you?"

Mary rolled up the banner, grabbed a roll of tape and headed to the front of the store. "I'm moving on."

"But...it's the Christmas shopping season. And everyone loves Lighthouse Lit. We need you!"

Mary shook her head. "I'm very replaceable. Someone else will open a bookstore."

"You're not replaceable!" Amber watched Mary struggle to tape up one end of the banner and then went over and helped her hold it. "Is this because of Imogene?"

"Because of Imogene, and what she said. Everyone knows my past now. No one will want to shop here." She slipped past Amber, unrolling the banner as she went, and started affixing the other end of it to the window.

Amber stalked over and held that end for the older woman, too. "That's ridiculous. People don't believe what Imogene said. They believe you."

"I don't want to talk about it." Mary finished a hurried, sloppy tape job and then turned toward Amber, hands on hips. "What are you doing out in this cold, anyway?"

"Thinking," she said.

"About Paul?" Mary beckoned her to the back of the shop again and poured her a cup of tea without asking if Amber wanted it.

"About Paul, about Hannah, about a lot of things."

"But mostly about Paul, eh?" Mary raised an eyebrow as she perched on the stool behind the cash register. "The two of you really seem to be going somewhere."

"It's not going to work."

"Why not?" Mary's eyes were piercing.

Amber waved a hand. "Something happened in the past, and he blames me for it. And he's sort of right to blame me."

"Did you have a choice?" Mary asked gently.

Amber thought of Wendy, sick and crying, desperate to confess the sin that lay heavy on her heart. There had been no time to call a priest or counselor.

Had she had any choice, in that situation, but to hold Wendy's hand and listen, and then promise not to tell? "Not really."

Mary nodded slowly. "Life stinks sometimes."

"Yeah." Amber studied Mary. "I didn't take in everything your stepdaughter said, but it sounds like some things happened that you didn't have a choice about, too."

Mary pursed her lips and tilted her hand from one side to the other. "You're not wrong. There were parts of it I didn't have a choice about, but parts I did, and I screwed those up royally."

"Sounds familiar." Amber leaned on the counter and took a sip of tea. She looked around the store. "Do you really want to leave when things are pretty good in your life? I mean, you have your store, your friends, your new puppy—"

"I gave the puppy to Kirk." Mary's voice went husky on the last couple of words.

"No!" Amber stared at Mary. "You love that puppy!"

Mary nodded, her eyes shiny with unshed tears. "I love her, and that's why I gave her away. I don't know where I'm going and I can't put a dog through that."

"And you're punishing yourself." As soon as she said

it, she knew it was true, and Mary's wide eyes and raised eyebrows confirmed it.

Was Amber doing the same thing to herself?

"I'm just looking out for the dog," Mary said, but her protest sounded half-hearted.

"That dog loves you already. Don't you think you deserve to have a dog that loves you?"

"No!" The word burst out of Mary, and then she stared at Amber, her eyes getting suspiciously shiny.

Amber studied her. "Think about that," she said. "And why don't you think about this move a little longer, too?"

"My mind's made up." Mary wiped her eyes. "But you know what? I value your friendship and I hope we can stay in touch. You're a good person, Amber Rowe. A very good person."

She opened her arms, and Amber came around the counter for a hug.

And as she walked out of the store, as she made her way down to the waterfront and sat on one of the benches facing the bay, something broke through to her, just as the sun was trying to break through the clouds.

She had tried her best: with Wendy, with Paul, with Hannah. She'd made mistakes as a friend and a mother, of course. Maybe more mistakes than most. But it had never been out of bad intentions.

The weak December sun didn't warm her, but she felt a little warmer nonetheless, because she finally felt a new truth, felt it inside. She was worth loving as she was, mistakes and flaws notwithstanding, just as Mary was.

Unfortunately, she wasn't going to *get* love from the person she wanted it from most. But not only was she worth loving, she knew how to give love, and to give it in an active way. She glanced back toward town, then stood and started walking in that direction, pulling out her phone.

There wasn't any time to lose.

AFTER AMBER LEFT, Mary continued marking down books and adjusting displays until it was time to open the store. When she unlocked the door, several people were waiting—unusual for a Sunday, except maybe not, since it was the holiday shopping season. She let them in and greeted them, and they began to browse the store.

More people came in. Drew, Ria and their two teenage daughters said they were stopping by after their family's Sunday brunch. Julie and Earl showed up, too. "I know you said you didn't need me to work today," Julie said, "but we're here to shop, and I can help you if need be." She looked around the shop, but didn't mention the sale and store closing signs, which was odd. Mary hadn't told Julie about what she was doing, of course, but since Julie usually knew everything that went on at the store, she had to be surprised that such a big change had been made without her input.

More people poured in, and when Amber showed up in the middle of that group, Hannah at her side, Mary started to get suspicious. Had Amber told the others what Mary was planning to do?

All of a sudden, Amber nodded at Hannah, who pushed herself up to sit on the counter. Then she scrambled to a kneeling position and waved her arms. "Okay, everyone, are we ready? Who wants to start?"

Oh, no.

"I'll start," Julie said, waving a hand. "This is the best job I ever had, and I don't want the place to close."

"I'm sorry I didn't tell you," Mary said, looking around

to include her other friends in the apology. "It's all happened rather quickly. You and everyone else will get a nice severance package."

"You didn't tell me because you knew I wouldn't let you do it, right?" Julie asked, ignoring the mention of severance. "And you were right. I won't let you, if I can help it."

"I don't want Lighthouse Lit to close, either," Trey said. Mary hadn't even realized he had come in. "I like getting my thrillers here, not online. I like to browse in person."

A couple of other people chimed in on that one.

"As a college student," Hannah said, still kneeling on the counter, "I like having a bookstore in town. Sometimes I need a book last minute, and you're always able to get it quickly."

"Can I say?" came a kid's voice. It was Davey, here with his grandfather, who lifted him to perch on the counter beside Hannah.

He was so cute that everyone smiled. "Go ahead," Hannah said, putting an arm around him to encourage him.

"I like story time!" He got up to his knees, bouncing a little, and Hannah put a hand behind to steady him. "'Cuz it's okay if we don't sit still!"

Everyone laughed, and Ferguson leaned on the counter beside Davey. "I like the store, too," he said, "and my wife *really* does. She likes to spend our fixed income here."

That raised more laughter, because it was pretty obvious that Ferguson and his wife had the opposite of a fixed income and could buy anything they wanted.

Mary wanted to thank everyone, but her throat felt too tight.

"Your website is accessible to people with visual impairments," Drew called from near the windows.

Mary smiled at that. She'd had to learn a few things to

make her website more accessible, and she'd had Drew in mind when she'd done it, but it was a help to a lot of other people besides him. She'd done it willingly.

A pang hit her. All that work would be for naught when the store closed down.

A few more people came into the store, and when Mary saw Imogene among them, her heart sank. She just wanted. to escape the woman before she did more damage, either to the store or to Mary.

Trey, always alert, moved to the edge of the crowd, phone to his ear. His eyes never left Imogene, and at that point Mary realized that, most likely, Imogene was wanted by the police for vandalizing her store.

Then more people were saying what they liked about the store and pleading with her to remain open. Of course, it warmed her heart. Just having all these people around praising her business was wonderful. She waved a hand until everyone quieted down to listen to her. "You're all wonderful," she said. "I can't thank you enough, but it's likely that someone will open another bookstore in town."

"Not the same."

"It's you, your touch."

"We don't want another bookstore, we want you."

Mary put her hand to her heart and looked around, and her eyes came to rest on Imogene. Her face was a puzzle as she stared at Mary, a puzzle Mary couldn't interpret.

The shop door opened again, and this time, a uniformed Pleasant Shores police officer entered. He approached Imogene, who tried to step away, but Trey had come up on the other side of her and blocked her escape.

The slight scuffle drew people's attention, and Mary took the opportunity to go through the crowd to her stepdaughter. Trey had his hand on one of her arms, and the other officer held the other as he quietly read her her rights.

"Please don't treat her harshly," Mary said when the man had finished. "She's truly suffered in her life, and she has her reasons for blaming me."

"That may be," Trey said, "but vandalism is still a criminal act."

"You're so rich," Imogene snarled at Mary. "Why don't you share it?"

Mary drew in her breath. It felt fruitless to explain yet again why she wouldn't give Imogene money, how Imogene had squandered the money she'd inherited on drugs and alcohol rather than using it to fix her life.

"Mary does share, every day," Drew Martin said. "We have a new museum in town because of her."

"And the Healing Heroes cottage," someone else said.

How had *that* become common knowledge?

"She donates plenty to cancer causes," Amber said. "She's done so much for this town. She's incredibly generous."

Mary's face heated and she waved a hand. "Don't," she said. "I do what I can, but so does everyone else in Pleasant Shores."

Imogene stared at her, her face seemingly frozen in hostile lines. And then, suddenly, it crumpled a little, and her eyes got shiny with tears. "Why does everyone love you? You're just a rich old lady." For just a moment, genuine longing came into her voice. "How'd you get past what happened, when I couldn't?"

Mary studied her as the past thirty minutes replayed in her mind, nudging in all kinds of new awareness. She *was* loved. Despite all her flaws and mistakes, this community had embraced her. "I'm rich in friends and love," she said, gesturing at the listening group of people. "That matters more."

Imogene snorted. "You sound just like Dad."

Mary pictured Ben's kind face. "That's a huge compliment," she said quietly. "Your father was the best man I ever knew."

"He was," Imogene said, and suddenly, she sank to the floor, her shoulders shaking. "It's my fault," she moaned, rocking back and forth. "My fault."

Mary knelt beside her. "It's not your fault. Not even a little."

"But I called him," Imogene choked out. "I called him on his car phone and begged him to come home, and he did. And that's why…" Her words ended in a wail and she buried her face in her hands.

Mary sank the rest of the way down to the floor, feeling like she couldn't continue kneeling without falling over. "You *called* him? You didn't tell the police that. Are you sure you're remembering right?"

"I was afraid I'd get in trouble and be blamed," she sobbed. "So I lied."

Mary closed her eyes and put a hand on Imogene's shaking shoulder. If Imogene was telling the truth now, it would explain so much. Why Ben had returned so quickly. Why her mobster first husband had suddenly left her alone. In fact, he'd died soon after the incident, leaving Mary all of his wealth.

She'd never understood how he could put a hit on his own child. But if he'd intended it to be for Mary, who'd betrayed him by marrying someone else, or more likely for Ben alone…and then he'd found out he'd caused Daisy's death… She felt her shoulders sag as the pieces finally fell into place.

"Even if you called and caused your dad to turn around and come home," she said, leaning close to Imogene, her words for her stepdaughter alone. "Even if you did that, that doesn't mean your dad's death was your fault. It was the fault of the man who hit them with his car. And the fault of the person who hired him to do that."

Imogene had gone still as she was speaking, clearly listening.

"You just did what any teenager might have done." And, Mary realized dimly, she herself had just done what any confused young wife might have done.

They'd both paid dearly for their mistakes, if they even were mistakes. They'd just handled their guilt differently—Imogene by ruining her own life and now trying to ruin Mary's, Mary by endlessly working to make amends.

"Come on," the uniformed officer said to Imogene. "We're taking you in. You can come peacefully, or not, your choice."

Imogene let out a sound almost like a growl, but walked along with the officer toward the door, the crowd of people parting to let them through.

After she left, Amber put a hand on Mary's arm. "Will you stay? Keep Lighthouse Lit open, and keep living here with your neighbors and friends?"

Mary looked around at the group of townspeople, seeing so many beloved faces. It would be hard to leave, harder than she'd realized. "I'll have to think about it."

"Maybe this will help you think," Kirk James called from the back of the crowd. His deep voice was accompanied by a little yip, and then Kirk made his way through the crowd to her, holding Coco, now adorned with a big red ribbon around her neck. "I sure hope you'll take her back. Too much work for me."

The puppy struggled toward Mary, and Kirk set it in her arms. She cuddled it close, and as Coco licked her face, she let a few happy tears fall.

She wasn't going to make any rash promises. She still had to think things through. But she felt safe, as if all these people's caring had wrapped her in a warm embrace. That was worth changing her mind for.

CHAPTER TWENTY-FOUR

PAUL HELD DAVEY'S HAND and looked around the loud gathering of happy, slightly intoxicated people, all talking and laughing and hugging and kissing, and feared he'd made a mistake.

A Christmas Eve gathering at Bisky's big, rambling waterfront house was *not* the romantic setting he'd have preferred for what he was about to do.

He'd proposed to Wendy on the couch. But when he'd consulted Trey about how he could go big with this proposal, in order to make up to Amber for all the mistakes he'd made, Trey had insisted that Amber would love being asked for her hand at a party. When Paul had expressed his doubts, Trey had called Erica, who knew her sister better than anyone else, and she'd concurred.

As a consequence, here they were at Bisky's, spilling out into the yard and onto the docks under colored lights, for an occasion called the Feast of the Seven Fishes. Apparently, Bisky hosted the event every year.

They were, after all, in a fishing town. It was easy enough to get the food for seven seafood dishes. Bisky was half-Italian, so the Italian American tradition made perfect sense.

Paul had gone to church beforehand—he'd needed it—but the calm produced by the beautiful service dissipated as he approached the rowdy group. Was it even kid-friendly?

But then he spotted a couple of the families from Davey's class and realized adults and kids of all ages were here.

In fact, everyone in town was here. And he didn't want that much of an audience, but for Amber, he'd do it.

He sucked in a breath, inhaling the fragrances of fish and spicy tomato sauce and garlic, and plunged into the outdoor crowd, heading toward the house, gripping Davey's hand more tightly.

And there, on the other end of Bisky's long porch, was Amber.

She wore a sparkling red dress that clung to her slender figure, and she was laughing at something someone else had said. She looked like an exotic bird that a mundane creature like Paul could never hope to catch.

He didn't want to weigh her down, tame her fire, even if she *was* willing to be his wife.

"There's Justin! Can I go play with him?" Davey was tugging at Paul's hand.

Paul tore his eyes away from Amber, ascertained that Justin's mom was keeping an eye on several small boys and let Davey run to join them.

When he turned his gaze back to Amber, she was looking at him. And then someone stood up in between them, and when he looked again, the spot where she'd been was vacant. She was gone.

He wove his way through the laughing, loudly conversing people, or tried to. But Bisky stopped him with a hand on his arm. "Hey, glad you came. You're empty-handed. Let me get you a drink and point you toward the food."

"It's okay, I'll help myself."

"What kind of a host would I be if I let you do that? You have to eat." Bisky's words were ever so slightly slurred.

Paul had the feeling he wasn't going to escape her firm

grip unless he let her in on the reason he wasn't hungry. "Actually," he said, "I was hoping to find Amber. I have to apologize to her for something I said...something I did... that was wrong."

Bisky stopped still and faced him, frowning. She was a big woman, nearly as tall as he was, and her expression was as severe as his fourth grade teacher's had been. "Don't you *dare* hurt that woman."

"I did hurt her," he admitted, scanning the room for that red dress. "I want to make it right, but I have to find her first. Did you see her go by?"

She looked into his eyes, then nodded. "She's in the kitchen, I think." She gestured toward the back of the house.

"Thanks." He headed toward the kitchen, making his way through the crowd.

"Hey, my good man. Give me a hand with this?" Kirk James was about to pick up a large tureen of oyster stew that smelled fantastic. Paul needed to find Amber, but he hastened to grab the other side of the giant vessel, and the two of them carried it to the serving table. Immediately, people clustered around it.

As they walked away from the table, Paul asked Kirk how he was doing, figuring he needed to make some effort to be a decent party guest.

"I tell you what," Kirk said, "I'm a happy man because my neighbor Mary isn't moving away. I just wish I could make some progress with her."

"I know what you mean."

He must have said it in a heartfelt way, because Kirk studied him, then nodded. "Yes, I believe you do," he said.

"If you don't mind, I need to find Amber."

"She was in the kitchen a few minutes ago."

But when Paul finally reached the kitchen, filled with

bustling men and women, lots of talk and laughter, and amazing smells, Amber wasn't there.

"Anyone seen Amber Rowe?" he asked the group at large.

"She's right...no, she's not," someone said.

"She was slicing bread. She must have taken a tray out to the docks."

"She did," someone else said. "That's where they were asking for more."

"The docks?" There were *more* people out there?

"There's a table and tent set up out there, with gas heaters," someone else explained.

"Thanks." He headed that way, the ring in his pocket seeming to dig at him.

He wondered why Amber was playing a host role at Bisky's party. But then again, she was a great cook, and this seemed to be a community effort. And that was the kind of person Amber was. Despite her supposed party-girl image, she was actually a nurturer to the core.

He walked down the porch steps, waving to Hannah and Mary and a couple of other people he knew. He kept moving so no one would stop him. He was on a mission, and he wasn't going to relax and socialize before making one of the biggest moves of his life. With the most potential for embarrassment or failure.

"Daddy!" Davey's voice rang out from the front yard, and then Davey broke off from the small gang of kids to run over and cling to his leg. "There are *too* dogs here! I wanted to bring Sarge! He didn't get to have a party!"

"Sarge is better off at home," he reassured his son. When somebody's big gray wire-coated dog came over, too, along with a couple of little boys trying to ride him, Paul realized why Sarge had come to mind. "Boys, don't ride the dog."

They didn't look inclined to obey him, but he channeled Amber and Davey's teacher, Kayla, and went for a sideways distraction. "I think they just put out some cookies inside the house. They smelled good."

"Cookies!" Most of the boys ran off, and the dog sank down into the yard with a sigh, obviously worn-out by his young charges.

Davey, though, didn't seem to want to go with them. Instead, he snuggled against Paul's leg. Understandable, since it was getting close to his bedtime.

The trouble was, Paul wanted to propose to Amber. He'd envisioned doing it without Davey there.

When you thought about it, though, they were a package deal. If he was lucky enough to have Amber agree to marry him, she'd be agreeing to become part of Davey's family, too. Basically, to become his mom.

So it wouldn't hurt to have Davey at his side, or at least close by. Besides, his son was so cute, he might improve Paul's chances. He'd just have to time things in such a way that if Amber said no, Davey wouldn't hear it and be devastated.

He picked Davey up and walked down toward the docks, where the party seemed to be even more raucous. He scanned the crowd. Why was every woman wearing a red dress?

And then he saw her. Leaning against a post, looking out at the bay, a full drink in her hand.

Her clothes and hair were festive, her nails painted, her heels high. She looked every inch a party girl. But the expression on her face was pensive.

There was a sadness in her, or maybe just a depth, that he didn't see in very many people. She'd been through a lot, lost a lot. She'd learned that life didn't come with guarantees. And yet she went on, living and loving and caring and, most of the time, laughing.

He could recognize the sadness because he had it, too. He, too, had seen the dark side of life.

Beneath the surface attraction—and man, that was fierce—he felt drawn to her at the soul level. Like they could help each other grieve and grow. Like they could get through the hard times, not just the good times.

Davey squirmed against him, and he realized he couldn't just stand here gawking at Amber. He needed to make his move.

First he texted Hannah. At docks in five.

He spotted Kayla, now basically cornered by a heavy-set guy in a fleece jacket and cowboy boots. She looked like she wanted an escape, so he carried Davey over to her. "Would you mind hanging with Davey for a few minutes?" he asked, then felt guilty, because it would take well more than a few minutes to convince Amber to do what he wanted her to do.

"I'd like nothing better," she said. "Hi, Davey! Come sit beside me."

The guy in fleece looked disgruntled.

"Whenever you need to move on, if I'm not back, just tell Davey to run over to me. I'll be talking to Amber."

Kayla gave him a knowing grin. "It's about time," she said. "And no rush. I love hanging out with my man Davey." She handed Davey a cookie, and the man in the fleece jacket threw his hands up and walked away.

Game on. Paul straightened his shoulders and headed over to where Amber now perched on a bench near one of the heating lamps.

She was still looking out at the water and didn't see him coming, so he cleared his throat. "Hey. Amber."

She looked up at him. No smile. "Hey."

"Mind if I sit down?"

She hesitated, then lifted a shoulder. "Go ahead."

She wasn't exactly her warm, welcoming self.

But he'd expected that. He'd known he'd have to dive in and grovel. "I'm sorry for being such a judgmental jerk. I said some mean things when we last talked."

"You did." She shrugged again. "Understandable. You'd found out something awful, and I'd kept that information secret."

"For reasons I'm starting to understand."

"That's good." She sounded distant as she looked back out at the bay, dark but sprinkled with reflected sparkles from the lights strung along the dock.

The silence between them wasn't exactly uncomfortable, but it wasn't comfortable, either. "How have you been doing?" he asked finally.

She met his eyes then. "I'm fine." Her mouth twisted into a wry smile. "You know me. I'm always fine."

"Or you put on a show of that."

"Better than moping."

"It is." He swallowed. *Get to the point.* "Listen, I've missed having you around." *Geez, make it sound like she's an old jacket.* "I've missed talking to you, and laughing with you, and…" He trailed off because he wanted to say *holding you*, but he didn't want her to think it was all physical for him. It was that, but it was so much more.

She looked wary. "It's best, though, right? Because we aren't going to be a couple, even if you get over being mad at me about what Wendy did."

"I'm over it," he said promptly. "I never should have been mad. It wasn't your fault what she did."

She lifted her hands, palms up. "I feel like I could have

handled it all better," she said, "but I don't know how. Should I have shut her up when she started to talk? Or blurted it out when I first came in contact with you? Or told you when we started to..." She hesitated. "To get closer?"

"No. There was never a good time, and it wasn't your issue to begin with. It was mine and Wendy's."

"And Davey's," she said quietly. "How are you dealing with finding out you're not his father?"

"I *am* his father," he corrected. "I keep getting shocked by the fact that we're not biologically related, a few times every day, but it doesn't change the truth—he's my son."

"Good." She nodded as if satisfied. "Well. Was there anything else? Because I promised I'd help serve the dessert." She stood.

He couldn't let her get away. "Yes, there's something else. Sit down."

She lifted an eyebrow and then sat, looking at him warily.

"Amber," he said, calling back into his mind the phrases he'd planned out. "I've come to care about you so much in the past couple of months. I was a jerk when I learned this news, and I'm sorry, but I'm over it now. And it doesn't change that caring. I still feel it."

She dipped her chin, studying him through lowered eyelashes, not speaking.

His heart sank a little. She wasn't exactly jumping into his arms.

He couldn't bear to lose her. "You're an incredible person, and I've seen that more and more as I've gotten to know you," he said. "What you've been through...and yet you still put a smile on your face and help other people as best you can."

She waved a hand and looked away.

He cleared his throat. "I admire you, but it's not just that. I'm crazy attracted to you, Amber. You're…" He swallowed. Was he really going to say it? "You're the sexiest woman I've ever known. You're beautiful, and exciting, and a little bit wild, and I…I really, really want to be with you."

"Now you're making me blush." A smile tugged at the corner of her mouth.

He smiled, too, but only a little. He didn't feel confident of her response to what he was about to ask, not at all. "You've been wonderful to Davey, and he loves you for it. You're already a great mother to Hannah, and…" He looked over his shoulder, making sure she was there as planned. "And she's on board with this."

"On board with what?" Amber's eyes widened and she looked at her daughter.

Hannah gave them a big smile and a thumbs-up. She had her phone facing their way, videoing them. Not what Paul would have preferred, but no doubt Amber would like that.

Paul pushed on. "I haven't told Davey yet, because I didn't want to get him excited until I knew how you felt. But I know him, and nothing would make him happier than to have you as his mom."

She pressed a hand to her lips then, her eyes getting shiny.

"You're a mystery, and a puzzle, and I don't feel like I'll ever figure you out," he said. "But I would love to, I'd be completely honored to be allowed to try."

"Paul…" A shadow crossed her face and she pressed her lips together.

She was going to say no.

He had to go on, though. He had to see this through, to at least ask. "It's gotten to the point where I can't imagine a future without you. I want to be with you all the time.

Which is why I wanted to ask you…" He pulled the ring box out of his pocket and then sank down onto one knee. "Will you marry me?"

AMBER SUCKED IN HER BREATH. Had she heard Paul right?

She looked around and it seemed like a lot of people she loved were there, nearby, standing around, but they were out of focus. All she could see clearly was Paul, kneeling before her, holding open a box that seemed to have some kind of a ring inside.

He was watching her, his eyes resolute, like he wasn't going to give up and go away. She reached out and touched the sleeve of his shirt. Soft flannel.

So it was real, then. This was really happening.

But there was a barrier, a big one. "What about my health?" she asked him, keeping her voice low. "I'm good now, but there are no guarantees. What about Davey?"

Paul drew in a breath, let it out and nodded. "I know. But the thing is, he already loves you. And I do, too. And love's more important than fear, whether we have months or years or decades to love each other."

His words made her heart stop and then expand in her chest. She felt tears prickling in her eyes, and she couldn't speak. She just looked at his dear, strong face and thought about what it would be like to wake up next to him, every morning for the rest of her life.

He lifted an eyebrow. "Do you at least like the ring?" he asked.

The ring! She hadn't even looked at it, not really, and she leaned closer to see it through her tears. And she gasped. The band was twisted, like the rings she most liked to wear, with a heart at one end, and embedded all the way with diamonds. It looked handcrafted. She'd never seen an engagement ring like that, which meant he must have searched high and low for it, or paid a ton, or both. "I love it," she said, her words little more than a croak because her throat was so tight. She looked into his eyes. Paul was so steady, so humble, so *good*. What he was offering, what stood in front of them, filled her with joy. "What's important is, I love you." She tugged at his hand, wanting him to get off his knees and come closer.

Dimly, she heard the collective sigh as he rose and sat beside her and pulled her into his arms. "Thank you," he said. "At least you care. Can I keep trying? Can you spend more time with me and Davey and see if you might want to make it permanent?"

Yes, he was humble. She shook her head against his shoulder and felt him tense. "I don't need to spend more time," she said, lifting her face to his. "I already know that I would be thrilled and honored and completely happy to be your wife, and Davey's mom."

The happiness she saw on his face, just before he pulled her close, was surely mirrored on her own. And then he lifted her face and kissed her with all the tenderness in the world, a kind of tenderness she'd never experienced before, beautiful, rich and complex, interlaced with passion.

"Daddy, you're kissing Miss Amber!" Davey rushed over and threw himself against them. "Me, too! Me, too!"

Amber laughed through her tears as she wrapped an arm around this dear child and pulled him close. He cuddled against her, not questioning, full of a child's trust, a trust she knew she'd work to be worthy of for the rest of her life.

And then Paul lifted Davey onto his lap. "What do you think," he said, "about Miss Amber being your mommy?"

Amber cringed a little. What if Davey said he didn't want that, now, in front of all these people? Because she was starting to realize that there were a *lot* of people here, and not just because it was a party. All her friends and family were watching and listening.

"'Kay," Davey said. He yawned hugely and lifted his arms to her, and as she pulled him to her chest, felt the sweet weight of him against her, as she heard the collective "awwwww," she started to cry in earnest. She looked helplessly up at Paul, and he stroked her hair and smiled. "Told you he'd be on board," he said quietly.

"Mom." Hannah hurried across the open space to where they were sitting. She knelt in front of Amber. "You're messing up your mascara. Here." Carefully, tenderly, she blotted Amber's face with a tissue.

Amber transferred Davey back to Paul and put her hands on Hannah's shoulders. "You're good with this?"

Hannah nodded, her own eyes shiny. "You deserve to be happy. You've focused on me all these years. It's time for you to get love, not just give it."

Amber hugged her daughter tight. "Thank you for being your wonderful self," she choked out. Looking over Hannah's shoulder, Amber saw Erica smiling widely.

Hannah reached out an arm to Davey and Paul, and then they were all hugging in an awkward circle, laughing, as their friends clapped and cheered.

There were congratulations to be shared, and hugs. Bisky and Mary opened bottles of champagne and sparkling grape juice, and everyone toasted them.

Amber was surrounded by her friends and she loved it, laughed and cried and celebrated, hammed it up. But she kept looking over at Paul. He was definitely a part of the community, shaking hands and laughing and talking, but his eyes didn't stray far from her ever. Mostly, he just stood watching her and smiling. Hannah was holding Davey on her lap, and Amber heard the words *big sister* and *little brother*, and that made her tear up again. It was something she'd never been able to give Hannah, a sibling, and she was thrilled that Hannah was embracing it so joyously.

Finally, the party started breaking up. Some needed to get the kids home to bed, and others were headed to midnight mass. Bisky and Mary and Kirk cleaned up, but waved away the offer of help from Amber and Paul. "You two relax," Kirk said. "That's an exhausting experience."

"You should know," Mary said dryly. "How many times have you proposed to a woman?"

"Hey, now, that's classified information."

They moved away, clearing dishes and trash, amicably bickering.

Paul pulled Amber into his arms. And as she looked up at his handsome face, as she traced his strong jaw with one finger, gratitude and joy filled her heart.

EPILOGUE

SPRING CAME EARLY that year. Or maybe it was just that every day felt like spring to Amber. At any rate, Paul and Davey had been happy to go out for a walk on this balmy day. Davey was excited to go anywhere so long as he could ride his new bike, a gift from his grandparents. It was sturdy and bright blue, covered with stickers and mud just like the bikes his friends had.

It was a much more appropriate gift than the little car, which they'd ended up donating to a kids' charity after Davey had tired of it. Ferguson and Georgiana made a point now of checking in with Paul, and sometimes even with Amber, before they bestowed a gift.

By mutual consent, the three of them headed down toward the docks. It was beautiful there, and Davey had a friend among the fishing families that he played with often. And Paul always stole a kiss at the little bench where they'd shared their first kiss, so it was romantic for them.

Everything was romantic for them, it seemed. Right now, they were holding hands, watching as Davey pedaled his little bike madly a stone's throw ahead of them.

"Not too far," Paul called.

"I know," Davey called back. He slowed down ever so slightly, then sped up again.

Amber squeezed Paul's hand. "He's fine. Let him have a little freedom."

Paul wrapped an arm around her shoulders, pulling her closer to his side. "I should be glad for the privacy. Sometimes it seems like we don't get enough chance to be together."

"Be grateful for what we have. I am." Amber slid an arm around his waist and squeezed. It was true: she *was* grateful, every day, for the gift of Paul and Davey.

The beauty was that now, she felt like she deserved the happiness. That her mistakes of the past were just that, mistakes, not character flaws.

That she could have a new chance and a new life.

She breathed in the air of the shore, slightly pungent with salt and fish, overlaid with spring flowers. Those were out in abundance, the apple trees vying with pear and cherry for the beauty prize.

On the water, a lone boat chugged in toward shore. "Hey, that's Bisky," Paul said.

Amber waved big, arms windshield wiping over her head until Bisky waved back. "Wonder why she's coming in early?"

"Mary said she's been different lately. Doing a lot of reading. Quieter."

"I hope she's okay." Amber resolved to invite Bisky to dinner within the week.

"*You've* been doing a lot of reading, too," Paul observed as they passed Bisky's dock and headed toward the end of the peninsula. "I saw that you had a memoir of a woman who'd traveled to Nepal. Are you jealous?"

He sounded concerned, and she disentangled herself from him to give him a playful punch in the arm. "Stop it, you. I'm reading that because she went a lot of the places we went. And where Hannah's going to go this summer."

"You're sure? You know, we can travel again this summer. Ferguson and Georgiana want to take Davey to their summer cabin for a week."

Amber shrugged. "Maybe. Let's see how they do having him for a weekend." It had been a real leap of faith for both her and Paul to allow Davey to go for an overnight with his grandparents, but after they'd talked with the older couple's therapist, they'd agreed to give it a go.

"I just don't want you to feel restricted," he said.

She reached up and kissed his cheek. "I don't. My world got larger when you and Davey came into it."

It was the simple truth. Once she'd agreed to marry Paul, they hadn't wanted to wait, so they'd had a hurry-up Valentine's Day wedding. And then they'd had a spectacular, though short, honeymoon in the Far East. She was pretty sure Paul had gotten the travel bug; he'd loved the trip, and she'd loved being on it with him.

They kissed on the docks, slow and lingering, and then headed back. They waved to Harmony, the new occupant of the Healing Heroes cottage. Soon they were passing Amber's old place and then the new Victory Cottage, where Mary was planting flowers along the porch, and Kirk was painting trim.

"She's put you to work, has she?" Amber called, and the two of them waved. They both looked happy. Mary continued to insist that she wouldn't date Kirk, didn't want to date anyone. But it definitely seemed like they were spending more time together.

Imogene was well and truly out of Mary's life now, which was good. She'd done a little jail time for her vandalism and possession of drugs, and then Mary had paid for a stint of treatment for her. While in rehab, she'd met someone and they were living together on the West Coast, hopefully dry, both working.

When she, Paul and Davey reached their home, Amber smiled, feeling the warmth she always felt when she saw it. It wasn't fancy; it was a pretty little beach cottage, with a yard for Davey and Sarge to play in, and a glassed-in sun-room for Amber to do her writing projects.

Paul hadn't gone back to being a cop. He was working as a firearms instructor for now, but was retraining to become a high school teacher. He'd gotten over his distaste for being in a school. With his patience and his calm demeanor, he'd be great with teenagers.

Davey threw down his bike in the yard and came back to them, lifting his arms. "I'm hungry."

Amber bent down and picked him up. Having a five-year-old was better than any weight lifting program.

Was better than anything. "We'll let Sarge out and get some lunch," she said. "And then I think we all need naps." She winked at Paul, and nearly laughed when his face colored. He'd always be more reserved than she was, and that was fine. Underneath that reserve was a fiery passion that both surprised her and filled her with joy.

She'd always wanted to live an adventurous life. But underneath that, she'd always been searching for love and a home.

She had that, now, with Paul and Davey. Home and adventure and, most of all, love.

* * * * *

ACKNOWLEDGMENTS

As ALWAYS, FINISHING a novel reminds me of the debt of gratitude I owe to so many people. My publishing dream team, Karen Solem, Shana Asaro and Susan Swinwood, have been incredibly supportive with ideas, suggestions and encouragement. The art, sales and marketing teams at Harlequin are staffed with talented people who work hard, often behind the scenes, to get books into the right readers' hands, and I'm the beneficiary of their expertise. Writing these books for HQN has been a dream come true.

I owe a special debt to my writer friends. My Wednesday morning writers' group pushed me to make each chapter better, while my pals Sandy, Dana and Rachel listened to my complaints and encouraged me to get back to work. Nicole Peeler was a blessing, organizing online write-ins that created a supportive virtual community. And I'm especially grateful to Karen Williams, who read the manuscript and guided me toward a stronger portrayal of both cancer survivors and young children.

Nearest and dearest, I'm grateful to Bill for his unfailing support and ready smile, and for reminding me to stop working and have some fun. And finally, I am so thankful for my daughter, Grace, who fills my life with love and laughter.

Lee Tobin McClain's The Off Season series continues!
Read on for a sneak peek at the next book, coming soon!

CHAPTER ONE

"THAT'S A WRAP on oyster season." Bisky Castleman tied her skiff to the dock, fingers numb in the March morning chill, then turned toward the wooden shed that connected the dock to the land. She hung up her coverall on the outside hook, tossed her gloves in the bin and sat down on the bench to tug off her boots. "You coming?" she asked her sixteen-year-old daughter, Sunny.

"I'm coming. I'm just dragging." Sunny hung her coverall beside Bisky's and then flopped down on the bench beside her, letting her head sink into her hands. "Sure doesn't feel like a vacation day."

It was one of those teacher workdays they hadn't seemed to need when Bisky had gone to school. "I appreciate your coming out dredging and culling when most of your friends were sleeping in." Bisky slung an arm around her daughter and tugged her close for a quick side hug. "Come on, I'll make pancakes and then you can take a nap."

Sunny frowned. "No pancakes, thanks."

"You sure? You've been working hard. Too hard." Bisky paused, thought about it. "Maybe I'll see if we can hire some of the teenagers from around here to work the traps with us, come crab season. Heard Tanner Dylan dropped out of school."

"He's not going to want to work with us, Mom." Sunny's face flushed a deep red. "Please don't ask him."

If Tanner was one of the boys who'd been teasing Sunny

about her height and size, Bisky would tan him herself. She lifted her hands. "I said maybe. We need to find some help. If you have better ideas, tell me, because I'm not keeping you out of school."

Now that they were done oystering, the second half of March would give them a rare break. Mostly, they'd spend the next couple of weeks scraping down and repainting the hull of their boat and trading out the dredging rig for the simpler setup they'd use for crabbing season.

It was increasingly hard to find a crew to work the water, and Bisky worried about her family business. Worried about a lot of things.

At the outdoor sink, she and Sunny washed their hands, and then they both pulled their hair out of ponytails and shook them out. Bisky ran a hand over Sunny's brunette hair, removing a piece of oyster shell. "Don't worry. I won't ask Tanner if it embarrasses you. But if you think of anybody else who needs a job, send 'em my way."

If she could help out a needy teen in the process of hiring, she would. The community of Pleasant Shores had taken care of her and helped her out since she was a kid, and she tried to pay it forward.

"I'd know you as mother and daughter if I'd never met the pair of you before." The voice behind them came from Mary Rhoades, the energetic seventy-year-old philanthropist and bookstore owner who was one of Bisky's closest friends. She approached with her dog, Coco, a young chocolate-colored goldendoodle who was as tall as Mary's waist, but lanky. Coco let out a bark but remained at Mary's side. Clearly, her training was coming along.

"Hey, Mary." Sunny turned and smiled at the older woman. "No, don't hug me. I need a shower. And Mom needs one, too," she added, wrinkling her nose at Bisky.

Then she knelt down to pet Coco. The big dog promptly rolled onto her back, offering her belly for Sunny to rub.

Bisky pulled a plastic lawn chair forward for Mary and then flopped back down on the bench. "Have a seat. I'm too tired to talk standing up."

"I will, just for a few minutes," Mary said. "I'm supposed to meet the new Victory Cottage resident this morning. Hoping he'll take on the therapy dog program. If not, I'll have to advertise for someone." Mary was one of Pleasant Shore's major benefactors and had started many useful programs in town, including her latest, a respite cottage for victims of violent crimes and their families. Victory Cottage was a place for them to heal, volunteer in the community and find new hope.

"Don't advertise for someone," Sunny said with more energy than she'd shown all day. "I can do it. I can start the therapy dog program."

Mary patted her hand. "You're good with dogs, for sure. Just look how Coco loves you. But I need an adult for this."

"But—"

Mary cut off Sunny's protest. "There are legal requirements and regulations. And anyway, you need to be a kid, not take on more work."

"She's never had the chance to be a kid," Bisky said, sighing. "And it's my fault." Money had always been tight, and Bisky had the business to look after. Sunny had started early with cooking, cleaning, doing laundry and serving as Bisky's assistant on the boat. No wonder she was strong and assertive, just like Bisky was.

"It's not like you have people pounding down your door to work in Pleasant Shores," Sunny argued now.

"I have connections, if the Victory Cottage resident doesn't work out," Mary said.

"When he doesn't, and you can't get an adult to take the job, you know where to find me," Sunny said, just on the edge of disrespect. She gave Mary's dog a final ear rub and then headed across the street and toward the house.

"Sorry she's sassy," Bisky said. "Getting up at the crack of dawn puts her in a mood."

"*Aaanddd* the apple doesn't fall far from the tree," Mary observed, watching Sunny depart. "She got her sassiness from you, and it's a useful trait in a woman."

"It can be. I'm glad she's not afraid of her shadow like some kids."

Mary nodded. "You've raised her well. No doubt she *could* start a therapy dog program. She could probably run the high school or Salty's Seafood Company if she wanted to."

"You're right. She could." Bisky watched Sunny walk toward the house, holding her phone to her ear as she jabbered with one of her friends, and a wave of motherly love nearly overwhelmed her. "Raising her is the best thing I ever did."

"Of course it is." Mary's voice was a little pensive, and it made Bisky remember that Mary had had a daughter and lost her.

"So tell me about this new guy who's coming to Victory Cottage," Bisky said, trying to change the subject.

Mary ran a hand over Coco's furry head, and the dog sat down, leaning against Mary. "He's from here, actually. And like everyone who comes to the cottage, he has a sad story, but that's his to tell." She frowned. "I just hope that the support system we've put into place will work. He's set up with counseling, and the cottage is a dream, but I'm still unsure about what volunteer gig he'll be best suited for." Volunteering was an integral part of the Victory Cottage program, just as it was in Mary's other program, the Healing Heroes project.

At the dock beside them, an old skiff putted in, and eighty-year-old Rooker Smits gave a nod as he threw a rope to his five-year-old great-grandson, who'd been waiting to tie up the boat. Rooker waved to the boy's mom, who was dressed in scrubs, obviously headed for work now that Rooker was back to help with childcare.

Like many watermen from these parts, Rooker wasn't a talker, but he'd give the coat off his back to her or Sunny or any neighbor. Now he and his great-grandson tossed scraps from the oysters he'd culled into the bay. Gulls swooped and cawed around them, drawn by the remnants of a day's fishing.

The smell of brackish water and fish mingled with that of the newly fertile March soil. Spring was coming, Bisky's favorite season. Maybe she'd plant some flowers later today, if she could find the energy to get to the hardware store for seeds.

She stretched and yawned. "Boy, that change to daylight savings is a tough one," she said. "I'm like Sunny, probably going to need a nap today."

"You work too hard," Mary said. "And speaking of work, I should be on my way. Lots to do." She stood and hugged Bisky against her protests—Sunny had been right, Bisky needed a shower—and then she and Coco walked off toward town.

Bisky stood and stretched her back. At thirty-seven, she was starting to feel the aches and pains of a lifetime's physical work. She loved what she did, loved the water, but it took its toll.

She spent a few minutes wiping down her rig, did the minimum she could get away with and then called it a job done. Not well-done, but done. As she crossed the road, heading for her house, she glanced in the direction Mary had gone. A tall figure walked slowly down the middle of the road. So tall and broad-shouldered that she had to look twice at him, because it wasn't anyone from around here.

Or rather…

She stared, then took an involuntary step toward the man, unable to believe what she was seeing. It looked like her beloved childhood friend William Gross. Only, that wasn't possible. Because William had sworn—with good reason—that he'd never, ever come back to Pleasant Shores.

As WILLIAM WALKED the familiar and yet strange road toward the home he'd successfully escaped almost twenty years ago, he heard a man's shout. "Look out, boy. I told you not to play by those…"

William cringed, an instant flashback to his childhood here: his father's yelling and the likely painful aftermath. He snapped back to the present and turned in time to see a huge pile of crab traps teetering near a boy of five or six, who was poking at a small crayfish on the dock. The child didn't even glance up.

William bolted toward the child and swept him up just as the big wire boxes crashed to the ground.

A couple of the traps bounced against William's back, and he tightened his hands on the boy's waist, holding him high and safe. As the clatter died away, William blinked, studied the startled-looking boy to ensure he wasn't injured and then deposited the child in front of the old man who'd shouted. "Is he yours?"

"He's my great-grandson, and he's not to be playin' around this close to the docks or the water. And that's why." He gestured at the cluttered heap of crab buckets. "Come on, boy, you can help me clean up the mess you made."

Fair enough. William was just glad the kid wasn't going to get a beating. "Need any help?"

The old man looked at him. "No, the boy needs to learn. Sure do appreciate your pulling him out of harm's way."

He cocked his head, studying William. "You look like a kid who used to live here, name of Gross."

William held out a hand. "That's me, William Gross." He tilted his head to one side. "And you're...Mr. Smits?"

"Guess you're old enough to call me Rooker." The old man shook hands and studied William, curiosity in his sharp blue eyes. "Been a while." He limped over to the cluttered traps, ushering the boy in front of him.

"You sure I can't help you straighten out these traps?"

"We got it. Get to work, boy," he told his great-grandson, and then turned back to William. "Heard you're living in the city."

"Uh-huh," William said. "Nice talking to you." He wove his way through the fallen crab traps before the man could ask any more questions.

When he got back to the street, he stood a minute, processing what had just happened. Three college degrees and twenty years hadn't served to disguise him. He'd be recognized here. He'd have to figure out how to deal with that.

The sun was at its peak now, casting a surprisingly warm light that made William slide out of his sport jacket and sling it over his shoulder. Just being here made him think he shouldn't wear a sport jacket, anyway. He felt pretentious, dressed up, here on the docks.

"William?" came a soft voice behind him. A voice that brought him back to laughter on sparkling water, and catching crayfish, and good meals around the table of a family that actually liked each other.

He turned and studied the tall brunette who stood before him. She wore work clothes, and she was older than the last time he'd seen her, but he'd never forget the eyes and the smile of his childhood best friend. "Bisky Castleman?"

"It *is* you!" She flung herself at him and hugged him fiercely.

She was tall for a woman, and more muscular than she'd been in school. Still, it was the first woman he'd held in two years and the hug felt good. Having a friend felt good and was something he needed to try to cultivate, now that he'd sworn off love.

They let each other go, finally, and stepped back.

"Where have you been, and what are you doing back?" Bisky asked. "I heard you were teaching in a college."

"I was." The casual way she asked the question told him she didn't know what had happened. "Life's dealt a few blows, and I'm here for an R & R break." He tried to keep the words light.

She didn't buy it. "Come over here and sit down," she said, taking his hand and drawing him toward the same old fishing shack her family had always had. There was the same bench outside it, a little more weathered than he remembered. "Tell me what's going on, because I know it would take a lot to bring you back to Pleasant Shores."

"I appreciated your note when Mama died," he said instead of starting up the story of where he'd been and what all he'd been doing, what had transpired.

"I'm glad my note found you. No one seemed to have a recent address."

"I've lost touch." He looked out over the bay, watched a pelican dip, snag a fish and carry it away.

"Heard you had a daughter. About the age of mine, sixteen?"

She didn't know. He glanced at her and then shook his head. "Not anymore," he said through a tight throat.

It had been two years, and he still couldn't talk about it. Still hadn't really processed it, and that was why his

department head at the college had teamed up with someone from HR to find this program for him. It was his last
chance to heal before he'd lose his job that he'd gotten
worse and worse at.

He'd agreed to do the program despite its location, because Mama was gone and his father had moved away. He
wanted to heal for the sake of his students who'd come to
be his whole world.

But those of his students who'd gotten too close had
seen the ugly, damaged side of him, had scraped his emotions raw. He couldn't let that happen again. Couldn't let
anyone get too close.

He had to make sure that these people who'd known
him in younger days didn't worm their way into his heart.

"What happened to her?" Bisky asked quietly.

He'd dodged that question a million times, but for some
reason, he couldn't dodge it when it came from Bisky. He
cleared his throat, hard. "She was shot by an intruder who
broke in to steal a TV. She was taking a nap and surprised
him, from what the police could figure out."

Bisky's face contorted with horror she didn't try to hide.
"You poor, poor man," she said, tears in her voice and eyes.

"Don't feel for me. Feel for her." He didn't deserve the
sympathy of Bisky or anyone.

She ignored that. "As a mother, I can only imagine…
Oh, William." She leaned close and hugged him again.

Maybe it was because of the familiar, salty smell of her,
or the fact that she knew him from childhood, but something broke off inside William then, a tiny piece of his grief.
His throat ached and tears rose to his eyes, even though he
tensed all his muscles trying to hold them back.

"You can cry in front of me," she said, patting his back
as if *he* were the child. "It wouldn't be the first time."

She was right about that. He remembered, then, the rabbit he'd kept as a pet, what his father had done to it and how he'd beaten William for crying. William must have been seven or eight, and he'd run to his best friend for comfort. She'd hugged him and cried with him then, just like now.

He pulled out his bandanna, wiped his eyes and blew his nose. Then he smiled at her, a real if watery smile. "Thanks. I guess I needed that," he said.

"You're here for the Victory Cottage program." It wasn't a question.

He nodded. "The woman who runs it wanted to seek out people who had a connection with this place. I'm the perfect candidate according to her." He quirked his mouth to show Bisky he didn't think he was perfect at anything.

"You are," she said thoughtfully. "There are plenty of people who'll be glad to see you."

"That I doubt," he said. "My family wasn't the most popular."

"No, but most folks knew you were cut from a different cloth. Come inside." She gestured toward the house across the road, where her family had always lived. "I'll make pancakes and coffee. Sunny could use a meal, and I could, too."

The thought of sitting around the table with Bisky and her daughter—her alive and healthy daughter—tightened a vise around William's insides. "Thanks for the invitation," he said, "but I won't be able to. I need to get going." He ignored the puzzlement in Bisky's eyes as he turned and strode away.

He couldn't let himself get that close, feel that much.

Don't miss the continuation of Lee Tobin McClain's
The Off Season miniseries, coming soon!

IF YOU ENJOYED THIS BOOK WE THINK YOU WILL ALSO LOVE

LOVE INSPIRED
INSPIRATIONAL ROMANCE

Uplifting stories of faith, forgiveness and hope.

Fall in love with stories where faith helps guide you through life's challenges, and discover the promise of a new beginning.

6 NEW BOOKS AVAILABLE EVERY MONTH!

*What happens when a beautiful foster mom claims an
Oklahoma rancher as her fake fiancé?*

Read on for a sneak preview of
The Rancher's Holiday Arrangement
by Brenda Minton.

"I am so sorry," Daisy told Joe as they walked down the sidewalk together.

The sun had come out and it was warm. The kind of day that made her long for spring.

"I don't know that I need an apology," Joe told her. "But an explanation would be a good start."

She shook her head. "I saw you sitting with your family, and I knew how I'd feel. Ambushed."

"I could have handled it. Now I'm engaged." He tossed her a dimpled grin. "What am I supposed to tell them when I don't have a wedding?"

"I got tired of your smug attitude and left you at the altar?" she asked, half teasing. "Where are we walking to?"

"I'm not sure. I guess the park."

"The park it is," she told him.

Daisy smiled down at the stroller. Myra and Miriam belonged with their mother, Lindsey. Daisy got to love them for a short time and hoped that she'd made a difference.

"It'll be hard to let them go," Joe said.

"It will be," Daisy admitted. "I think they'll go home after New Year's."

"That's pretty soon."

"It is. We have a court date next week."

"I'm sorry," Joe said, reaching for her hand and giving it a light squeeze.

"None of that has anything to do with what I've done to your life. I've complicated things. I'm sorry. You can tell your parents I lost my mind for a few minutes. Tell them I have a horrible sense of humor and that we aren't even friends. Tell them I wanted to make your life difficult."

"Which one is true?" he asked.

"Maybe a combination," she answered. "I *do* have a horrible sense of humor. I *did* want to mess with you."

"And the part about us not being friends?"

"Honestly, I don't know what we are."

"I'll take friendship," he told her. "Don't worry, Daisy, I'm not holding you to this proposal."

She laughed and so did he.

"Good thing. The last thing I want is a real fiancé."

"I know I'm not the most handsome guy, but I'm a decent catch," he said.

She ignored the comment about his looks. The last thing she wanted to admit was that when he smiled, she forgot herself just a little.

Don't miss
The Rancher's Holiday Arrangement *by Brenda Minton,*
available November 2020 wherever
Love Inspired books and ebooks are sold.

LoveInspired.com